Until I See Stars

by Marisa Recker

DORRANCE
PUBLISHING CO
EST. 1920
PITTSBURGH, PENNSYLVANIA 15238

Dorrance Publishing Co
585 Alpha Drive
Suite 103
Pittsburgh, PA 15238
Visit our website at www.dorrancebookstore.com

ISBN: 978-1-6376-4290-0
eISBN: 978-1-6376-4606-9

Dedicated to my sister.
I love you, always.

Ad astra per aspera
To the stars, through difficulties

Prologue: Then

They all sat in the living room in silence. Dan cleared his throat and sat up a little taller. "I wish you had told us earlier," he said with a sigh. He glanced at his living room where two large suitcases seemed to overshadow the room.

"Why didn't you just tell us?" Karina questioned. She too couldn't ignore the glaring fact her daughter was moving out and this was the first they heard about it.

"I didn't know what to say. I knew you wouldn't agree with my decision. I just didn't want to make anybody upset," Kayla responded in a cautious tone. It was hard enough to build up the courage to leave the only home she had ever known, but she knew that she would not be able to handle getting into a brawl with her family hours before her plane was scheduled to depart.

"Of course we're upset. You are moving to a big city halfway across the country with no job, no security, and no backup plan. Not to mention you didn't communicate with anyone in your family that you were leaving in the first place. It's…it's cruel!" Karina snapped and stood up to walk out of the room.

"Karina!" Dan retorted. He stood up and pulled her into their kitchen. The only sounds Bethany and Kayla could hear were angry whispers from their mother and stern whispers from their father. When they came back into the living room a few minutes later, Karina's arms were folded and she slumped into the chair in silence. "We support you, Kayla. We're just worried about you. That's all," Dan spoke softly and reached for his daughter's hand but was left with his hanging in the air for a few moments, and then awkwardly placed it to his side.

The last thing Kayla felt from this conversation was support. True, she did blindside her family by booking a ticket in secret, packing her suitcases in the middle of the night, and calling a family meeting to tell everyone the day she was supposed to leave. She was eighteen, and even though she believed she had everything figured out, she still needed to work on her confrontational skills. While she told them she wasn't sure what to say, the truth was, even though she was confident in her decision to leave, she still hated disappointing them.

Bethany remained quiet for the duration of the family meeting. However, when Kayla stood up to leave, Bethany did as well. "How about I walk you to your car?" Bethany gently suggested, and Kayla agreed.

Kayla expected her sister to react more vexed, but she seemed to be the calmest out of the whole family. Kayla hugged her tearful mother and strong but concerned father goodbye. Once the front door was closed and the two sisters found themselves standing on the sidewalk next to Kayla's car, she was met with Bethany yelling in her face.

"This isn't what family does. Family doesn't leave family!" Bethany cried as she stood with her arms crossed.

"I'm not leaving, I'm *living*," Kayla said and clutched her suitcases even tighter. "I'm not you. I'm not going to spend the rest of my life living and dying within the same town lines. There is an entire world out there, begging to be seen. I'm young and I have nothing tying me down. I want to go see it."

"You are dividing our family. You're dividing us," Bethany cried and grabbed one of Kayla's suitcases. "Stay. Build a life here where you have people who love and support you," she pleaded and beckoned to the familiar neighborhood Kayla had grown tired of seeing years ago.

Kayla yanked her suitcase out of her sister's hand. "I'm not dividing us, Bethany. You had no problem doing that yourself when you lied to me," she huffed and searched for her keys in her stuffed backpack. Once she found them, Kayla unlocked her old, white Subaru Legacy and stuffed her suitcases inside. She looked down at her one-way ticket to Chicago and gripped it tightly in her hands. This was it. Her one chance to escape the small town she had been trapped in her whole life. She may not have had her sister's support, but she didn't need it. This wasn't for Bethany; it was for her. It was her ticket to freedom, and she was determined to use it.

Prologue: Now

Kayla,

I hope you are doing well. I am reaching out once again to make you see reason. You have made a lot of decisions in your life that I have not agreed with, but I have handled this issue on my own for years now. He is getting worse, a lot worse. You have avoided him long enough. It is time for you to grow up and look beyond yourself and focus your attention on him. You need to come back. I'm not asking this time.

Love,
Bethany

Chapter One: Then

"Bethany! Kayla! It's time to come inside!"

The two young girls pretended not to hear their mother as they continued to run around in the yard. The girls were too invested in playtime to be ready for dinner. This day was princess and knight. While both girls wanted to be the princess, since Bethany had the upper hand by being the older sibling, she took precedence and forced her younger sister to be the knight who rescues her when she is trapped by the evil dragon.

"Princess" was not one of the common games the girls liked to play because, again, fighting over who was the princess often ensued. Typically, they liked playing race car driver with their dad, but their dad was overseas, so they were stuck entertaining themselves. This was a strain on both girls, but especially a strain on their mother.

Karina worked as a special ed teacher at the girls' school, so it seemed like they could never escape each other. It was convenient to be able to take them to school every day and work in the same building, and it made it a bit easier after school since the girls could play in the classroom while Karina worked in her classroom, but that also meant Karina never got a break from being a mother. Even though she loved teaching children with special needs, every moment of her life involved taking care of another human being. On top of that, the person who was supposed to be taking care of her was thousands of miles across an ocean in another country for business.

Dan Fitzpatrick enlisted in the military immediately after he graduated from high school. He didn't really have a choice in the matter. His parents were very poor and told him once he graduated high school, he would have to learn how to support himself. Since he knew college was not going to be an option, unless he wanted to enter the adult world in debt, he viewed the military as the best way to support himself and perhaps see a bit of the world he always dreamed of seeing. However, while he waited to start basic training, something unexpected happened: he fell in love, and when he realized there was no escaping his fate, it made being deployed even more difficult. So, he did what many other young and lovesick boys do: when he got a break during his deployment, he married her.

While he was serving overseas, Karina discovered she was pregnant, and that became the first of many milestones Dan would miss because of distance. Karina went through the majority of her first pregnancy alone and only saw Dan for short bouts of time when he was allowed to come home. But, when Bethany turned two years old, Dan had served his time in the military and was able to come home for what he thought was for good. However, the military never left him, in fact, connections he had made overseas followed him home and begged him to return. A special operations force he had connected with while serving had offered him a high-paying job. The only catch: it was in Germany, and Karina was pregnant again.

This was when the first splinter happened. Dan wanted everyone to relocate to Germany, but Karina did not want to move their young girl and her soon-to-be baby sister to a foreign country. After many long nights of arguing, Karina finally gave up. Dan moved to Germany, and she stayed in Plymouth. They stayed married, and he lived with the family for half the year, but nothing was ever the same for Karina. Even though the job paid well, she felt the weight of being a single mom for at least half the year, and the moments Dan missed were ones he would never get back. More importantly, they were moments she had to experience alone when she should have been spending them with him. The hardest part for Karina, besides lying in bed alone many nights, was when one of their daughters would do something wonderful, and she would have no one to share in that joy with. Sometimes she even caught herself turning to tell someone who wasn't there.

It was a strange life for all of them. Bethany and Kayla had lived a huge chunk of their lives without their father, and yet they remained incredibly close and loyal to him. Perhaps his being away allowed them to create more of a fantasy than a real person, but they were okay with that at the time.

Every time Dan came home, he spent all his time with his girls. This created resentment in Karina's heart. She felt like she never got to spend time with her husband, but he felt like he never got to spend time with his kids. The emotional ties in their marriage were ones that perhaps they wouldn't even fully understand, and so they accepted the bumps and viewed it as okay enough. And besides, Karina often assured herself he was a wonderful father to Bethany and Kayla when he was home. She spent a lot of time convincing herself that was enough. One day she would learn it wasn't.

While the girls didn't fully understand why their dad was gone so often, Karina repeatedly assured them it was because of his love for them, and his hope that they would have the brightest future they could dream of. It was an easy answer for a far more complex situation.

When their father wasn't there, it meant the girls were forced to play with each other, which was often a conflict. Bethany and Kayla may have only been two years apart, but their core beings were vastly different.

Bethany was steady. Her greatest desire was to build up Plymouth to be something greater. She wanted to start her own family there, and perhaps her own business. Her world was not greater than Plymouth, but Kayla's was. Their dad always told them to dream big, and she took that to heart. She wanted to go off and see the world and explore things beyond her small town. She had no desire to settle down; all she wanted to do was move and breathe new air and see new things with her own eyes. Her young, wanderlust heart often called her outside her yard, so she consistently begged her mom to take them to a park or a forest so she could explore someplace new.

Bethany was not as inclined to leave her safe backyard. She believed she could create all the adventures she needed without leaving her own house. This caused many conflicts Karina was left to solve on her own. Almost every day, she had to decide whether to give into Bethany's demands to stay home and play pretend or Kayla's demands to go to town and tromp around any-where else. She often did not have the energy to force them to compromise, but typically gave into whichever voice screamed the loudest. She knew it wasn't good parenting, but it wasn't like she had anyone there telling her differently.

So, like this day, even when it was raining outside, they continued to play princess and knight in the backyard. Kayla's heart kept pulling her past the fence, but Bethany's heart kept them grounded in their fantasy world.

As they toyed with their sticks and worn-out princess dresses, Bethany had her first revelation. Even at eight years old, Bethany had a wise heart that seemed to stretch far beyond her years. She was a quiet soul who liked to sit, listen, and observe the world around her to be able to fully take it in. When she did choose to speak, it was after careful thought and consideration. She also had a perception of people that went far past what her sister or even her parents could understand. She was incredibly attuned to other people's thoughts, emotions, and their approaches to a situation. But it was when Kayla ran up to their backyard fence when she saw a bird fly by that Bethany realized for the first time her life was not going to be like that forever.

Perhaps everyone has a moment in their childhood when they realize their temporal experience is not permanent. Or maybe, for some, it is a slow real-ization that comes in a swirl of little moments. No matter how it occurs, there is a natural question that follows: what will my life be like after this? This is typically when dreams, goals, and aspirations find their way into our midst.

For Bethany, there wasn't a dream that answered that question but a fear. Her sister's dreams were going to look vastly different than Bethany's, and even though on the surface she knew this fact, that day was the first time the reality of it seeped into her heart. It was this moment, the first of several that filled her with a desperation to hold onto her sister as tightly as she could. While Bethany viewed these moments as reminders of why it was her responsibility to hold on and care for her sister, it may have been these revelations that caused the ruptures in their relationship. When Bethany was grabbing onto Kayla, Kayla was grabbing onto the whirlwind of a world around her, and Bethany's grasp didn't comfort her but suffocated her, even at an early age. But they wouldn't realize the weight of either grasps until later. This day, they would run inside for a large helping of spaghetti, forget to say thank you, and continue to play princess and knight in their bedroom until they got tired and went to sleep.

★ ★ ★

Dear Dan,

The rain does not seem to stop. I hope the weather is prettier in Germany than the grey that faces me every time I walk outside. The girls miss you terribly. They keep talking about wanting to play race car with you, but, unfortunately, I can't seem to get the motor on the toy car to work, and besides, I don't think they would want to play it with me anyways. The way they love me does not quite compare to the way they love you. I keep reminding myself having you live overseas is the best decision for our family, and I know you are making more money there than you would here, but it is still difficult to live day after day without you here.

I've been having trouble sleeping lately. I lie awake for hours wondering what you are doing, what you are thinking, and I can't help but wonder if you miss me as much as I miss you. Every day I look at our girls, it makes the grief I feel in my heart that much heavier. All I want so desperately is to wrap you in my arms just for ten minutes, just to feel your heartbeat in my ear as I lean my head against your chest. But I don't know when that day will come. I don't even know if that day will come. I guess all this is just to say I miss you, and you living away is hard on all of us. I hope that one day soon things can change.

Love,
Karina

"Kayla, wait up!" Bethany yelled as Kayla ran out of the car and bolted into the ice cream shop. This was one of the days Karina had caved and took the girls to get ice cream after hours of begging had worn her down. Kayla's sticky hands left her fingerprints all over the glass case that housed the ice cream the girls had spent hours craving. Immediately, she knew exactly what she wanted. By the time Bethany and Karina had caught up to her, Kayla already had two scoops of Very Berry Sunrise in a cone and a big smile on her face. Bethany went for something simple, one scoop of vanilla and one scoop of chocolate, and then sat next to Kayla on a bench right outside the ice cream shop. Karina stayed inside and talked to the owner of the shop.

"Maybe I'll buy this ice cream shop when I'm older," Bethany remarked.

"Why would you stay here and own this ice cream shop when you could go to Italy and own a gelato shop?" Kayla asked.

Bethany rolled her eyes.

Kayla had recently gotten into reading about different places across the world. She may have only been six, but she was determined to learn as much about the world as possible, even if the world was being presented through children's picture books. Her latest interest was Italy. Last week, Karina took the girls to the library, and Kayla got a stack of picture books all about different places in Europe. She still struggled to read a lot of the words, so it was sometimes Karina or Bethany who filled her mind with the wonders of the world. Kayla's biggest takeaway was that Italy was nothing like Plymouth. It was filled with yummy food and old, crumbling buildings she desired to see purely because it was something new and different.

Since Bethany was two years older, she enjoyed reading a series of chapter books about one dog's adventures. It wasn't anything exotic or fantastical, but she was okay with that. Kayla, however, thought that these books were utterly boring and lacked adventure.

"I don't need to go to Italy, Kayla. I like it here. I don't want to leave," Bethany told her.

"Ugh. All I want to do is leave. I want to be with Dad. I bet he's on a big adventure right now," she sighed and imagined her father driving through a beautiful countryside, or trying new foods even he wouldn't be able to pronounce.

"I think Dad's just working. He's trying to take care of us. I don't think that's adventure, that's just being an adult," her sister sternly reminded her. Even though she herself wasn't aware, Bethany was always subconsciously trying to steer her sister away from her fantasies and towards a life she thought was best. And that life was in Plymouth.

"I don't like your idea of 'adult.'" Kayla complained. "I like the heroes in stories who get to go and have fun and save people. All you want to do is be like Mom."

It's true, Bethany did admire her mom a lot. Karina was raised in Plymouth and didn't leave because she couldn't afford it. She went to the closest community college she could find and got her degree in special education. After college, she moved right into teaching. There was no gap year to go and see the world, and even though Karina had a desire to go on a grand adventure, it just didn't seem possible. The grandest adventure she had experienced was when she went to the Bahamas for her honeymoon. However, Karina had higher hopes for her kids. She wanted her kids to have everything she didn't, but Bethany struggled because her most prevalent example of success was her mom who didn't go anywhere.

Meanwhile, as the young girls debated where they wanted to go in their lives, Karina leaned up against the glass display case to talk to her friend William, who owned the shop.

"I just don't know what to do anymore. I'm so tired of waiting. I've spent my entire life waiting. I feel like I've spent my entire marriage without a husband. He is gone most of the year, and when he is here, he isn't here for me, he is here for the girls," she complained. Karina was not typically an over-sharer, especially to an honest acquaintance, but lately she had been feeling so overwhelmed that she needed to talk to somebody, and William happened to be that somebody.

William reached out and touched her hand. "I know, I hear you. I can't imagine what you're going through. I can't even imagine being married, honestly," he said with a chuckle.

William Stewart, indeed, had no idea what being married was like. He had not been able to hold onto a steady relationship for more than six months. Although it was mostly because he chose women who weren't a good match for him. His first adult relationship ended because she had never been serious about marriage, and he had, but he pursued her anyway. The second relationship wasn't much better, they were just too different.

But while Karina innocently enough complained about her marriage to an old high school friend, William found himself looking at the woman before him in a way he knew he shouldn't.

When Karina was finally ready to take her girls back home, William decided to take a risk that, deep down, he believed was a bad idea. But he grabbed her receipt and scribbled a note on the bottom anyway.

2 Scoops (Cone) 4.99
2 Scoops (Cup) 4.99

Tax: 0.62
Total: 10.60

I'm here if you want to vent. Anytime.
(508)-555-0131
        -William

Karina decided to give in and dial William's number. She wasn't sure what she was going to say or why she was even calling in the first place, but she found herself listening to the incessant ringing until he finally picked up.

"Hey! This is William," he answered in a chipper tone.

"It's Karina. Sorry for calling so late." The girls were already asleep and Karina was sitting alone in her bed with only the lamp on her nightstand to illuminate the room.

"I gave you my number for a reason, right?" he responded, even though both were cautious as to what that reason was.

"It's just been a long night and I wanted to vent to somebody," she admitted and groaned out of exhaustion from a day that had taken everything out of her.

"Well, vent away," he said and leaned back in his armchair. As with most of his nights lately, William was spending this one alone, drinking a beer in his chair and watching a movie, so he embraced the phone call as a welcome change from his pitiful routine.

"The girls and I got in a fight today. They are just missing their dad and I'm so tired of making excuses for him," she started. Karina thought about leaving it there, but then decided to be honest with herself about why she was calling. "I guess I just feel really alone right now."

"I can't imagine what you're going through. But I do know one thing: you are not alone." Even though William meant it as a comfort, it struck a bit of fear in Karina. It wasn't fear of not being alone anymore, it was the fear of who was keeping her company. For a moment she wondered if she should've even called William, but her desperation for support provoked her to continue talking.

"I guess I just feel like I can't lean on anybody," she confessed. "I don't have my husband and, if I'm being honest, I don't even know if I would be able to lean on him if he were home. I don't know if I've ever really leaned on anybody," she said with a deep sigh.

"Well, if you want to, you can lean on me. That's what I'm here for," William replied.

This time, Karina took comfort in his words. Maybe he could be a friend to her, perhaps that was exactly what she needed.

The two continued to talk, and it wasn't long before Karina was sobbing on the other line of the phone. "This isn't what a marriage is supposed to look like," she wailed after talking about how depressed and isolated she had felt lately.

"Okay, what do you want your marriage to look like?" he asked.

Karina let out a long-suffering breath. No one had asked her that question in a long time, if ever. "I want a husband that's home," was the first thing she said. That much was obvious to everyone except Dan, it seemed. "I don't want everything to be about the money. I keep telling myself we are doing this to give our kids a better future, but maybe you don't have to go across the world to give your kids a good life. I just keep feeling like it doesn't have to be this way," she said.

After a moment of silence, William encouraged her to continue, and so she took another breath and did just that. "I've looked at so many families like mine, and even though some of them struggle a bit financially, they seem happy. I know so many kids who have received full-rides to college even without their parents' support, and I know it's my responsibility to give my kids their best chance, but I'm not so sure living like this is anyone's best chance."

There was a long bout of silence on the other end, and Karina felt the panic and weight of what she had said sink into her chest. Every moment that William didn't respond to her cry for help, her heart raced a little more. Finally, there was a deep breath.

"Karina, you deserve better than this. You deserve someone who wants to be there for you every day. You deserve someone who is going to put you first. One day, your kids are going to grow up and go off on their own paths, and what are you going to be left with? A husband who's a stranger to you? You deserve better than that. Your partner should be the one who looks at you and thinks of you as their whole world. You deserve so much more than what you've been given."

There weren't any more words that could be said in the conversation, so Karina sat and sobbed until at some point she hung up the phone altogether. She sat in the corner of her bedroom for hours, replaying the words William said, repeatedly in her mind. She went back and forth from believing he was right to believing that she was crazy, and she couldn't figure out which one was the truth. Didn't she deserve better? Or maybe she should be happy with what she had. She had two children who loved her, and she had a husband trying to give those children a better life. That was more than what she got. She had two parents deeply in debt, and conned their way into living. But was her measurement of success just to be a little better than her own crappy upbringing? And William was right. One day her kids were going to leave, and then whatever she built between now and then was what she would be left with. Then she had another realization: Dan was seeing the world without her. He was living his dream while she stayed home alone. It wasn't him making the sacrifice, it was her. It was as if one phone conversation had unraveled years of abandonment she had suppressed every time she thought of it, and during all of that, one question stood at the forefront of her mind: What was she going to do now?

Chapter Two: Now

Loud music pulsed in her ears as she pressed up against the sticky bar counter. Work had been exhausting, per usual, and now all she wanted to do was to have a drink and try to forget about the rest of the world. And she thought she could do that. Maybe she could come to one bar and have one moment of not worrying about anything else. However, she already had one sleazy man use a cheesy pick-up line on her and now she either had the choice to continue to look away from the stare another man three barstools down gave her, or pick up her things and just go home. She almost chose the latter option until, out of the corner of her eye, she saw him. It was her boss.

Normally, people do not enjoy running into their employer after-hours, and Kayla was in that boat, but the problem was she didn't just see her boss, she saw something she was not supposed to see, and now she would not be able to erase it from her mind. But she decided to try to ignore it by talking to the guy a few barstools away. Her boss was on the other side of the bar, it was dark, the music was loud, he couldn't have possibly noticed her. But, just to be sure, she took her hair out of her bun, fluffed it up with her fingers, and scooted those couple seats down.

"You come here often?" he asked her. This was undoubtedly one of the worst opening lines she could think of, but Kayla rolled with it anyway out of her desperate desire to block out what she saw as much as possible.

"Yeah, I come here sometimes to get a drink and get my mind off work," she stated, unbeknownst to her suitor that the only thing on her mind at that moment was her work.

The two continued in casual conversation until the inevitable question came:

"Do you want to get out of here?"

Kayla hesitantly agreed, grabbed her bag, and walked out the door with a stranger wrapped around her arm, and she hated it. She hated every moment of it, not just because she knew it was a foolish choice, but because this guy was a terrible match. He could barely hold a conversation and had zero life aspirations. He seemed like every other guy who set foot into the city she had higher hopes for. But she went back to his place and woke up the next morning and still had her boss on her mind. There he was, the man who seemed so smart, confident, and even a little sexy, being just as stupid as every other guy in St. Louis, and she couldn't tell anybody about it. If she did, she would be fired at best, at worst, he could destroy her career. And so, she walked into her cold, empty apartment, sat at her desk, and started to write a letter to her sister.

She hated it had to be this way. She hated that their relationship had gotten to a place where the only way they could amicably communicate was through a few letters back and forth, but it was honestly a miracle it had gotten there in the first place.

A few years ago, they didn't know if they would speak to each other again. Even still, there was a large part of her that missed her sister, and wished she could take back some of the things she had said. She longed for when they were kids, and wished more than anything to live one more day like that. Unfortunately, life doesn't work that way. She felt like her and Bethany's relationship was crippled and hobbling along pretending like it was normal. But the only reason they were writing letters was because they knew they would not be able to have a phone conversation without screaming at each other and hanging up. That was the sad truth: both knew this, and neither of them acknowledged it. So, they continued to write letters and pretend like everything was okay when it was not, a decision too common among society for comfort.

But every word Kayla had to write on the beautiful stationary her sister had sent her on her birthday felt like a farce. It didn't look like that on paper, of course. If someone read her mail, they never would have guessed there were years of pain wrapped up in simple words.

She wrote until she decided it was time to change out of last night's clothes and start another day.

She couldn't eat that morning because of how anxious she was about going into work. She was terrified her boss was going to say something even though she swore he didn't see her last night. But still, there was a nagging voice that whispered doubt and made her question everything. Maybe when she went into work, he would confront her, or harass her, or fire her. He was a powerful man and could get away with all three easily without a word from the board. And so, she ironed her shirt as her hand shook, poured a cheap cup of coffee she would probably only take two sips of, got in her car, and went to work.

The work environment was tense, but that was because of how nervous she was. She was going to avoid Benjamin as much as possible, and while she didn't know if avoidance would make matters better or worse, she hoped if she didn't look at him, he wouldn't engage. Even when they had their team meeting and he asked her to present some of her latest ideas, she continued to avoid direct eye contact with him and picked out one of her nasally-congested coworkers to narrow in on. Luckily for her, the day went on and he didn't say anything. She hoped she was in the clear, but still that small, nagging voice inside her head told her she wasn't.

"I have two scoops of raspberry sorbet, two scoops of chocolate, and one scoop of birthday cake. Will there be anything else for you?" Bethany asked as she tugged at her itchy apron.

"No, that will be it. Thanks so much," the tired mother responded, and a young boy and girl whined for their ice cream. She spoke in hushed tones to them and then flashed a fake smile at Bethany.

She was used to it. People always tried to act like they had it more together than they did, which was natural for most of the population who feared the judgement of others. Bethany herself had been guilty of this many times, especially after becoming a mother. Her entire world changed when she realized everyone had something to say about how she raised her child.

After the sweet family left, Bethany flipped the *Open* sign on the door to *Closed*, and then began the process of shutting the shop down. It was a peaceful time that Bethany quite enjoyed: she played soft music she loved, swept the floors, cleaned all the equipment, emptied the trash cans, wiped down the counters, and then counted the tips for the day and put them into envelopes for her few employees. It was tedious work, but that was where Bethany thrived, especially if it meant a couple minutes of quiet time before coming home to the hustle and bustle of family life.

Of course, eight-year-old Bethany had no idea she would own the ice cream shop she frequented as a child. But that was exactly what she did. When she was twenty-two, after she graduated college with a degree in business, she decided, instead of going into a stale corporate office, she wanted to move into a more entrepreneurial field. Ironically enough, the owner of the ice cream shop was putting it up for sale at the same time she was looking for work, and for Bethany, it felt like a Godsend. By some miracle, because of her degree and because she knew everyone in town, including the owner, she was able to secure a loan at the bank and purchase the ice cream shop for herself.

But that was a while ago. Now she was a successful business owner and worked at the shop to keep her busy and involved with the business. She didn't want to be the type of owner who was hands-off; she wanted to be someone involved in the day-to-day operations while always keeping the big picture in view. She was able to find three sweet employees to have on her team, and she respected each of them greatly.

Nancy was a single mom who worked in the shop and often had her kids playing at the table outside or creating chalk masterpieces on the sidewalk. It was the only job she could find where she didn't have to find a babysitter for her three children after school, and it had become a lifesaver for her.

Maxwell was a college student studying mathematics at the local college and often worked the later shifts at the shop. Bethany adored him because he was shy, but loved kids.

Sirena worked at the ice cream shop on the weekends to make a few extra dollars. She was the most reserved out of the small team Bethany created, but she was a great problem solver.

While it appeared Bethany had thrown together a ragtag team of people to work at the shop, they all brought something special to her small business, and that was one of the reasons why she loved it so much. Plus, having only a few employees gave her the opportunity to work during some of the gap shifts, and take them out to dinner once a month to make them feel appreciated.

She had also done many things that grew the business to even greater heights. The shop was represented at all the town's festivals, and she was even offered the chance to serve ice cream at a movie festival in Boston. But, in terms of the day-to-day, it was mostly the locals who stopped by to get the ice cream. In the winter, to continue to generate a steady income, they served her husband's famous homemade hot chocolate.

For Bethany, this was the image of success, but Kayla had a very different view of what success looked like. She found success not by settling down but by seeing the world around her, although, as she soon realized, seeing the world cost more than pipe dreams. But at least she got out of Plymouth, which was more than Bethany could say. Neither of them wouldn't have it any other way, at least on that day.

Chapter Three: Then

"Alright fellas, this next round of drinks is on me!"
The whole beer hall seemed to cheer as Dan slammed down some marks on the counter.

"Dan, I think you are the only one keeping me in business, sir," said the barkeeper, Emerson.

"Well, if that's the case, I'm happy to do so, my friend. This is the only bar that gives me a cheap, good-quality beer and doesn't harass me for being an American."

Emerson laughed and continued to pour pilsners for the crowd when another man approached the counter.

"*Guten Abend,* Dan!"

"Jonas! *Wie geht's?*" Dan replied in German that still sounded a tad American.

"Ah, just some problems at home. The wife wants me to spend more time at home, but I don't think I'm ready to settle down like that yet. I don't know how you keep your woman, Dan."

"I'm not keeping anyone, Jonas. Karina and I decided a few years ago this was the best thing for us. I wouldn't be able to find work out there that pays me this much and lets me take off so much time to go back to the States. If I did what every other middle-aged suburban man did, I would be working a pointless nine-to-five job, and then by the time I would get home, I would feel too exhausted to spend quality time with my girls. Living this way gives me the chance to do something I love, and to go back home and devote all my attention to them," he explained and took another sip of beer.

Jonas signaled to Emerson and took a large gulp of *pils* before responding. "But what about your wife? Doesn't she have a problem with you being away most of the time? I mean, what kind of marriage is that?"

Dan's immediate response was going to be defensive, but instead, he reminded himself Jonas was a lot blunter than Dan personally agreed with, and let it slide. "Yeah, Karina and I have had our problems, but I know, at the end of the day, we have a solid foundation. She'd be honest and tell me if she couldn't handle this anymore."

Jonas rolled his eyes and took another gulp. "And she's never told you that, *freund?*"

"Sure, we've had a few discussions of me quitting this job and looking for another one in America, but we usually end up coming to the same conclusion: making this much money is going to give our girls their best chance, and so we have to make it work."

"Well, you have one understanding wife. I don't know any woman who would be content with having their husband gone most of the year and stay faithful. Surely no *frau* I know."

"Karina is something special. She is fiercely loyal, and I've never seen a mother work as hard as she does."

"Well, that's high praise for a woman you barely see," Jonas remarked and then sauntered off to a young woman a few tables over.

Dan rolled his eyes and slouched back in his seat. He knew his friends didn't understand or even agree with his marriage, but that was because most of them didn't have a problem flirting with whatever young thing came their way, married or not.

Dan worked with four other men from America who moved there for the special ops team. The rest of the people he worked with were locals. He loved the work he did, and felt like he was doing something valuable for German-American relations. Throughout history, America and Germany had a love-hate relationship, but it was programs like what Dan led that continued to strengthen relations between the two countries. However, some Germans did not view it that way. There were many Germans who were bitter about Dan and his team being there, so in order to fit in with the crowd, Dan often had to keep his mouth shut and let some of the behaviors he didn't agree with slide. But his heart went out for the women his coworkers were married to. They deserved more than men who weren't loyal to them.

Loyalty meant a great deal to Dan. He valued it because of his time in the military. Loyalty to his country, his commanding officer, and his fellow soldiers were what developed them into one solid unit. Having loyalty was sometimes the defining difference between life and death. That desire for loyalty poured into every other aspect of his life. He hoped to instill that same sense of loyalty in his girls too.

After having a few more drinks than he probably should have, Dan headed back to his measly *dachgeschoss* and found a letter from Karina. Often, he found these letters were her working through the emotions of him being gone, so he took a lot of what she said with a grain of salt. It was also difficult because the letters came at least a week after they were written, so sometimes what she said felt like old news by the time her words got to him. He debated about writing a reply, but decided he should probably sober up a bit before writing anything. Instead, he put on some music he rarely got to hear on that side of the world, and went to bed.

A week went by before Dan decided to respond to his wife. He had gotten so wrapped up in a project he and his team were working on that he had forgotten she even wrote him in the first place. This made him feel a pang of guilt when he saw her letter on his desk a week later, and he still hadn't responded. So, at that moment, he sat down with a pen and paper and began to scribble a response.

> *Dear Karina,*
>
> *I miss you too, dear. The team and I are knee-deep into a project, but I don't want to bore you with the details. Let's just say I am really excited about the progress we have made and how hard my team members are working. Once we tie up some loose ends with this part of the project, I should be able to slip away for a couple weeks and be there for Kayla's birthday. But don't tell her just in*

case it doesn't work out. I don't want her to be disappointed. Maybe we'll just call it a happy surprise.

Sorry the weather has been rainy there. It has been decent here, although I don't spend a ton of time outside. I often find myself either at the office or at the local beer hall. I have bonded a bit with the barkeeper, Emerson. I went over to his family's house for dinner the other night. He has three girls. Can you imagine having another little one brought into the mix? B and K cause enough trouble on their own (but you know that better than I do). His youngest daughter, Elsa, reminds me a lot of Kayla. She has that same adventurous spirit our girl has. Being around them makes me miss our girls even more. I can't wait to come home and wrap you all up in lots of hugs and kisses. But, until then, I hope this letter finds you well.

I love you.
Dan

And with that, he folded up the letter, carefully put a stamp in the corner, and headed out for another day at work.

From: william2scoops@hotmail.com
To: karina.fitzpatrick@psd.org
Subject: Hey

I want to see you.

From: karina.fitzpatrick@psd.org
To: william2scoops@hotmail.com
Re: Hey

I'm working today. I could get away during lunch, but that's all I can do.

From: william2scoops@hotmail.com
To: karina.fitzpatrick@psd.org
Re: Hey

Meet at Al's parking lot at noon.

Karina's hand shook as she stared at the email on her computer. Her heart and soul were overwhelmed with grief. She and William had started talking more since Karina broke down over the phone a couple weeks ago. Even still, she knew what she was doing was wrong. She was getting too involved with another man while she was still married to Dan. But even though she knew this, William provided her with comfort Dan couldn't, and it wasn't because Dan was overseas. Even when he was at home, Dan wasn't there for her, he was there for their girls. Ever since she started talking with William, some of the resentment she felt towards her girls started to fade, because she finally had someone putting her needs first. It was that reason that led Karina to pull next to a blue Subaru Outback in a hardware store parking lot on the edge of town.

William got out of his car and slid into the passenger seat of her white van. For a few minutes, they didn't say anything, they just stared ahead at the hardware store in front of them. It was William who decided to break the silence.

"I just really wanted to see you."

Karina took a deep breath and nodded. "I wanted to see you too. That's why I'm here. I just don't know why I want to see you."

"Yes, you do," William said matter-of-factly. "Karina, I think there is something here you have never had with your husband."

She shook her head. "William, I don't even know if that's true. I don't know if I could have that with my husband because he is never here! I'm not around my husband enough to build that kind of connection, and I don't know if I ever will be, but shouldn't I at least give him a chance?"

"Karina, he has chosen money and security instead of you time and time again. When are you going to let someone choose you first?" he pressed her, grabbing her hand tightly.

It was then that she grabbed his collar and kissed him. It took only a few seconds until she was filled with a guilt that seemed to darken the world around her. "This is wrong. This is wrong," she repeated as she tried to deny what had just happened.

"No, what your husband is doing is wrong. You're just trying to get your life back," he argued.

Images of her husband flooded Karina's mind as she continued to shake her head. She thought back to the moment they got married, when she looked him in the eye and promised she would be faithful. She thought about his smile, his laugh, the way they would chase each other around the house and get into laughing fits that seemed to last forever. All of these memories were in her head only for a moment, but they were enough to remind her that her husband was not just who she had made him out to be in her head, he was a real person, and even if she didn't feel happy with him anymore, she had to tell him.

"No. You're wrong. It's not fair to him. He needs to know. If I end things with him, then maybe I could find some ounce of happiness with you, but I can't do that until I tell him the truth."

William grabbed her hand and squeezed it. "I'm here for you, Karina. Whatever you need to do, I'm going to respect that. But I'm not going to sit here and deny the feelings I have for you and how badly I want to kiss you again. I'm not going to sit here and pretend the moment I get in my car I won't replay what has happened and try to work out ways in which I could have done things differently. I'm not going to sit here and not say this is the realist thing I have ever felt in my life even though I know it is wrong in some way..." his voice drifted off and he took in more air. "Karina, I care about you more than I've cared about anybody in my whole life, and I hope you'll let me show you what that kind of care looks like."

Karina silently nodded and gripped her hands on the steering wheel, which was William's signal to leave. Even after he pulled out of the parking lot and she was left in her own silent despair, she still didn't turn the car on. She couldn't, because turning the car on meant she had to continue with reality as if nothing had happened. She would have to go back to work and pretend like she did not just kiss a man who wasn't her husband. She would have to pick up her girls from their class in a few hours and pretend like their lives were not going to completely change. It was in those few minutes that she sat in the car and pretended like none of it was real before she would have to embark on a whole new path of reality. Karina knew more than anything that, one way or another, what had occurred in that car was going to change the entire course of her life.

Chapter Four: Now

"Has he eaten much today?" Bethany asked with her notebook ready.

"You don't need to keep notes, dear. I keep track of all his eating, sleeping, and behavioral habits. One of the reasons you hired me is so you wouldn't have to carry this part of the burden. Let me keep track of that stuff for you, okay?"

Bethany nodded and tucked the notebook back into her handbag. She glanced over at her dad in the other room. Every time she visited him it was obvious she was never really going to be with her dad again. Sure, it was his body, and when she held his hand, it was the same hand that let her go when she learned to ride a bicycle or when she got scared of the monsters in the closet, but when she looked into his eyes, he wasn't all there. There were very few people who had the experience of looking into a loved one's eyes and not seeing them there. But if they had, they would know that one look had the ability to rip their heart right out of their chest. It only took one glance to change someone she used to be so familiar and comfortable with into a stranger looking back at her. All she had left was this empty vessel of someone she loved so dearly, and no way to bring him back. Perhaps what was even worse was what happened after that first glance. Every day after she tried to remember as much about him as possible, because every day that she looked into those unfamiliar eyes, she feared she was going to forget what his real eyes looked like.

That is what Bethany feared most when she visited her father. She feared the more memories she made with someone who looked like her father, but wasn't quite him, the harder it would be to remember the man she loved and looked up to her whole life. And yet, she visited him anyway, because the last thing she wanted was for him to be alone, even if he didn't remember who she was, and he didn't most of the time. Occasionally, he was able to piece together memories, and sometimes he knew it was Bethany, but other times he thought it was her mom, and sometimes he didn't even know who he was. That was what happened with diseases of the mind. They slowly ripped away who a person was and left them with someone so utterly confused and scared about why they were there.

Bethany didn't wish for Kayla to experience this. She wouldn't have wished her worst enemy to experience something like this, but she thought it was necessary. She didn't think it was fair she had to shoulder this heavy burden alone. Just because she was the one who stayed in Plymouth did not mean she was the natural caregiver of their parents. Kayla should have stepped up. She should have been there, and she never felt that more than when her dad would ask where Kayla was, or would think Bethany was Kayla. It was in those moments she felt her blood boil at the injustice of telling her dying father his other daughter wasn't there, and couldn't give him an explanation as to why.

But Kayla didn't understand any of that. Kayla was living in her own world with her own problems that she was blind to the fact she was so close to losing her father. Or maybe she did know, and she just didn't want to deal with the trials Bethany faced daily. She didn't imagine her sister to be so selfish, but in the last few years, she hadn't imagined her sister to be a lot of things.

Today, all he could talk about was his wife. He was so enraptured with how beautiful she was. He mumbled stories about how sometimes they would stand in the kitchen and dance to no music, and how they would write letters back and forth when he was overseas. He talked about the first moment he saw her, and that he immediately knew he loved her and wanted to marry her. The one good thing about someone losing their mind was sometimes all they could remember was the good stuff. That was the state he was in that day, because all he wanted to talk about were the happy moments he and Karina shared. Bethany relished in those moments, and even in those times she wished

Kayla was there too. If only she could hear how their father talked about their mother. If only she could have these last experiences of hearing little details about their love story…

But alas, it was Bethany sitting alone in her dad's favorite rocking chair and listening to him ramble on and on, and sometimes mumble to the point of incomprehension. In those times, she would just nod and smile and he would continue talking, because at least at that moment he was happy.

She spent a couple hours with him before deciding it was time for her to go back home to her own family. This was one of the days he struggled with her leaving. He begged and cried for her not to go because he didn't want to be left alone. Still, she had to summon up all her strength to plaster on a smile and promise she was going to be back soon. Even though she knew that he was probably going to forget her leaving anyway, she still sat in the driveway and sobbed. It killed her to have to leave him every time. She couldn't imagine being in his shoes, constantly forgetting who you were and then remembering again, and amid that roller coaster, feeling alone or being around nurses who were strangers to you.

When Bethany got home, her husband greeted her with a smile and hugged her immediately. Like her, Huxley had an acute awareness of knowing when something was wrong with someone, especially his wife.

"Do you want to talk about it?" he asked and wrapped his arm around her.

"It was just another one of those days when he didn't want me to leave," she said with a sadness that carried further than her words.

Huxley promised the next time she went to visit her dad, he and their son, Henry, would tag along too.

Henry didn't remember much of his grandfather before he was diagnosed, which was another heartbreaking thing for Bethany. She knew her dad would have made the best grandfather and he never even got the chance. The only grandparents Henry knew were Huxley's parents, but they lived across the country, so they only saw each other once or twice a year. Bethany couldn't help but feel like Henry was being deprived of something even she felt deprived of for part of her childhood. She never imagined Henry might be left with the same Dan-sized hole in his heart that sometimes crept up in her own. But now, that was inevitable.

"Kayla, can I see you in my office for a minute?"

Instantly, Kayla's heart rate spiked. It had been a week since she saw her boss at the bar, and she thought she was in the clear, but he rarely ever asked anyone to come into his office (often it was the team asking to speak to him), so this put her immediately on edge. But she happily agreed and cautiously closed the door behind her as she walked into his office.

Benjamin Weedle's office was not one to be shown off in the magazines. All that hung on the walls were his degrees, one picture of him and his wife, and a cheap landscape painting that looked like it was picked up at a thrift store.

"Go ahead and take a seat," he said and gestured to the empty chair that sat across his desk.

"What's this about?" Kayla asked casually.

"Well, as you know, you are a valued member of this team, and I just wanted to check in and see if there was anything you wanted to talk about."

Kayla hesitated. Had he seen her at the bar? Was this his way of giving her a chance to confess what she had seen? Or was this his way of determining if she had noticed him at all? Or maybe this had nothing to do with the bar and he was just genuinely checking on his employees. But since Kayla did not know which one it was, she had no idea how to respond. "Is there something specific you are looking for here?" she casually questioned with a modest smile.

"I'm not looking for anything specific. I'm just checking in with the team members and seeing ways we can continue to foster a work environment that encourages honesty, humility, and team participation," he paused. "How do you feel about me and my wife as employers?"

This question made Kayla even more guarded. "Well, since the day I started working at CodeX, I've been incredibly grateful for the opportunities I've gotten. I loved working on the Handy Heart app, and I'm excited for some of the things we have in the works now," she responded, and this was all true. Kayla had started working for CodeX six months ago, and even though she was not qualified to be working at a medium-sized tech company, they hired her anyway and she believed she had proven herself a lot through her work on the Handy Heart app. The app was designed to check people's heart rates and oxygen levels with an aux cord plugin on someone's phone. It was Kayla who created the momentum the app needed, through her idea to send the data it collects directly to the person's doctor. But CodeX was a cutthroat company. They were constantly competing with their competitor BlockWorks for the latest coding, technological developments, and new apps and ideas that came down both pikes.

"As for you both as employers, I couldn't be happier." She laughed timidly.

"Uh-huh," Benjamin replied, clearly unimpressed with Kayla's answer. He put his hand to his face and seemed to ponder his response. "Are there any ways you think we can improve the company? Or stand out among competitors?"

"Well," Kayla began and nervously tapped her finger on her thigh, "I think the way we can really sell people is to be one step ahead of the game. Block-Works is working towards the same goal we are, and the only way we beat them is by being ahead of them. As for our clients, I think the work we produce is the best way to convince them we are the right company to go with."

"Those are all good thoughts. Is there anything else you want to add?"

Kayla racked her brain for what she could say in response. What was he looking for? She didn't know the safest way to play it, and so she just continued to play dumb. "No, I think we've covered it. Unless you need anything more from me, I should probably get back to work."

"Yes, go ahead," he said and gestured toward his door.

As Kayla walked out the door, the knot in her stomach was almost unbearable. Perhaps to a stranger, the conversation would have seemed to go smoothly, but Kayla knew Benjamin. He was smart, and she couldn't shake the feeling that the only reason she was called in there was for him to try to collect information. If he knew she saw something, it made sense he didn't say anything about it. He wanted *her* to confess to it so he could trap her and have the control. That was the dirty game Benjamin played. She had watched him play it with other employees.

Two months ago, there was an employee who had worked at CodeX for years, but it was clear Benjamin wanted him gone. No one really knew why, but Benjamin shifted in the way he started talking to him, and never gave him any assignments. He even went so far as to accuse him of selling confidential information. Once he planted that seed in the team's mind, no one wanted to work with him, and he eventually ended up quitting because he knew Benjamin had placed him on his own sinking ship. Kayla was terrified Benjamin was gearing up to do the exact same thing to her.

When Kayla went home that night, she was tempted to write to her sister again. She wanted to explain her fears to Bethany and remind her how important this job was to her. Even though she had only been there for six months, it was the only thing Kayla had, and she would be lost if she was fired. But she knew in her heart she couldn't go to her sister about this, because she already knew what Bethany's answers would be. "Come home. Build a life here. Stop running away from all of your problems." She had told her that so many times Kayla had lost track. If only Bethany knew that matters were so much more complicated than she understood.

Kayla carefully curled the last piece of her hair and zipped up her favorite pair of ruby red heeled boots. This was her second date with Peter, and she had these nervous butterflies in her stomach she had never experienced before with someone, and it was only the second date. There was something mysterious about him that left her dying for more. This was terrifying for Kayla, because she normally did not allow herself to want for anything, especially a person. She didn't like relying on people like that. She had learned that lesson the hard way.

They met up at a classy Italian restaurant in the heart of downtown. His smile grew wider when he saw her. He opened the door for her in the restaurant and pulled her chair out to sit in. She had never encountered someone with such chivalry. They made light conversation at first, but then there was a moment Peter looked at her with such intensity they both paused.

"What is it about you that draws me to you more than I have ever been drawn to any other woman?"

Kayla felt her face grow tomato red. "I don't know if I have an answer for you. I mean, my whole life I have been trying to explore and break away from small towns and small minds. Maybe all my wanderlust spirit has rubbed off on you." In her head, the words sounded a lot better than how they seemed to clumsily stumble out of her mouth. Even still, Peter didn't seem to notice.

"It's something more than that. Something deeper. You have an overcoming spirit. You don't back down from things," he told her. The only other person who had said things like that to her was her father. But this was different. This was someone she barely knew but felt like she had known forever. And here he was saying things about her she didn't even believe herself.

"Well, if it counts for anything, I think you are pretty great too," Kayla told him, and he gave a coy smile and then they flowed right back into the casual conversation they were having earlier. It was strange. She didn't know a lot about Peter or his history, but when they talked, they felt like old friends, and she hadn't really felt that with anybody before.

It was a couple months later that Kayla learned the truth about Peter. She had only been to his house one time, and he always opted to go to her apartment instead. A few of her friends remarked that maybe he was hiding something, but she couldn't bring herself to believe that. However, her friends' voices were a little too loud, and she decided to show up at his house unannounced one day. When she knocked on the door, she got a face she was not expecting. It was a woman, just around Kayla's age, with beautiful auburn hair, a soft face, and emerald eyes. She was a vision, and she was also his wife.

When Kayla stood on that doorstep, it did not take long for her to realize the truth and watch her entire little world she had made with this man come completely unhinged. She had to play it off and pretend like she was one of Peter's coworkers and was picking something up from him. She gave his wife a fake name and went on her way. She drove about a quarter-mile before she pulled over on the side of the road and started crying. Sure, she had only known him for a couple months, but they were talking every day. They saw each other at least a few times a week. She felt like she was really starting to have feelings for him, and even got a glimmer of hope she could have a future with him.

Immediately, she wanted to call him, yell at him, ask him how he could screw her over like this. But she didn't. She waited for him to reach out, and sure enough that night he texted her casually with no idea she had learned the truth. She decided to meet up with him because she wanted closure. But probably more than that, she wanted answers.

That night she sat on the bench of their favorite park. He came up behind her and touched her shoulder, and greeted her with a warm smile, but she immediately tensed up. He could instantly tell that something was wrong.

31

"What happened?" he asked casually.

"I know Peter."

"Know what?"

"I know about her."

Peter let out a deep sigh and tried to reach for her hand, but she pulled away. "I'm not happy with her, Kayla. I'm going to leave her."

She rolled her eyes. It was at this moment she was filled with so much anger that she had become one of those women. She never thought she would be one of those girls hearing a guy she cared about give a crap explanation as to why he was married. And yet here she was, scraping together some response for him.

"So all those things you said to me...did you just not know how to be with your wife? You can't stay with one woman? Am I just a pawn to fill some void in your life?"

"It's not like that at all."

She started to get up but Peter grabbed her hand. "Wait, Kayla, please. Let me explain."

"What is there to explain, Peter?" she yelled. There was no one in the park since it was so late, but she still felt self-conscious about drawing more attention to herself than she wanted. But soon her anger overtook her, and she found herself filling the park with her angry shouts. "You're married! You pursued me when you were married! There's no coming back from that."

"Kayla, I'm not happy in that marriage. Please just sit down and let me explain," he pleaded and gestured for her to sit back down on the bench.

She probably shouldn't have allowed him to speak at all, but she couldn't deny she had real feelings for Peter. And so, she stood with arms crossed, hesitantly waiting for his so-called explanation.

"Laurie and I met in high school. She was my first love, and then we got married a year after we graduated. We were young, and we didn't know what we were doing with our lives. All we knew was that we loved each other. But after we got into the real world, our lives changed a lot. We realized we wanted different things in life. I want to settle down, and she isn't there yet, and I don't know if she ever will be. She doesn't even know if she wants kids, and I do.

"I'm going to leave her, Kayla, and even before I met you, I knew that. I never expected to have feelings for someone else while I was still married, but from the moment I saw you, I felt something in my soul come alive. It was like nothing I had ever felt before, even with Laurie. She is a good person, but she deserves someone fully on her

team, and I'm not that person anymore. We've talked about getting a divorce for a couple months, we just haven't gotten the papers. But we both agree it is the best decision."

At this, Kayla rolled her eyes. She couldn't stand listening to her married ex-boyfriend's speech any longer, but something in her kept quiet. Maybe it was because she didn't know what to say, or that she was tired of yelling, or maybe the smallest part of her hoped he would say something that would make what he did okay enough for her to stay with him.

And so, he continued. "I know what I did was wrong and that I betrayed the trust we were starting to build. It's just, when I first met you and started talking with you, I didn't want to be living the life I had chosen. I wanted to be a single man who could pursue you fully and fall in love with you without all the baggage I knew I would be dragging behind. So that's what I let myself be. But it was so wrong and I am so sorry," he said as tears welled up in his eyes.

Kayla sat down on the bench beside him. She wanted to cry over how heartbreaking the situation was, but she held her composure. She didn't want to feel the heartbreak because it just confirmed the deep feelings she had for him. So, instead, she masked her heartbreak with more anger, because that was the only thing she was comfortable with feeling at that moment.

"Peter, I wish I could tell you your story brings me some sort of comfort or understanding, but it doesn't. At the end of the day, you still pursued someone while you were married, and if on the slight off chance we were going to end up together, how could I ever trust you wouldn't do the same thing to me? Because I can bet Laurie has no idea I even exist!"

When Peter looked down, Kayla's suspicion was only confirmed. "You know that I have not had a lot of serious relationships in my life, but I took this relationship with you very seriously. This wasn't me playing in a pretend life. These were my real feelings, my real heart on the line... You've made it very clear you would have rather lived in a fantasy than be with me in real life, and we can't come back from that."

When Kayla got home that night, the first thing she wanted to do was to call somebody, but she didn't even know who. And besides, she felt too ashamed to tell anyone.

Even a year later, when she sat in her apartment holding a keychain he had gotten her on their first date, nobody really knew. The truth she told people wasn't quite the whole truth. All that Bethany knew was that she walked away from someone who was ready to settle down and commit to her, but no one knew he had committed to his wife first. But that was a shame she was not ready to bear to anyone else.

Chapter Five: Then

Karina tapped her foot anxiously as she swung around to the pantry to grab flour from the top shelf. It was Kayla's birthday, and Dan was still not there. In fact, she wasn't sure if he was coming at all. His last letter indicated he would try to get there for her birthday, but she hadn't heard anything since then. She thought maybe an email would have been nice, but Dan didn't really operate at her consideration. If he was going to come, he was going to make it a grand surprise for his daughters. Which, for them, was sweet and magical, but, for her, it was just stressful.

She was busy in the kitchen early in the morning making a birthday cake so when they all came home from school, they would be ready to celebrate her. Kayla wanted some big, extravagant party with all her friends, but Karina was able to compromise with a few friends coming over after school. She put the cake in the oven, and then continued with her own morning routine before the girls woke up. She made herself a cup of chamomile tea and went out on the back porch to watch the sunrise. It was a routine she was fond of that had started when she realized she didn't sleep as well without Dan there. She thought it was ironic that even though she spent most of the year without Dan there, she still couldn't seem to adjust to sleeping in a bed by herself. It was a stability thing for Karina. Her entire childhood was filled with instability, and Dan felt stable. Even during the military leave, and even when he went to

Germany, she still felt a sense of stability when he was home. Of course, that stability had faded over the past couple years. She had grown accustomed to a life without him in it, at least on a day-to-day level.

She hadn't spoken to William since the day in the parking lot. There were so many times she was tempted to reach out because she knew he would listen, but she didn't, knowing it wasn't fair to Dan. Even though she was angry at Dan, she was angrier at herself. He deserved to know what happened.

That was the reason she was so nervous. If he showed up today, she would have to face her new reality. She already felt guilty enough for lying to the girls and pretending everything was okay with her and their father, but it was going to be even more difficult to tell him the truth. She knew he deserved better. Despite the hell they had been through, she still knew kissing William was not the answer. She had prayed so many times for God to give her guidance on what to do next, but didn't find any direction. She didn't think that was because God wasn't there, but merely she didn't have the ear to listen.

The girls woke up an hour later and Kayla was filled with the kind of energy every young kid has on their birthday. All she wanted to do was get school over with so she could come home, eat cake, and play with her friends. She raced to eat breakfast and was at the door a half an hour before they needed to leave. The kind of energy Kayla brought on this particular day was unmatched by anything Bethany felt, even on her birthday. But that was in line with Kayla's energetic spirit.

Karina's heart still raced, even as the girls buckled in, and they were on their way to the school. Maybe Dan would surprise them there. She wouldn't put it past Dan to do some grand gesture like that. But when they got to the school and no one was there, she took a deep breath of relief. He wasn't coming today, or at least, not at her place of work. So, the day dragged on like any other day, that is, until three other kids were huddled with Kayla and ready to get into Karina's minivan after school. Karina had already talked to all the parents who were all planning to pick up their kids in a couple hours from Karina's house, but until then, five kids were her responsibility and she was not prepared one bit.

When Karina pulled into the driveway, she knew he was there. She couldn't see him, but felt Dan's presence, and when they walked through the front door, sure enough, there was Dan with a fluffy stuffed horse and a big 'Happy Birthday' banner. Again, those big gestures fit Dan to a tee. Kayla squealed and screamed with joy, because who wouldn't want their dad surprising them on their birthday?

Dan wrapped up both of his girls with big open arms and then faced Karina. She plastered on a fake smile and Dan wrapped her in an embrace. "I've missed you, baby," he whispered in her ear.

"I've missed you too," she responded, and she did, but not in the same way anymore.

After all the kids went home and Bethany and Kayla were sound asleep, Karina took a deep breath. From the moment she saw his face, the guilt she was already consumed with seemed to dance around her. She couldn't hide from it and couldn't pretend it away anymore. Now was the first chance she had to get the ghost that haunted her out in the open. But before she had a chance to speak, Dan spoke up first.

"You feel a little off," Dan said casually as he took off his shirt to get ready for bed. While he sensed his wife was upset, he never could have foreseen the bomb she was about to drop on him.

"There's something I need to tell you," Karina said in a voice only a little louder than a whisper.

Dan looked up at her inquisitively and dropped the bed sheet in his hand.

"I kissed someone else," she stated plainly, but then quickly continued. "I am so sorry for doing this to you, but I am not happy anymore, Dan, and I want a shot at happiness."

Dan took a few steps back in shock. "You're...you're having an affair?" he asked, with more emotion than Karina had heard in a long time.

"No, it's not like that. It was only one kiss, and I haven't talked to him since then, because I wanted to talk to you first." Karina's mind was racing and she hated how her words sounded. Even though she denied it then, she would later realize she did indeed have an affair. Maybe not a physical one, but she was emotionally reliant on William, and that was just as terrible.

"When?" he asked harshly.

"It was a couple weeks ago."

"And you didn't think to reach out to me? You didn't think to let me know of this development as I took off time and planned a trip to come see you?" Karina huffed. Her guilt quickly shifted to anger, or defensiveness, or perhaps a mix of both. "You didn't come here for me! You came here to see *them*! It's never been about me, Dan. Once you took that job in Germany, you threw our marriage in the trash. No one can have a healthy marriage when their husband chooses money over being with their family."

Dan was floored at what his wife just said. After all the conversations they had about Germany, they always went back to their daughters and the life they could give them with a job like that. He had no idea that everything had changed for her. The reason for moving to Germany, the job, everything. "It was never about the money. It was about us giving our kids a better future than we got," he stammered. His hand started to shake and his breathing quickly became labored. Suddenly, his head felt lighter and he grabbed the dresser to stabilize himself. Karina didn't take notice. She was still busy trying to justify her choices, but to herself or to him, even she wasn't sure of that answer.

"Well, Dan, I still have a chance to have a happy future, and I think the girls could too, money or not. They could still get scholarships, and they could still be happy. Bethany doesn't even want to leave Plymouth right now, and I'm not going to force her. And, sure, Kayla wants to go out and explore the world, but we can't fund that. She's going to have to learn how to make it on her own in some ways too."

Dan was shaking his head in disbelief over everything she was saying. There were a million questions crammed into every part of his mind but he couldn't even ask one. He didn't even know what to say or how to react. He had spent years staying faithful to Karina and judged men who continually cheated on their partners, and he never would have imagined Karina would have done something like this to him. It was a kind of disbelief that left a person instantly numb. That was what he felt.

He started to ask a question, but then he stopped himself, because nothing felt sufficient. Instead of all the questions and pain he wanted to scream at her, the only thing that came out was a quiet whisper. "So, what now?"

Karina had thought about the answer to that question ever since she had started talking to William. Once she realized she wasn't in love with Dan like she used to be, she knew something would need to change, she just didn't know quite what that meant.

"I just want a chance at a happy ending, and I know that might sound cheesy or naïve, and maybe it is, but I know I have spent my entire life giving to other people and allowing everyone else to choose other things before me. More than me needing someone else to put me first, *I* need to put me first. So, I want to get a divorce."

The harsh word rang in Dan's ear.

Divorce.

Divorce.

Divorce.

He couldn't make it stop.

He brought out sheets to sleep on the floor of their bedroom for that night. He didn't want to alarm the girls if they woke up in the middle of the night to find him on the couch, and it was clear Karina had no interest in sleeping in the same bed with him anymore.

If Dan had known his life was going to be flipped upside down, maybe he would have done things differently. Maybe he would have written to Karina more, or he wouldn't have taken the job in Germany. But the problem was that he never even saw this coming. There was never even a shadow of doubt in his mind he was going to spend the rest of his life with Karina. The thought of that not happening left him shell-shocked. He lay in bed that entire night and replayed the conversation repeatedly in his head.

When he woke up the next morning, Karina was at the edge of their bed braiding her hair.

"I just...I thought I was your happy ending," was the only thing he could bring himself to say to her.

There was no reply. She had nothing left to say.

"We finalized everything last week," Karina told him, and William observed her guarded stance. It had been a grueling four months for Karina. Even though Dan didn't fight the legal yellow tape, it still took a long time to get everything finished. She never imagined there could be so many rules and guidelines needed with the girls, and yet there were, and she was exhausted.

"I'm not expecting anything from you. You know that, right?" he told her and she relaxed her shoulders a little bit.

"I just don't know what I feel right now, but I didn't want to leave you hanging because I do have feelings for you. It's all just really unknown territory for me."

"How have the girls been taking it?"

That was a question Karina was not fully equipped to answer because, if she was being honest with herself, she was in denial about on how the girls were doing, which, in a few words, was not good. The divorce hit Kayla a lot harder than it hit Bethany.

For Bethany, while she loved her dad, nothing felt any different. Her dad wasn't living with them that often anyway, and so the only difference was when he did visit, he wouldn't be sleeping there.

For Kayla, she felt like her whole world was being ripped at the seams. She had this vision of her dad moving back home and their family living happily together and going on adventures as a family. Now, all those years of fantasies had completely vanished, and she never even saw it coming. As far as she had known, her parents seemed happy, and then suddenly they weren't. Kayla was so consumed with fear that she would be judged by her friends and classmates, and anger because Bethany wasn't more upset about it. She felt like there was something she was missing. None of it made sense, and all she knew was that her little heart was breaking and there was nothing she could do about it.

But Karina brushed a lot of it off. Not because she didn't care about her girls, but she couldn't carry the weight of her children's pain, at least not at that point. Every morning she woke up, she felt so terrible for how blindsided Dan was by everything that had happened. Part of her had assumed he was unhappy too, but he was devastated and shocked. He kept asking her questions to understand where he went wrong, and she didn't have many answers to them. All she knew was there came a point where she wasn't happy living apart from him, and maybe she didn't convey those feelings enough, or maybe he didn't want to come back enough, but there was a disconnect that couldn't be repaired.

Karina had grown up believing marriage was something sacred. Her parents told her the only reason for divorce was adultery, but she never imagined she would be the one committing it. In her heart of hearts, she believed it wasn't God making her feel so terrible, but her own consuming guilt that constantly weighed her down.

She had asked Dan for his forgiveness and she had repented and felt the weight of the decisions and actions she made. In all reality, there was nothing more she could do. She made a mistake and, of course, after she made it, all the "what ifs" filled her mind. What if she had told Dan earlier how she was feeling? What if she had given him the ultimatum: he needed to come home or he would lose her? What if she had told him never to take the job in Germany in the first place? What if she had given their marriage a fighting chance even after she kissed William?

However, the "what ifs" weren't doing her any good, because the "what is" had already taken place. And yet, even amid so much pain, she had a glimmer of hope that maybe she could have happiness after that. She didn't know if William was part of that picture, but she believed breaking away from a marriage she was deeply unhappy in gave her the opportunity for something better. And so, in the middle of constantly grappling with the guilt, the pain, and the searing grief she felt, Karina tried to hold onto that hope.

Chapter Six: Now

Huxley buckled Henry into his car seat and grabbed Bethany's hand when he slid into the driver's seat. "We're here for you. You don't always have to carry this alone, Beth. That's why you have a family here."

She twiddled with the loose string on her handbag. "I know, I just feel guilty," she said and glanced back at Henry, who was flipping through a book he barely knew how to read, and then spoke in a hushed tone. "I know Henry doesn't understand a lot about what's going on, and I feel bad for dragging him along to sit in a stranger's house. And I hate that he sees me so emotional too, but I can't seem to help it. Every time I see my dad, it hurts."

Huxley nodded. "And that's okay. It's not a bad thing for Henry to see his parents get emotional, and when he is older, he'll understand why. I think he might even thank you for letting him get to know his grandfather, even if it isn't how you want it to be."

She silently agreed and they continued to drive to his house. There had been a lot of vacillation for Bethany about whether to put her dad in a nursing home or hire a couple live-in nurses. While it was a bit more expensive, she opted to hire the nurses so he could stay in his own home. They took good care of him. She remembered the hours she spent vetting the men and women she would hire to be with her father during his final days. She and Huxley went through at least fifty candidates and none of them felt good enough. At the time, none of them were because, at that point, her father seemed well enough to be on his own.

Before the live-in nurses, it was Bethany coming over every day to ensure he was doing little things like taking his medication, checking the mail, or turning off the stove. At that point, he was functional and she felt closer to him than she did as a child. She was grateful for that time, and even though she now struggled to be the only child carrying the weight of losing her father, she would have rather been the one doing it than the one missing out. Bethany believed Kayla was going to regret the decisions she was making now. She had to. But Bethany's problem with Kayla was that she was selfish. She was always more interested in making her own dreams come true, no matter who had to sacrifice in the process.

But none of that mattered now. All that mattered was her getting out of the car, grabbing her son, and feeling her husband's arm wrapped around her as they walked up to the familiar door.

A friendly face answered, "Hi, Bethany. He's not doing so great today," Gianna, Bethany's favorite nurse, told her.

Bethany looked down at her shoes. Every time they came, she hoped he was having a good day, even though she knew there were going to be some bad days. This day was a particularly bad one. For the first few hours, Huxley stayed in the kitchen with Henry and played the games they had brought along while Bethany sat in the living room and tried to soothe her father after he had thrown a plate of food across the room.

"It's okay, Dad. It's Bethany. I'm right here. It's all going to be okay." She repeated the soothing words that were both for herself and for him, but she knew they were falling on deaf ears. Today it seemed Dan was too lost in his own mind and couldn't find his way back to reality. He was angry because he was confused, and it broke Bethany's heart to see him in such a state.

They ended up spending most of their Saturday with Bethany on the couch reading while her father stared blankly at a wall. She sent Huxley and Henry home after two hours; she didn't want them wasting their Saturday indoors. Huxley hesitantly agreed out of respect for his wife.

Huxley had been so good to Bethany during this time. She knew being the sole caregiver for her father was not what he signed up for, and yet he carried it with such grace beyond Bethany's own understanding. He was always gentle and patient with Bethany's mood swings, and even her father's. He was by her side and gave his own input while she grappled with whether her father should be put in a caregiver facility. Huxley stood by her when they had to sacrifice family vacations and constantly adjust the budget in order to pay for her father's care. Again, not what he signed up for, and yet he never complained. But that was the spirit he had their entire relationship. He was built on a foundation of self-sacrificial love beyond any person Bethany had encountered.

When Bethany met Huxley, it was on a ski resort in Colorado. It was rare that Bethany left Plymouth, but on a whim, she decided to go with a few friends for a winter break trip they saved up for a few months to go on. He was visiting from California because all he wanted to do was see snow during Christmastime. She didn't fall for him initially, and they didn't even share any romantic moments during the trip itself. They spent a lot of it joking around and learning about each other during the evenings. When the trip ended, they exchanged contact information and planned to keep in touch over the phone. But slowly, as each of them got back to their normal routines, they ended up talking to each other a lot more than they anticipated. Eventually, he flew across the country to tell her he loved her. It was that grand gesture that reminded her so much of her father that made her love for him grow even stronger. So, after about six months of long-distance dating, he moved to Plymouth, and they moved in together. Shortly after, they got engaged, got married, and the rest was history.

She didn't know a marriage could be so good. She always feared her marriage would be full of turmoil and arguing and heartache, and while they did have their fair share of arguing, most of the time they were grounded in their love for each other. It helped that they were similar in many ways, so they understood each other deeply.

Even on their worst days, like when Huxley and Henry picked up Bethany from spending the long day at her father's and Henry told her what a good mommy she was, Bethany was reminded of her two greatest blessings.

45

"Can I get a large hot chocolate with extra whipped cream and a sprinkle of cinnamon?" Bethany asked as she fished for change out of her heavy coat pocket.

"Absolutely! I'll have that right out for you," the cashier replied and turned around to prepare her cocoa.

Someone stood behind Bethany, and his ears perked up listening to her order. He cleared his throat to get her attention.

Confused, Bethany turned around.

"I met you, right? On the slopes?"

She thought for a moment and tried to picture his face with big ski goggles on, and when she could, their conversation dawned on her. "Oh, that's right. How was skiing?" she asked as she grabbed her drink.

"It was fun! I've learned I am a terrible skier which makes sense because I don't have a lot of experience around snow. The bruises on my body may say differently, but I had a good time," he timidly told her as they made their way towards a couch by the fire.

Bethany laughed. "And what are your plans for the rest of the evening? Healing?"

He laughed. "Actually, I was planning on talking to you," he said with a fake confidence that masked his rapidly beating heart.

A smile grew on Bethany's face as the blood rushed to her cheeks.

"That is, if that's okay," he quickly added.

She nodded. "Okay."

The two ended up talking by the fire for hours. When it started to get late, and the employees of the lodge seemed a little eager for them to return to their respective rooms, he struggled with how to say goodbye.

"Well, um, I guess I'll see you on the slopes tomorrow?"

"Yeah! I'll probably find you flat on your face somewhere, right?" she teased and he burst out laughing.

The next evening, they found themselves on the same couch, now with hot chocolates in both of their hands, talking about everything under the stars.

"Okay, I have a hardball question for you," he started. "What has been the most difficult relationship you've had in your life?"

Bethany's gaze went immediately to the mahogany floor below her. "That's an easy one. My sister. She and I have had our fair share of conflicts, and they haven't been over easy stuff either. We had a pretty big falling out a few years ago, and we haven't been able to really recover since then."

"Do you mind if I ask what happened? I mean, you don't have to share if you don't want to."

She smiled a little at how nervous he was. "It's okay," she sighed. "Our parents divorced when I was nine years old, and she never really recovered from it. But the divide was my fault. I made a mistake. And it doesn't help that I don't agree with a lot of the life decisions she has made. I think she has put a lot of unnecessary strain on our parents, and sometimes I just wish she could learn to think about someone other than herself."

He nodded. "I can understand that."

She nodded in agreement.

"In terms of her perspective, I mean."

Bethany's eyes widened and, immediately, her walls came towering up.

"You think I'm in the wrong?" she asked defensively.

He felt his face grow red, and he found himself stumbling over his own words. "No, no, I wasn't saying that. I just relate to being young and wanting to do something with my life," he said and twisted a pillow tassel in between two fingers. "When I was younger, I wanted the same thing, and it wasn't until a couple years later that I learned my desires put a financial strain on my parents. At the time, all I knew was that I wanted to go beyond the world my parents had given me, and I felt a sort of justification that they should help me get to the next stage in life. It took some years of being on my own to learn the kind of weight I had created. But I can still understand where I was coming from then."

"Huh," Bethany pondered what he had just said. Perhaps he was right. "But I've told Kayla about what a burden she was putting on our parents," she rebutted.

"Yes, but it was you telling her. I think there are some things we just have to learn on our own. We won't be able to hear them from anybody else."

Bethany took what he had said to heart and was filled with gratitude for the depth of the conversations. She hadn't experienced a friendship like this before, one fueled by merely wanting to know another person. She was filled with a bit of sadness that in just two days, he would be getting on a plane, going in the opposite direction. But she had hope that they would keep in touch.

However, it was on the last day, when they hugged goodbye, that Huxley knew he had fallen in love with Bethany. She wasn't there yet, but by the time he hopped on the plane, he was already figuring out how he would find his way back to her. And that was exactly what he did.

★ ★ ★

"I think I'm going to call her," Bethany stated and set her coffee mug firmly on the counter.

"Are you sure that is the best idea?" Huxley asked her as he rinsed his own mug out in the sink.

"Well, my letters aren't making a difference, and she needs to come home. She needs to spend time with Dad before he dies or she will regret it every day for the rest of her life," she stated. Even saying the words "death" and "Dad" in the same sentence made tears well up in her eyes.

Huxley gave her a tender smile and grabbed her hand. "Beth, you know I'm going to support you no matter what. But you can't force her to come back here. I think you should look at this call as your last attempt to get her to come home, not an ultimatum."

Instead of listening to her husband, Bethany wrote off what he said and dialed the familiar number. It rang a few times. She thought she was going to be sent to voicemail until she heard a click on the other line.

"Bethany?" answered a confused Kayla.

"Hey. I know we haven't talked much on the phone lately, but I wanted to hear your voice and have an actual conversation about Dad," she said gently and plainly. She wanted to be as civil as it took to get her sister home, even if that meant suppressing all the pain she felt when she heard Kayla's voice.

"Bethany, I can't deal with this right now. My entire life is falling apart," she replied exasperated.

"I know, I know. But he misses you, K. He asks about you, and I don't know what to say to him. I think you should at least come and see him. Even if it isn't permanent. Just so you can have a chance to say goodbye."

There was silence on the other line for about a minute, and then heavy breathing. "Bethany," Kayla's voice cracked, "I'm not ready to say goodbye to our dad right now, okay? I have to go, I'm going to be late for work—"

She seemed ready to hang up the phone, but Bethany started talking instead. "Kayla, please, if you'll just hear me out…I've spent a lot of time with Dad over the past couple of years, and you haven't come once. I think you owe it to him to come, just to let him see you."

"He won't even remember me, B!" she said, her voice racked with emotion.

"That's not the point. Please, please come home," Bethany pleaded.

Kayla hung up.

Bethany sobbed.

Huxley wrapped her up in his arms and said a few familiar words to her. "Sometimes people must learn lessons on their own, love. There is nothing more you can do."

Kayla hung up the phone, chucked it onto her bed, and yelled at her four walls. "Why can't she just accept I can't handle this right now?" she exclaimed to no one.

Kayla had just gotten home from a stressful day at work. That morning, she had started to look for other jobs after she convinced herself she was getting fired. She now had it in her head Benjamin had seen her at the bar and knew she had witnessed something she was not supposed to, and he would fire her for it. She just hoped she would be able to find somewhere else to work that paid the same so she could keep up with her rent. The jobs were slim, and she didn't qualify for any of them. She was lucky to have gotten her job at CodeX with only having an associate's degree in computer science. She applied to some entry-level coding positions and hoped, by some miracle, they would accept her without a bachelor's degree or much experience. If they didn't, her only other option was to move out of her apartment, get a smaller place, work a minimum wage job, and go back to school for her bachelor's degree so she could get a better job in the future. But all of that was too overwhelming for her, and so she went to work and ended up getting lunch with one of her coworkers.

Kayla struggled to make friends with her coworkers because she was intimidated by how smart they were. They all had bachelor's and master's degrees, and she felt completely inept to have intellectual conversations with them. She did understand the basics of coding and picked things up rapidly, but that didn't change the fact they had years more of expertise than she did. The reason Kayla did so well at CodeX was because she was good at thinking outside of the box, and then was able to leave it to her more experienced coworkers to work out the details. Even still, she got lunch with Elena, who had been working there a year longer than Kayla.

"What do you think about the diet app?" Elena casually asked.

"I don't know. I don't think it's anything revolutionary, but Melinda is really determined to get it off the ground."

Melinda was Benjamin's wife and the cofounder of CodeX, and she was brilliant. She had a degree in computer engineering and in business, so she was extremely skilled at convincing clients to choose them instead of their competitors. Kayla was left constantly amazed at the projects they were able to obtain, even though BlockWorks was the bigger company. But, somehow, Melinda was able to convince major clients to go with a smaller, less prominent company for their apps and programs.

Their latest project was a weight loss app designed to encourage smaller portions instead of constantly counting calories. Melinda loved it because it was focused on positive encouragement and affirmations as the motivators, not tracking pounds lost.

Encouragement and affirmation were ideas Melinda worked hard to integrate into her own company as well. Every month, each employee was assigned one of their coworkers to positively affirm during that month. Some of Kayla's coworkers thought it was stupid and cheesy, but she thought it was a sweet effort. But she wasn't too sure about this new app. It seemed like they were entering into a very flooded market, but Melinda told them sometimes flooded markets were good because that's where all the people were. You just had to capture them with something different. And so that's what they were trying to do with this app, even if they weren't quite sure how to do that yet.

After the two had carried on with polite conversation over their salads, they headed back into a workspace that was uncharacteristically quiet.

Elena leaned over and whispered in Kayla's ear, "Do you know what's going on?"

"I have no idea."

Melinda came out of her office and looked directly at Kayla. "Kayla, in my office. Now."

Kayla's face went white, and she was terrified over what she would find in her very near future.

"We have a problem," Melinda said as she paced around her office. Kayla's face was filled with concern. "Someone is leaking information to BlockWorks."

Kayla's eyes widened. Would Melinda blame her?

"I need you to find out who is doing it, and I need you to figure it out quickly. There is a rat on our team, and they must be stopped. They could bring my entire company down if they aren't."

"Why me?" she asked inquisitively.

"I trust you, Kayla, and other people around here do too. If there is anyone around here who could figure it out, it would be you."

The music pulsed as Benjamin slid into a booth on the dimly lit, far-side of the bar. He waited fifteen minutes before she arrived in a tight, scarlet dress. He immediately ordered two old fashioneds and settled into the seat.

"Why are you doing this?" she asked in the middle of the conversation.

"I have to look out for my best interests. And, right now, you are my best interest," he said coyly. But when he spoke, a familiar face caught the corner of his eye as she walked in. Kayla Fitzpatrick, looking exhausted from what was probably a long day at the office, but instead of her typical pinstriped blazer, she was wearing a leather jacket over her blouse. When he saw her, he froze for a moment. He racked his mind to figure out what needed to be done now that she was here. He couldn't acknowledge her, and he surely couldn't take the risk and hope she didn't notice him. Things had gotten outside of his control, and he had to get it back. He was so close to having everything he ever wanted, and he wasn't going to let some measly employee stand in his way.

Chapter Seven: Then

Dan walked into the coffee shop with an aura of shame around him. This was the last thing he wanted to be doing right now, but all his friends continued to tell him it was necessary. It had been six months since his divorce was finalized, and now here he was, at a small coffee shop in Paderborn, going on his first-ever blind date.

Dan had been given several pep talks before walking through the front door: Don't compare her to Karina. She isn't Karina. Don't think of her as your future wife, she probably won't be that either. Think of this as branching out, exploring, meeting someone new, and having a new life experience. Don't tell her you just got out of a divorce. That is not first date material. Keep it casual, light, airy.

He tried to remember all the instructions in his head as he searched for someone who matched the measly description he received from his coworker: short, blonde hair, tan skin. That was all he had to go by. Luckily, the coffee shop was near empty, and he was able to spot her rather quickly, and she looked up at him with a kind smile.

"Dan?" she asked tentatively.

"Yeah, that's me. You must be Petra." She had a thick German accent but still spoke English well, which was a good thing considering Dan's German skills were poor at best. "How do you know Brian?" he asked casually.

"Oh, his wife and I went to Goethe-Universität together and we've kept in touch ever since.

"That's great!" Dan replied. He racked his mind in search of some conversation starter, but suddenly they had all vanished from his head.

Luckily, she piped up.

"How long have you lived in Germany?" she asked.

"For about six years now. I was in the military for a few years and made some friends with locals here and got offered a job I couldn't refuse."

"Well, you must not have had much tying you down in America," she joked.

Dan immediately felt defensive.

"Actually…" he began, but he then stopped himself. "I do have some things back there, but it was a really great opportunity," he said, remembering the voice that told him to keep it casual. He figured it was probably not the best opening line that he had left his pregnant wife and child behind to take said job. He knew how bad it all sounded.

Dan had spent the past several months trying to forgive himself for the choices he made. It took a lot of honest self-reflection to realize he didn't go to Germany purely for selfless reasons. He did believe he was doing what was best for his family. He thought he and Karina both believed that, but he also did enjoy living in Germany. Coming from a small town, Dan wanted the chance to see the world, and being in the military opened him up to that opportunity. It was a craving he wanted to satisfy. That's why he wanted to move Karina and the girls out with him. But he realized now it was selfish to ask that of Karina. After all, he could have probably gotten a job in America. While he had no degree to his name, he could have found something, and sure, it probably would have paid less and they would have been strapped financially, but, as he now realized, he would have been with his family. Instead, he missed out on so many important moments he now wished he could have experienced. Not only did he have many self-realizations, but he also had to grapple with the guilt that came from them: guilt for abandoning his wife and leaving her to be alone, leaving his kids fatherless for most of the year…there was a lot to be ashamed about, but he knew God forgave him for it all. Now he just had to figure out how to forgive himself.

Part of Dan was tempted to move back to the States and try to have a life with Karina again, but she had made it very clear over the divorce proceedings that their marriage was beyond redemption. He may have lost Karina, but he could still try to give his girls a good future. And perhaps even then it was self-ish of him to stay. He continued to go back and forth over what the best decision was.

"Well, it was really nice getting to know you," he told Petra after an hour of conversation that was too surface-level for his liking. They exchanged phone numbers and planned to get together in the future, but he wasn't sure if he would follow through. None of it felt right, and his friends warned him he would probably feel this way, because no matter how hard he tried, he couldn't help but think of Karina when he spoke with Petra.

Throughout the coffee date, he continued to think of the little things he had with Karina, like the inside jokes they shared. Even when they were arguing, they could tell each other one of those jokes and instantly make the other laugh. He had taken much of their marriage and wrapped it up as something better in his mind. He didn't want to remember all the fights, struggles, and turmoil they suffered. He wanted to remember all the good, pure, perfect moments in his mind. It was like he could walk through his own little museum of Karina, and see all these memories on display and relive them without an ounce of the negative things that may have surrounded those moments.

Dan had also started going to counseling a few months ago when he realized he didn't have all the necessary tools needed to process things. His counselor suggested writing a letter to Karina to explain all the ways in which he realized he was wrong. He didn't need to send it, but perhaps it would help him heal and move forward. He still hadn't brought himself to write it, but after going on this date, the only thing on his mind was to sit down at his desk and put something into words.

My dear Karina,

Immediately, he stopped and erased the words.

Karina,
I don't want to make this letter about me, but I want to validate
some of the things you have said to me about my actions and choices.

You're right. It was selfish of me to take this job in Germany, and it was selfish of me to keep it for as many years as I have. I fooled myself into believing I was doing the right thing, even though I could tell you wanted me to come home. I think when you tell yourself a lie so many times, eventually you start to believe it. I'm not making an excuse for my actions, but I want you to understand where I'm coming from.

This may come as a surprise to you, but I did consider coming back home about a year ago. In fact, I applied to a few jobs in Plymouth, but I never heard back from them, so I figured it was God telling me to stay. I think it was my insecurity of leaving that kept me here. I grew comfortable in my life here, and a part of me was afraid of what it would look like to go back to a normal routine of being married and being a father. I was insecure in my ability to handle that kind of responsibility in my day-to-day life, but it was absolutely and completely unfair of me to put all that on you to avoid my own fears.

The day you became pregnant with B, you and I made a commitment to care for her, and I have gravely failed in my half of that commitment. For that, I am forever sorry. I see the ways in which I've failed in our marriage, and I'm not writing this to you to fix things with us, but I just want you to feel heard. I know it's a long time coming, and it's probably too late, and I will carry that burden, but I wanted to you know these things.

I'm sorry.

Dan

Tears were streaming down his face by the time he finished the letter. They were revelations he already made, but it was an entirely other matter to put them onto paper. He still wasn't sure if he was going to send it to Karina or not. He felt like she deserved to know, but he wasn't sure if he felt that way for her sake or for his own. So, for the time being, he just left it on his desk and tried to get some sleep.

★ ★ ★

Karina had decided it was finally time for her to go on a date with William. She still didn't know if she had given herself enough time to grieve the loss of her marriage, as that would probably come in ebbs and flows for a while, but she also felt she needed to give her past self, the person who started this journey in the first place, a chance to be with someone she connected with.

The girls were over at a friend's house for a sleepover, and so she decided to have William over for dinner. She was more than a little nervous to have him come into her home, but she also wasn't ready to publicly declare her current circumstances, so she thought it might be better to keep it at home. He arrived fifteen minutes early with a bouquet of flowers and a bottle of wine in his hands. He was wearing a light blue button-up, and a very nervous smile on his face.

"Come on in," she said.

"You look beautiful," he observed, and rightly so. It was the first time in a long while Karina had put so much effort into her appearance. She even straightened her hair and put on a little more makeup than usual. In that way, it felt exciting for her, and she even experienced a flash of giddiness in getting dressed up for someone. It was those kinds of things she was deprived of in her marriage, so it felt good to experience them now.

She welcomed William in, and they awkwardly hugged, not knowing what to do. Of course, for William, he had never felt this way about someone before, and for Karina, she hadn't dated someone in years, so it was new for them both.

When they sat down for dinner, William nervously tried to open the conversation. "So, what have you been up to lately?" he timidly asked.

"Well, this week hasn't been very busy. I've just gone to work, and I packed up and shipped the last of Dan's stuff…. Oh crap," she muttered under her breath. "I'm sorry. That's probably the last thing you want to hear about right now. I don't know what to say," she admitted.

He laughed. "It's okay. This is real life. I don't want to pretend you didn't just go through a really traumatic experience in your life," he reassured her, and straightened the silverware in front of him, as he was also unsure of how to act.

The pair was as awkward as two high school kids who had been flirting for months and finally decided to go out. Even amidst the cumbersome exchange, there was no denying the chemistry and even whimsical feelings that they both had.

"Can I suggest something crazy?" she asked to move in a different direction, and he eagerly nodded. She abruptly got up and walked into another room.

William nervously folded and unfolded and refolded the napkin in his lap. They hadn't even started eating dinner yet, so he had no idea what she had in mind. She came out a few minutes later with an old, worn board game in her hands. "I know this can be the cause of many a strife, but I love Monopoly. Would you maybe want to play it?" she asked and he laughed. He nodded and cleared away a space to play it on the dining room table. So, they did something neither of them expected to be doing on a first date: they ate their meal and played a classic game of Monopoly.

It was strange. Karina had played the game so many times with her girls, but this time it felt very different playing it with an adult. Dan was not a big fan of board games, so it was something she had to give up in their marriage because she loved them. Every Friday night, she and her family had time set aside to play board games, and they alternated who picked the games. Her girls loved them too, probably Bethany more than Kayla, but Kayla put up with them for the most part. While her girls would get frustrated over losing, she still loved playing with them. In Monopoly, Karina was always the top hat, and so she relished getting to move her little hat across the board and buy a property just like she did when she was a kid.

William, on the other hand, hadn't played a board game in years. Growing up, his family didn't play a lot of board games. He was usually left to entertain himself because his parents were too exhausted when they came home from work, and he was an only child. This usually resulted in him playing a lot of make-believe and creating magical worlds with imaginary friends to keep him company along the way.

Karina had to teach him how to play the game since it had been so long since he had played it. But once he got the hang of it, it felt like he was getting a childhood experience he never had, and with it, a childlike joy filled him. He loved getting to laugh when he went to jail three times in a row and even relished in Karina making money off him when he constantly landed on her properties. It felt pure and innocent for them to get to share in a fun experience together instead of engaging in serious and emotional talk. As much as they both appreciated being able to have that with each other, doing this was just as needed.

Chapter Eight: Now

"I *trust you, Kayla."* These words rang in Kayla's ears and made her feel even more guilty. Her boss, a woman she greatly admired, trusted her, and here was Kayla, withholding the truth from her. Melinda had no idea Kayla had seen Benjamin getting cozy with a woman at a bar late at night. While Kayla did not know exactly how deep Benjamin was in his lie, she had enough experience with affairs to know what one looked like. And before, she could've pretended she didn't see anything, out of fear of losing her job, but now a woman was coming to her in confidence when Kayla was hiding something she deserved to know.

While Kayla laid in her bed, too stressed to go to sleep, and too upset to do anything productive, she thought about Laurie, and when she thought about Laurie long enough, then she thought about her dad. Here was the thing: Kayla didn't know why her parents had broken up until years later. When she found out about William, it was like her entire reality had been shattered, maybe even more than when she found out they were getting a divorce in the first place. At least when they got a divorce, she didn't understand what the nail in the coffin of her parent's marriage was, but when she did find out she felt like she would never be able to look at her mom again. At the time, she could not understand how anybody could forgive her for what she did. She sometimes imagined how blindsided her dad must have been because the only thing she had to compare it to was how blindsided she was by Peter. But that was a short-lived relationship. She couldn't imagine committing your life to someone and then finding out they threw that promise away. This was why she felt so torn about telling Melinda or not.

Benjamin and Melinda Weedle had been married for ten years. They met in college, they started CodeX together, and then they got married. Even though Kayla never got along with, or even particularly like Benjamin, she always viewed their love story as something so tender and beautiful. Kayla didn't have very many examples of good marriages in her lifetime, and it was devastating to find out this, too, was a sham. Then, of course, Kayla had the fact Melinda chose her to trust. Out of every employee at CodeX, she picked her. Was this all God's way of encouraging Kayla to tell Melinda the truth?

Of course, when Kayla went down that path, she was filled with doubts and questions of what could go wrong if she told Melinda. The worst thing, even a little bit worse than Kayla losing her job, would be if Melinda did not believe her. Why would she? Even if Melinda said she trusted Kayla, it was an entirely other matter to have someone approach them and accuse their spouse of having an affair. And if Melinda didn't believe her, Kayla would surely lose her job for overstepping every employer/employee guideline there was, and, even worse, Melinda would be trapped in a marriage she did not deserve. And so, Kayla settled on another option. She had to find out the truth. She had to prove Benjamin was really cheating, even if she had no idea how she was going to do that.

The next day when Kayla went into work, her two major investigations sat at the forefront of her mind. At present, Kayla needed to figure out who was leaking information. She met that morning to talk with Melinda about what she knew. Melinda had learned from an undisclosed source that data, codes, and projects from CodeX were being delivered to BlockWorks. There were only a few employees who had access to that information, so the suspect pool was small.

"How reliable is your source?" Kayla asked.

"Why do you ask?"

"Well, if they are plugged in with what's going on at BlockWorks, we could try to give each employee a fake code and see which one surfaces."

Melinda pondered the idea for a moment. "That could work." And so, two computer nerds tried their hand at criminal investigation for the day as each of them wrote out different codes that were then dispersed into the right hands. Now all they needed to do was wait and hope Kayla's plan worked.

Bethany loaded a few of Henry's toys and a game they could play for the day. It had been a week since Henry and Huxley had joined Bethany to visit her father. She didn't like taking them there too often. She knew, even though Huxley offered to go with her every time, it was a burden on everyone. In her reality, who would want to go visit their dying in-law? The drive there was quiet, but that was mostly because Bethany didn't have a lot to say lately. After she called Kayla and Kayla still didn't come, she was filled with a new sense of disappointment in her sister. There was a piece of her that hoped her call would inspire Kayla to come and be with her family, but it was clear now there was nothing Bethany could do to talk sense into her sister.

When they got there, Gianna greeted Bethany and told her her father was doing better than usual, which lifted Bethany's spirits a bit when she walked through the door. When she saw her father, he had a smile on his face and was tapping his foot to music. Gianna explained she was playing music when he woke up that morning, and he wanted her to keep playing it. At that moment, a Beatles song was playing, which was Dan's favorite band.

"Bethany!" he exclaimed and greeted her with a smile. It was rare that he addressed her by name, and even more so that he recognized her right away. It usually took about an hour for him to realize she was even there and then process who she was. It was like a switch had gone off in his brain and suddenly he seemed a little more like his old self than other days.

When Henry walked in, Dan's face lit up. He pointed at Henry and looked at Bethany with a confused face. "This is my son, your grandson, Henry," she told him, even though he had met Henry at least a hundred times.

"Henry," Dan repeated slowly, and then another smile grew on his face. Huxley brought the rest of their stuff into the house and got settled into the living room with her father. After he "met" Henry, Dan settled into another bout of staring in silence.

Bethany asked him a few questions, but he merely responded with mumbles or nods. But she was okay with that. She preferred nothing as opposed to him being angry or confused or lost, as he sometimes became.

After some time passed in silence, Dan looked over and beckoned Bethany to come and sit next to him. She obliged, and once she was sitting next to him, he leaned over and asked in a hushed tone what Henry's name was again. Once she reminded him, he called Henry over to sit on his lap. Henry was cautious at first since he was young enough to still only be comfortable with a handful of people, but once Bethany encouraged him, he slowly made his way over to Dan. Once on his lap, Dan smiled and was silent for a moment, but then started speaking again.

"You know, Henry," his shaky voice began, "when your mom was younger, she was so smart and wise. She always knew things about people, even when people didn't tell her what was wrong, she just seemed to know…" His speech was butchered and drifted off a bit, and even though Henry didn't fully comprehend what Dan was saying, Bethany did. "Your mother also loved playing games. Do you want to play a game with me?" he asked, and Henry nodded.

Dan looked to Bethany and she was still in shock with how the interaction had gone. She couldn't remember the last time her father wanted to do…well, anything. It was always her asking him to do things. She searched their toy bag and found a deck of cards Henry had played Go Fish with many times.

All four of them played Go Fish together in a circle in the living room until Henry grew tired of playing. He ended up lying on Dan's lap and falling asleep, and then shortly after, Dan fell asleep as well. Bethany leaned on her husband's shoulder and relished seeing two of the most important people in her life spending time together. It was one of the most precious moments she had witnessed between her father and her son. It was also an experience she would never get to see again, and she hoped Henry would remember it too. He may have only been four years old, but she hoped maybe this would be the memory he held onto of his grandfather. But, even if he didn't, she would be there to remind him. It may seem small for an outsider looking in, but it would be a moment Bethany would never forget.

★ ★ ★

Dear Bethany,

    I'm sorry our conversation did not go well the other week. I wish you could understand where I'm coming from, but I know you can't and, in the same vein, I know I can't understand where you are coming from either. So, I guess I just wanted to tell you that I'm sorry for hurting you. I don't want to disappoint you, and I know you think it would be best for me to come and see Dad, but I can't handle death right now. I can't handle much of anything right now, so I'm sorry.

Love,

Kayla

Kayla held the sloppily written letter in her hand. Before she even got the chance to read it over, she crumpled it up and threw it in the trash can. There were no words that could express her feelings over the situation with her father and sister. So, instead, she hastily threw her hair into a bun and headed to work.

When she pulled into the familiar CodeX parking lot, she sat in the car for a moment to collect her thoughts before going inside. She still was no closer to figuring out who was stealing the confidential information, and Melinda was becoming even more anxious. On her other front, she was also no further in figuring out if Benjamin was having an affair. She had frequented the bar where she spotted him, but never saw him again. Part of her was not surprised, because Ben was smart. He knew not to go to the same place twice, especially if he saw Kayla there. She thought about popping into random bars across the town, but she knew that would be aimless and a long shot at best. It was in the middle of her workday that she had a foolish idea. *I'll just follow him,* she decided. *And then, for better or worse, I will know the truth.*

So, when the workday ended, she got in her car and decided to take the huge risk she thought about all day. She tried not to think of all the ways it could go wrong, but even if she had, she probably would have gone through with it anyway. She was tired of the not knowing, and today she planned to get some answers. She waited in her car for a few minutes while she waited for Benjamin to come out of the building. Ben and Melinda rode in separate cars because one of them often stayed late or one came in early some mornings. Luckily, today was no different, and he came out of the building and hopped into his car. He quickly pulled out, and shortly after, Kayla pulled out as well. She hooked the same right Ben made, and her heart raced as she barreled onto the freeway. She stayed a couple cars behind him, but she was always keenly aware of his silver BMW. She couldn't tell where he was going at first, but after a little while following him, she realized he was going towards a cluster of bars on the outskirts of town. These places were certainly not popular hangouts, which made sense if Benjamin wanted to take his shady activities there.

He parked on the side of the street and casually walked into the bar. Kayla pulled over on the other side of the bar, and that was where her plan ended. She couldn't just go in after him, but she also didn't have the answers she needed yet. His going into a bar meant nothing unless she knew he was meeting a woman. So, Kayla was forced to think quick on her feet, and luckily her conniving personality thought outside of the box. She didn't need to go into the bar at all. All she needed was someone else to do it for her, and she knew exactly how to make that happen.

She leaned against the outside of the bar until she spotted her target: a young, cocky businessman in a cheap suit with an arrogant smile. She unbuttoned the top button of her blouse, fluffed her hair, and flagged the man over. "Excuse me," she said as she plastered on a fake and innocent smile. He strode over to her gladly. "I know this is going to sound kind of strange, but my sister and I are really close, and I think her boyfriend is cheating on her. He's in that bar right now, and I know if he sees me, it'll be some big thing, and I really don't want to cause any problems... I think I'm just in over my head and I'm wondering if you'll do me a huge favor?" she asked him in the ditsiest way she could muster.

His arrogance preceded him. "For a pretty woman like you, of course. What do you want me to do? Beat him up?" he teased and flashed a toothy smile.

"Oh no, nothing like that. I don't want him to get hurt. I just...I don't know," she dragged on. "I was hoping maybe you could take a picture of him, and then just, I don't know, send it to me? I know this is really weird and un-comfortable and it's a lot to ask a stranger—" she said, but he interrupted her.

"Babe, it's not a big deal at all. You're just trying to be a good sister," he responded.

Even though the word "babe" made her skin crawl, she nodded and touched his arm. "Will you really do it? You will be my hero," she added, just to solidify the deal. A huge smile grew on his face and he agreed. She pulled out a picture from the CodeX website to show him. He walked into the bar on a mission, and Kayla laughed as she stood outside and waited. Men like that were so easy. They were so desperate to be a hero and cocky enough to think they could be, which made bending them to her will a little too simple.

When ten minutes passed by, she started to get a little nervous her "hero" had gotten distracted, but a few minutes later he came out with two beers in his hands.

"I hate to be the one to tell you this, but I saw him in there with another woman."

Kayla's face looked visibly upset, even though on the inside, she was not surprised. "I just have no idea how I'm going to tell her. I hope she believes me," she said with a sigh and looked off into the distance.

"Well, of course she will. If you'll just give me your number, I'll send you pictures that prove he is not the type of man worthy of her."

"You really are my hero. Thank you," she said with a fake grin and put her number into his phone. And, just like that, she had ammo. Benjamin Weedle was going down.

Chapter Nine: Then

"But I don't want to do homework. School is boring," Kayla groaned.
"I know, but it's important that you get it done. These are crucial things you will need to know for the rest of your life," Karina reminded her.

Kayla groaned. There were only a few more weeks until summer vacation and Kayla was chomping at the bit to be finished with school. It was sunny and warm outside, and all she wanted to do was play at a beach, or play at a park, or even play in her yard. Anything that would take her away from the dreadful math homework sitting in front of her.

Bethany, on the other hand, was content to do her schoolwork. Her teacher had given her a summer reading list and Bethany was thrilled to go to the library and start reading. In fact, that was her only plan for the summer. She would tag along with her sister to the various places she would make them go, but she was most excited to sit out in their yard and read while the sun warmed her cheeks.

"Mom, when I finish with homework, can we pleeease go to the beach?" Kayla begged and gave a classic puckered lip to further her point.

Karina thought for a moment and then gave in and agreed. She had done that a lot more lately, but that was honestly because she still felt the guilt of flipping her girls' lives around. Even though it had been several months since the divorce was finalized and she was excited about the beginnings of her relationship with William, she still couldn't let go of the guilt she felt. Part of it was she couldn't really give the girls an explanation as to why she and Dan got divorced in the first place. She couldn't tell them about William and she couldn't tell them about the problems she had with Dan, because the last thing she wanted to do was create animosity between her children and their father. So, when she told them about the divorce and they continued to ask many questions about it in the following months, she said things like: "Sometimes people just grow apart" or "We still love each other, but we think we are better off as friends." It was complete BS, and Karina knew it. That was why she tried to listen to the girls and go to the library or to the playground when they wanted to; she believed the least she could do was make them happy by doing things they wanted to do.

Kayla rushed to finish the math problems she still didn't fully understand. While Kayla did that, Bethany sat snuggled up on the couch reading the last book in the newest trilogy she was enthralled with. Once Karina packed the necessary bag of things (towels, snacks, extra changes of clothes, sand toys, etc.), they headed out for the beach.

Luckily, the drive was short, and so they were able to settle onto a sandy part of the beach. Once Karina laid out towels and stuffed the beach umbrella into the sand, she settled onto a towel and picked up her book. Kayla immediately ran to jump into the water, and Bethany followed slowly behind her. The beach was not as crowded as it usually was, which made sense since school was still in session for the district, but they knew in a few weeks, this same beach would be filled with kids eager to play in the sand and run around outside.

Karina wasn't much of a reader, but about a month ago, she decided to pick up one of her favorite childhood series, *The Chronicles of Narnia*. She was able to get through them quickly, which was good because her schedule did not allot much time for her to read anyway. She was on the fourth book already, and reading them had brought back a few happy childhood memories. She had to hold onto them tightly since happy childhood memories were few and far between.

Last week, Karina finally gave in and shared a little about her past with William, which was not a pleasant time for either of them. She hated having to share how her family earned money for several years of her childhood, by conning people. It was shameful for Karina to admit her parents ran a series of cons before her father was caught and sentenced to ten years in prison for wire fraud. Most of the cons were small; they usually tricked people into thinking they won sweepstakes, and it was a trick more people fell for than Karina cared to admit. She didn't even know what they did until her father was caught when she was a teenager. Since her past was filled with a lot of pain, it meant she held on tightly to those weekly board game nights and books like *Narnia* her mom used to read to her when she was younger.

William was understanding and kind when he learned the truth. Of course, he couldn't imagine what going through such a childhood tragedy must have looked like, but he wasn't judgmental in the slightest.

As Karina continued to read through *The Silver Chair*, Bethany and Kayla had picked up a few large sticks and started sword fighting.

"Take that!" Bethany yelled as she swung her stick around to whack Kayla in the leg. Bethany may have been the quiet bookworm of the family, but she wasn't afraid to throw a few swings at her sister occasionally.

After a few rounds of fighting, Kayla desperately wanted to go swimming again. "Come on, B! It's not that cold. Let's just swim for a little bit," Kayla pleaded with her sister.

"Kayla, no. You know I don't like the water," Bethany begrudgingly replied.

But Kayla ignored her sister and tromped over to climb to the top of the jetty so she could jump into the cool water below.

"Kayla, don't do that. It's too deep," Bethany warned her.

"It's fine. It's not like I don't know how to swim," she yelled back. In a moment, Kayla jumped off the rocks and was in the water.

Bethany rolled her eyes at her sister's stubbornness. After about twenty seconds, she realized her sister still hadn't come up for air, and she immediately started panicking.

"Kayla?" she screamed, and when she didn't see any movement in the water, she screamed for her mom. Before her mom could react, Bethany was already climbing onto the rocks and jumping in herself.

The cold impact of the water was overwhelming for a moment, but Bethany was determined. She may have hated the water, but she forced her eyes open and stayed still so she could see the water as clearly as possible. The water was only around ten feet deep, so it didn't take long for her to spot her baby sister unconscious at the bottom. She swam as fast as her legs could carry her towards Kayla, and once she scooped her up, she used all the strength she didn't know she had to bring them back to the surface. Once her eyes adjusted to the sun, she noticed her mom standing on the rocks in a panic.

"Kayla!" she screamed, and pulled her daughter up onto the rocks. She carried her off the rocks and onto the sand. Kayla still had a pulse, but she was unconscious and didn't show any signs of breathing. Karina's emotions were scattered across the beach, but she was able to begin CPR as tears were pouring out of her eyes.

All the while, Bethany stood a few feet away in silence. She didn't cry or pace, but she didn't take her eyes off Kayla. It didn't take long for Kayla to cough up some water and for Karina to take what felt like her first breath in a lifetime. Once she saw Kayla was okay, Bethany fell to her knees and started sobbing. The next bit of time was blurry for Bethany. She remembered them going to the hospital and staring at the tightly checkered linoleum flooring of the waiting room. She remembered hearing something about a concussion due to the impact of her sister hitting a rock when she jumped off. But she didn't remember screaming in the car at her mother, which she did. She also didn't remember chucking a cheap magazine across the waiting room, another thing she did. Karina never brought it up because she knew what her daughter faced would be something that would stick with her for a long time, possibly for the rest of her life. And it did. Even though her mother told her that she had saved her sister's life, that wasn't what she took away from that experience.

Bethany categorized that day in her memory as the day she almost lost her sister, and it fueled the protectiveness Bethany already felt towards Kayla to an even greater degree. The bottom line for Bethany was in a promise she made to herself when she saw her sister in a hospital bed: that she would never take the risk of losing her again.

Chapter Ten: Now

Kayla was nervous when she entered work the next day. It wasn't going to be easy to tell her boss her husband was cheating on her, but at least now she would look like one woman looking after another woman instead of an employee throwing accusations at her employer. But when Melinda was the one to call her into her office, Kayla grew even more concerned. They still hadn't gotten anything back from the coding trap, so she was clueless as to why she was being called into Melinda's office in the first place.

When Kayla walked into the office, Melinda was visibly upset. Had she found out about her husband before Kayla had a chance to tell her? Questions like this were rushing through Kayla's mind, but Melinda didn't even notice her. When she did, she beckoned for Kayla to sit down. Melinda took a deep breath and prepared herself to say whatever it was she was going to say.

"We lost the app."

Kayla's eyes widened in a panic. "What do you mean? Did they steal information about what we were working on?" she asked, hoping she had misunderstood.

"They didn't just take some information. They took all the information and presented it to our clients and got them to drop us and go with them instead. They screwed us, and I don't know what I am going to do," Melinda cursed and started pacing the room. "I don't know how I am supposed to tell Ben about this," she exclaimed.

"Wait… he doesn't know about any of this?"

Melinda paused and looked up at her in anger. "I thought we could get it under control. But it's gone too far now. We are drowning. I destroyed the company we worked so hard to build." Melinda sank in her office chair.

Kayla's heart raced. She wanted so desperately to tell Melinda the truth about her husband and to relieve some of the guilt that she was feeling, but she feared she had waited too long, and now Melinda might never know the truth about who she was lying next to every night.

Melinda picked up the magazine on her desk and huffed. "Can you believe this is the woman who is going to take me down?" she said and threw the magazine in front of Kayla. "Some young blonde who's only succeeding because it's her daddy's company."

When Kayla saw the cover in front of her, her entire world shook and her mind raced a million miles an hour. Suddenly, puzzle pieces that didn't even belong in the same picture were fitting together perfectly. It all made sense now. She was so wrong, and yet she was so right. Her palms started to sweat. Now more than ever, she knew exactly what she had to do.

"Melinda, there is something I need to tell you," Kayla started. "I think I know who has been leaking the information." She sighed and wondered how she was ever going to tell Melinda how she knew this information. But Kayla learned a long time ago that the best way to help someone was by telling the truth. No sugar coating. No trying to come up with a better explanation. She just needed to be honest.

"Melinda, if I'm being truthful, I have no idea how to tell this to you," Kayla started and took a deep breath. "A few weeks ago, I noticed your husband at a bar with another woman. I have dealt with my fair share of affairs in the past, so I was very firm in the belief he was cheating on you, but I didn't want to come to you and risk you not believing me…" she continued and let out another deep sigh. Kayla felt a sense of shame that she knew about this for so long and was only telling her now. "So, last night I followed him to a bar on the outside of town, and he was with the same girl. But I don't think he is cheating on you. I think he has been the one selling the information to

BlockWorks." She pulled up the pictures on her phone and Melinda was speechless. In the photos, it was not just some young, dumb girl, but Jayna Starnes, CEO of BlockWorks.

When Benjamin walked into the bar that night, he certainly was not expecting the night to go in the direction it did. He met Jayna in their typical corner booth on the darkest side of the bar. This had been their new meeting location since their last one had been compromised by a pesky employee who happened to be in the wrong place at the wrong time, and who was now going to gravely suffer for it. When he settled in with her, they began discussing plans. Ben would become the CEO of BlockWorks, and all Jayna had to do was sit back and get a paycheck, without all the pesky work of leading a company she did not fully understand. That was when he noticed an eager young man taking pictures of him. If Ben acted like he noticed, he would lose the advantage, so, once again, he had to handle the situation delicately.

He leaned over to Jayna and whispered, "My wife is going to find out about us, and apparently sooner rather than later. I guess she is smarter than I gave her credit. So, this is what we need to do. Operations need to be sped up. I am going to give you the key to the kingdom, Jayna, and you are going to take action immediately. Tomorrow morning, we are throwing the grenade into CodeX, and I will watch my company burn."

"I can't believe this. He wouldn't do this. This is our company, and we have worked way too hard to get here," Melinda spoke while Kayla was still in her office.

Kayla had no idea what to do in the situation, because her heart broke for Melinda.

"I have to talk to him. I have to find out if it is true. Wait here," she demanded.

Kayla sat awkwardly in Melinda's office for fifteen minutes until Melinda returned, her face as white as a ghost. She never told Kayla exactly what Benjamin said but, from her reaction, Kayla gathered it wasn't pretty.

After watching Melinda's heart break, she decided to speak up. "I don't know what you are going through, but I do know what it feels like to be blindsided.

You are going to question everything, and you might even blame yourself for not knowing sooner, but if you can remember anything from me, please know this is not your fault. There was no way you could have known," she assured her, and Melinda nodded. Kayla knew Melinda wasn't going to be able to do anything with what she said that day, because she was still in shock. But there was going to come a day she would need to hear those things, because those words were what Kayla needed to hear so desperately on two terrible occasions.

Melinda went home early that day, but Kayla was left pretending like nothing had happened. It felt purposeless, sitting at her desk, working on an app they were going to lose sooner than any of them knew. Sitting there, Kayla realized how bad the situation truly was. She had opened Pandora's box, and it contained a much greater evil than she had initially realized. All she wanted to do was save Melinda from suffering the same fate her father and she did, but she ended up dragging the company down with her.

While Kayla knew logically that Benjamin probably would have taken down CodeX eventually as part of whatever plan he had, it felt like it was Kayla who set it all in motion. And she knew, in the process, she had destroyed her own career. If Kayla had been fired, that would have been one thing, but now there would be dozens of employees looking at the same jobs Kayla was, but were way more qualified. There was no way any employer would pick someone with an associate's degree over someone with a bachelor's or even master's degree in this field. Somehow, in the effort to do herself and her father justice, she ended up obliterating her own career aspirations.

CodeX Company Scandal
by Bailey McConnell

Tech company CodeX has shockingly crumbled in what is sure to go down in history as one of the biggest betrayals that St. Louis has ever seen. Benjamin and Melinda Weedle founded CodeX while they attended Washington University. The company quickly grew to be a strong competitor in the technology field. But in a recent revelation, Benjamin Weedle has been appointed the newest CEO of BlockWorks, arguably CodeX's biggest competitor, and left his own company (and wife) to fall to pieces. When asked about the scandal, employee Elena Martinez spoke out. "I never could have seen this coming. Mr. Weedle seemed so devoted to CodeX, and was constantly working to develop and grow it. This really came out of left field for me and the rest of my co-workers," Martinez told us.

Now the thirty-seven men and women who worked for the company are left jobless. A few of them told the Post they were going to apply to work at BlockWorks. "It's the most logical next step for the situation. Of course I am not happy with the way things ended with CodeX, but I know my talent could be used at BlockWorks," said an anonymous source.

Kayla closed the tab on her computer because she couldn't bring herself to read anymore. News articles had started to pop up in Midwestern newspapers, and she even had a few of them reach out to her for a quote. This was especially hard for Kayla as all she could think about was Melinda.

A few days after everything went south, Kayla ended up writing a short email to Melinda. She told her she was sorry, and if she ever wanted to talk, Kayla was available to listen. Melinda never responded, but Kayla didn't expect her to. She hoped Melinda had a support system of her own, but just in case she was in the same boat as Kayla had been, she decided to make herself available to be there for her.

Kayla ended up spending a lot of time thinking about Peter, reflecting on the pain he caused her. Seeing Melinda's shock and disbelief brought back a lot of those feelings for her, and she found herself struggling to get him out of her head. But she had to. Peter was in the past, and she had to focus on her quickly changing future.

Seven unopened voicemails were sitting in Kayla's cell phone. It had been two weeks since she sat on a cold park bench with Peter, and she hadn't spoken to him since that day. But she let her phone ring every time she saw his face on her screen. Several times she held it in her hand and felt the vibrations as she cried, and other times she didn't even notice he had called. But what she hadn't been able to do for the past two weeks was listen to the voicemails he had left. However, it had been a few days since he last

called, and it seemed he had quit reaching out, so she decided it was time to listen to the voicemails and then try to let him go.

"You have seven new voice messages. First message:"

"Hi, Kayla. It's me. I know you said you didn't want to hear from me anymore, but it's been a couple days since I saw you, and I wanted to reach out again. First, I just want to say again how sorry I am for what I did. I feel like there were some things left unsaid between us, so I would really love the chance to talk to you again. Please call me back."

"Message complete. If you would like to delete this message, press seven, to save, press nine."

Kayla hit seven and continued with the next message.

"Hey, Kayla. Clearly you don't want to talk right now, but I just need you to know I really do care about you. I know you are furious, and rightfully so. But I don't ever want you to think I pursued you just to pursue something. As I told you that night, my marriage has been broken for a long time, you were just the one who showed me I could have something greater. If you want to talk, I'll be here."

"Message complete. If you—"

Kayla hit seven before the automated message could continue.

"Kayla, I don't know what I'm doing. I miss you, and I know I probably shouldn't even miss you right now. But I wanted you to know I told Laurie about you. I'll spare you more details, but I wanted you to know you are not a secret. Everything is on the table now. Okay, bye."

Seven.

"Hey, I know it is probably foolish of me to keep calling when you aren't answering, but maybe one day you will hear these when you are ready. You are a great person, Kayla. I don't want you to think of yourself as anything other than that. That's all."

Seven.

"Hey, Kayla, I'm just really not having a good day right now. I know I shouldn't even be leaving this message, but I just wanted to hear your voice, even if it's just in a recorded message I've heard dozens of times before. I'm sorry."

This time, Kayla hesitated to delete the message. Peter's voice was shaky in that message, and it even sounded like he might have been crying. But Kayla needed to get through the messages, and so she deleted it and continued. Only two more left.

"Hi. I just wanted to apologize for my last message. I was in a dark place that night, and I couldn't get you off my mind. But, even still, it was wrong of me to do that to you. I'm sorry."

Seven.

"Hi, Kayla. I've spent the last week and a half reflecting on everything, and I have come to some important realizations about myself and my own feelings. I am calling because I wanted you to know how special you are to me. In a really short time, you have changed my life. I guess I'm still holding out hope that one day you will be able to forgive me. I love you, Kayla, and I know this isn't something I should be saying over the phone, and it certainly isn't something I should be saying in a voicemail after what I did to you, but I needed you to know. It was all real for me, and I realize now more than ever how special you are. Okay, bye."

Kayla's hand hovered over the seven, and for a moment, she thought about saving the message. However, she knew if she saved it, she would be holding onto him, even if it was just a piece. If she was going to move on, she had to let him go completely. So, she deleted the message, and then wept in her bed. The reason it hurt so much was that somewhere, deep inside of her, she knew she loved him too. But there was no way she could move forward after what he did. But even with that knowledge, it didn't take away how painful it all was.

After Bethany left her dad's house, she didn't get very far driving home before she pulled over to the side of the road next to an empty field. It had been one of the rougher days with her father. He was very emotional. Sometimes her dad would get stuck in moments of time, and that day he was stuck in finding out about William. He couldn't seem to remember anything past that or what happened since that time, but he was stuck like a broken record of learning about William, and Karina telling him she wanted a divorce. He seemed to sway in between self-hatred and anger. He either talked about what a terrible father he was, or he got angry at William's existence, or angry about how things turned out. Bethany tried to remind him of happier things past that time, but he wouldn't hear it.

This was hard for Bethany, not just in the typical way of seeing her father struggle through his memories, but watching him in so much pain, specifically about the divorce. It was a stark reminder of what she went through with her sister. The troubles and questions her dad had about the divorce were very similar to the thoughts and feelings Kayla had at that time. It also filled Bethany with a familiar sense of guilt over how she dealt with the divorce and how much Kayla struggled with Bethany's reaction. But there was one thing in particular her dad said that struck her enough to sit in her car on the side of the road.

"I want to go back," he wailed. "I want to go back and prove I am worthy enough to be the man she always wanted to marry."

It took Bethany back to a conversation she had with her dad a long time ago.

"Are you sure he is the one?" her dad asked after she told him how in love she was with Huxley.

"Yes, Dad, I know he is. I've never been treated better by someone than I have by him. He is so many things I want to be. I've never loved anyone like I love him."

"I just…" her dad looked down at his loafers for a moment and frowned. *"I just want you to be sure he is worthy enough to be the man you've always wanted to marry."*

"He shows me every day he is," she assured him.

And he had. Huxley consistently proved himself to be a man worthy of her heart. Oftentimes, it was Bethany who didn't feel worthy of his. She yelled at him and got angry way more than he deserved, but they didn't often fight because he never let them. He handled their marriage with a kindness she did not understand. But Bethany did not know at the time her dad was referring to himself so many years ago. In fact, she hadn't made that connection until he said the very same phrase that day. She always thought he was just being a protective dad and wanted to make sure his daughter didn't end up with a scumbag. But Bethany now realized it went a whole lot deeper than that. He wanted to make sure she didn't end up with someone like *him*.

She fiddled with her wedding ring and thought about how lucky she felt to have Huxley. At the same time, she wished so badly that her dad could have known how much he had grown and changed since the divorce.

But while the phrase Dan used caught her off guard, the emotion he displayed did not. She caught him that emotional about the divorce once before, a few months after it was finalized. Dan came back to the States for Bethany's birthday and stayed in a hotel. Kayla really wanted to stay with him, so Karina decided to have both girls spend the night with him. They went to his hotel, and since the hotel had a pool, Kayla's only plans that night were going to be in the water. This was before Kayla's beach accident, and so Bethany was okay with leaving Kayla at the pool for a few minutes while she ran back to the hotel room to grab a book to read. But when she came in, she found her dad sitting on his bed, sobbing. Of course, he tried to pull it together when he noticed her, but there was no hiding what she had already seen. Bethany, even at that age, came over and wrapped him in a hug, which made him cry even more. The only thing she asked was if it was about Mom, and he nodded. But Bethany didn't know what had gotten to Dan that night.

Dan's initial plan for that night was to take the girls to get ice cream, but he wanted to make sure the ice cream shop was open, so he called them to check. The phone rang and rang until a message played:

"Hi, you've reached William at 2 Scoops Ice Cream Shop. Our regular operating hours are...." and then Dan tuned out the rest. Never in Dan's wildest imagination did he think he would have to hear the man who replaced him on the phone. He hung up the phone and then fell apart. To Dan, it was like losing Karina all over again when he heard that man on the other line. It made him real. Before, *William* was just a name. A faceless person that didn't mean anything to Dan. But now, he was a voice. A real, living person whom Karina saw something in that she did not see in Dan. He wanted to feel that grief, but the pain was interrupted by his daughter seeing him in a state he never wanted her to see him in.

Now it was twenty years later, and she was still seeing him in states he never would have wanted her to see him in. He just didn't fully realize it.

After that day in the hotel room, Bethany never saw her dad cry about the divorce again. Well, that was, until that day. While at first Bethany was upset seeing her father so broken, it took a sudden shift into anger. She banged her hands against her steering wheel and yelled at God for putting her family through this. "How dare you?" she looked up and questioned aggressively. "He didn't deserve this. How could you do this?" she yelled. Somewhere in the yelling, she asked God if He could just let her dad come home. Not to Bethany, but to God. As morbid as it was, she wanted her dad to be done with the personal hell that was Alzheimer's. She wanted him to be set free from losing himself.

But he wouldn't be, not yet anyway, and that filled her with so much anger she did not know how to handle. But she didn't want to put her husband through such anger, and so she sat in her car on the edge of a field for an hour before deciding to come home. He had been through plenty of Bethany's emotional breakdowns about her father, he didn't need to go through this one too, especially with how volatile Bethany's anger was in those moments.

When she arrived home, she told her husband it hadn't been a great day, but expressed hope it was a new day tomorrow, and hopefully, her father would be in a better place then. But there was still a wave of lingering anger at God that stuck with her for much longer than she wanted.

Chapter Eleven: Then

D an got to the bar and already regretted being there. After going on a few dates with Petra, he decided to part ways. But then he ended up going to a bookstore and connecting with the clerk. Unfortunately, she was very flakey and canceled on him multiple times before he finally decided to give up pursuing her. Then, when his friends discovered he had given up on dating because every option was disappointing and would never compare to Karina, they encouraged him to go on one more blind date. He did not want to do it, and after weeks of dodging commitments, he finally gave in and said this would be his last blind date.

This was what led him to stand outside a bar and contemplate whether he should go inside. He had not had a good day at work and had no desire whatsoever to do anything except to lie in his bed and cry. But he mustered up enough strength to walk into the bar and meet the mystery woman his friends believed would sweep him off his feet.

It wasn't hard to spot the mysterious redhead. Robyn was from Ireland and was living in Germany for a work-study program. She was a little young for his taste, but he had no more energy to fight his friends' valiant efforts to make him happy again. Dan threw on a devilishly fake smile and got to know Robyn. They talked for about an hour before she made a compelling case for him to go back to her place. Dan hadn't slept with any women since Karina, but she was persistent, and he was tired, so he haphazardly agreed, and, before he knew it, they were in her soft, cotton sheets. After they hooked up, something different happened to Dan. He felt a pressing need to get out of her home, so he rushed out of there without an explanation.

On his drive home, all he could think about was how everything felt wrong, and he didn't know how to piece together the *why*. When he got home, he did what his counselor recommended when he felt a panic attack bubbling up inside of him, which was to write down what he was feeling. So, he wrote out fragments of sentences that didn't really make sense to the common eye, and then he closed the notebook and went to bed.

When Dan woke up the next morning, he opened his notebook to read through what he had written. Scribbled notes filled the page in every direction with phrases like: "I can't do this anymore," "I don't want to live without her," and "I want to be with my girls." But amidst all the scrawls lay the answer he had been searching almost a year for: he had to go back to the United States.

Most of Dan wanted to return to the U.S. so he could be with his girls. He was tired of living without them. He felt so guilty for being such a terrible father for so many years, and now he finally had a chance to be something different. But then there was this other, small fraction of him that whispered another reason he wanted to go back. The whisper said he wanted to get his wife back. But Dan stuffed that fraction so deep inside him he pretended it didn't even exist. Those feelings wouldn't be beneficial to anyone, but especially not to him. They could end up doing way more harm than good. Instead, he told himself he was going back for his girls, and only for his girls. Logistically, there was a lot of work to be done before he could hop on a plane and be with them again, but at least that day he had an answer. He finally felt like he had a purpose and a path, and that path was straight towards two beautiful girls.

Karina was anxious about the day that awaited her. It was the first day William was going to take the girls on his own. Even though they had been dating for five months, a few weeks ago was the first time he was even allowed to meet them in the context of being Karina's boyfriend. The day they were all set to meet, she sat down with the girls and explained she had met someone else. It was a conversation she was nervous about having, mostly because she knew it could yield a very negative reaction from them both, but especially Kayla. It seemed Kayla still held out hope her parents would get back together, and Karina didn't know which was worse: to squander that belief, or to let her hold onto hope.

However, in terms of William, neither of the girls had a strong reaction to her news. She assumed they had already known she was dating somebody, which was exactly the case for Bethany.

Bethany started to catch on last month, and she told Kayla about her suspicions. So when Karina finally admitted she was seeing someone else, it didn't faze them like it should have.

For Kayla, she viewed this man as a temporary stop, or a rebound for her mother, as the rom-coms had taught her. She may have been young, but she already became obsessed with the romantic comedies her sister was starting to dabble in. Kayla was probably too young to be watching such things, but Karina allowed it because she didn't have the energy to fight it. But there was one thing Kayla knew for sure, the couple meant to be together always ended up together by the end of the movie.

For Bethany, she just wanted her mom to be happy. She would still see her dad every few months, and the only thing that could change would be being forced to spend time with a stranger like William, but Bethany could easily distract herself and enter a different literary world if she needed, so that wasn't a problem for her.

When the girls met William, it was a very casual interaction at Karina's house. William came over and ate dinner with the whole family. Karina had spent several hours preparing a lasagna enjoyed in relative silence on the girls' part. They answered William's "get-to-know-you" questions briefly and without elaboration. They weren't trying to be rude, but Bethany didn't particularly enjoy talking to a stranger, and Kayla didn't care enough to make any more effort than she did. But since there weren't any mental breakdowns, Karina considered it a success.

Now they were going to William's house to learn how he made the ice cream for the shop. It was his idea because he wanted to do something the girls might be interested in, and when Kayla heard the words "ice cream" it didn't matter whose house it was, she was sold.

Even still, Karina was reluctant to leave her kids in William's care. It was one thing to eat and have dinner at their house, and it was a whole other matter to be responsible for them and make parenting decisions, even if they are small. William did not have any experience with parenting kids, or with kids in general, and the fact Karina had to stay home while her kids were at her boyfriend's house was a scenario she had never imagined.

Karina dropped the girls off at noon. After they ran into the house, she stood at the door and gave William intense instructions about a bunch of things he didn't need to know. Even though Karina had left her kids with many high schoolers trying to make an extra buck, she seemed more terrified to leave them with an adult man who also happened to be her boyfriend. Perhaps it was because she truly questioned William's capabilities. While he was sweet, he did have a childlike quality about him, which made her nervous about his ability to be strict and firm when needed.

However, William was adamant about taking the girls, not just because he wanted to spend more time with them, but because he wanted to prove to Karina he was able to step up and handle the girls, at least for a few hours. If they were going to spend their lives together, he would have to learn how to be a good stepfather, and that was something he never imagined tackling. But he needed to try.

After Karina left, things were going smoothly for a while. They were able to settle on making chocolate ice cream, and loaded all the ingredients into the machine and ran around outside while the machine churned the ice cream. However, once the ice cream was finished, things went a bit downhill. He scooped out some of the freshly made ice cream into two bowls for the girls, but Kayla immediately threw a fit about how she wanted more. William didn't fight it and walked over to the freezer to get her more ice cream, and that was when Bethany got upset. She did not agree with William's decision to give her sister more ice cream and tried to parent him on how he was handling the situation. She said he was being irresponsible and Kayla would be wired on sugar for the rest of the night if he decided to give her more. While Bethany was not an extremely emotional person, apparently disagreeing with a man who could quite possibly be her stepfather set off something inside of her.

"I know her better than you do. You've been in our lives for a minute compared to how long I've known my sister." It was a sass even Bethany herself was not familiar with. But she was getting to that age where tween sass was starting to make an appearance.

William, on the other hand, was not expecting this. Karina consistently talked about how level-headed and wise Bethany was, so parenting her was not something he could have prepared for. To make matters worse, Bethany's reaction made him doubt himself. Maybe Bethany was right. She did know Kayla better, and maybe he was the one being irresponsible. But when he stepped back, he realized listening to an eleven-year-old was not the right call. When he followed through and scooped more ice cream into Kayla's bowl, it resulted in Bethany crying in the bathroom.

When Karina came back to get them, it was not as smooth a handoff as William had hoped for. Kayla was content with her sugar high, while Karina had to go into the bathroom and talk to Bethany. But what Karina didn't know when she walked into the bathroom to comfort her daughter was that a fatal word slip would occur, and it would make a small crack in Bethany's little world.

"Honey, I know you want William to do his best, but he has to make his own choices. It was a small thing, and even if he doesn't always do things the way you think he should, that doesn't mean he's wrong. You may know your sister, but he knows a thing or two also. Maybe you could learn something from him too."

"Mom, he hasn't even been in our lives for that long. Who does he think he is?" Bethany snarked.

"Honey, he's been in our lives for years. I think he knows a bit more about you girls than you give him credit for," Karina reminded her.

Bethany took a moment to process, and when she didn't say anything, Karina realized the mistake she had made. Karina had told the girls they had been dating for five months, which was true, but, of course, she didn't mention they had been talking long before then.

Bethany realized this too.

"Were you dating him when you were still with dad?" Bethany accused.

Karina immediately panicked, but decided she had to lie to her daughter and try to brush it off. This was not something she could deal with right now.

"No, no, no. I just meant we were friends before, and he learned about you girls just like any of my other friends know about you," she casually said even though her heart was racing.

Bethany accepted this, but, as everyone who knew Bethany knew, she was perceptive. That slip of the tongue and moment of questioning her mother would stick with her, and would eventually lead her to learn a lot more about the situation than Karina ever intended.

William was petrified at the task that lay before him. He had been planning it for weeks, and with the ice cream fiasco that had occurred a couple weeks ago, he was even more terrified to follow through with his plans, but he was going to anyway. He told Karina to meet him at the ice cream shop before they went out for their annual Friday night dinner, the only night Karina splurged on getting a babysitter for the girls. But he did not plan on taking her out to dinner. Instead, he covered the floor with so many candles it was surely a fire hazard. In the back of the ice cream shop, he had a picnic blanket laid out with assorted sandwiches, and a wine and cheese platter in the middle of it.

He held the small box in his hand as it shook with anticipation. There was a possibility this plan could go poorly, but the optimistic part of him was giddy with excitement.

When Karina pulled up, she was tired from a day of working at the school and handling some particularly frustrating children. But she put that aside because she wanted to have a good dinner with William. When she pulled up to the ice cream shop, she felt something shift in her, and wondered if her subconscious knew something she didn't. That feeling was confirmed when she opened the door and saw the display of candles. She walked into the shop towards William, who stood in the middle of the room. She grabbed his sweaty hands and asked what was going on, even though she already knew the answer.

"Well, when you came here three years ago, I felt like it was the first time we really connected." He reached into his pocket and handed her the store copy of the first receipt he had written his number on so long ago. "You see, I don't often keep my receipts, but I held onto this one. I know it's silly and sentimental, but I want you to know you have never left my heart since that first day. So, I thought it was fitting to come back to the place where I first caught a glimpse of how wonderful you are, and ask you something." He got down on one knee, and Karina covered her mouth in shock. "Will you marry me?" he asked her with a big, hopeful grin.

"I...I," she stuttered and unknowingly, her fight or flight response kicked in. Without thinking, she ran out of the shop and into her car. She wanted to cry or even drive away, but she couldn't bring herself to do either, and so she sat in silence.

A few minutes went by before William knocked on her window. She unlocked the car and he sat down in the passenger's seat.

"Do you want to talk?" he asked.

"I don't really know what to say," she replied without making eye contact with him.

"Well, I did ask you a question," he teased, and she gave a slight smirk.

"William, all of this is so beautiful, but it was also really unexpected. I guess I don't know what to do," she replied with a sigh. At that moment, all Karina felt was heartbroken. This wasn't the reaction William was hoping for, and all she could do was squander his beautiful gesture. But instead of responding in anger or devastation, he spoke to her with kindness and understanding.

"That's okay," he assured her. He pulled the box out of his pocket. He took the ring out and handed it to her. "I want you to hold onto this, and when you have an answer for me, I'll be waiting," he said and opened her hand to place the ring inside, gently closing her fingers around it. "I love you, Karina."

"I love you too," she responded softly.

With that, William got out of her car and left Karina alone again. She drove home in utter silence. She didn't think about William, or the girls, or anything else of the sort. All she did was stare at the road in front of her. She looked at the different shades of green the trees were and glanced at how the yellow road stripes curved as they wrapped around a corner. She spotted the dilapidated house she drove by every day and wondered if someone was ever going to fix it. She read the names of the streets and thought about how silly some of them sounded. Then she pulled up to her mailbox, grabbed the mail, and walked into her home. She typically threw the mail on the counter and dealt with it later, but that day she decided to welcome the distraction and read through the envelopes. She tore up two advertisements, but then came across a letter she was not expecting. Even though it didn't have a return address, she recognized the handwriting immediately.

Dear Karina,

I know this letter may come as a surprise to you, but I wanted to reach out to you personally beforehand so you are aware of the changes I am making in my life. Ever since we split up, I have been going back and forth about whether I should move to the States. On the one hand, I want to bolster our savings for the girls' future, but on a more realistic, and far more important hand, I realize I've spent way too much of their lives without them, and I don't want to miss another moment.

In the past months, I have been in the process of quitting my current job and looking for an apartment and job in Plymouth. As you know, Plymouth is a small town with not a lot of either, but I did find a job in Marshfield working in human resources. It wasn't the job I was expecting, but I suppose my work of leading a team for so many years has paid off, even with no degree.

So, when you receive this letter, I will either be on an airplane or just getting settled in the States. I haven't seen the girls yet because I don't want to blindside you, and I want to give you the opportunity to mentally prepare. Also, if you plan to talk to the girls beforehand, I wanted to give you that opportunity. If not, I would love to talk to them about why I decided to come back to the States and why it has taken me so long to get here. I know this is a long time coming, but I'm here now, and I want to be a real father to our girls. I hope you will let them spend some weekends with me, and I can pick them up some days after school. The apartment I rented is a two-bedroom, so one of the rooms can be theirs.

I hope you are doing well. You are still in my thoughts, and more than anything, I just hope you are happy.

Love,

Dan

For Karina at that moment, she didn't think about what had just happened or what she had just read. All she wondered was: *What are the odds both these things would happen on the same day?* And because she knew the odds were so small, what then, was the reason? Karina believed there had to be some purpose behind having her boyfriend propose to her and receiving a letter that her ex-husband was moving back to be a father to their kids on the same day. She just had no idea what that purpose was.

After sitting with that question for a while, the reality of the two situations started to flood her mind and consume her thoughts. She didn't even know which one to mentally tackle first, but she decided on the latter. She imagined all the changes that would take place in having Dan move back. Not only would she have her girls less (which would be a tough adjustment), but Bethany and Kayla would also have to learn to be parented by their father. They had spent most of their lives being parented by Karina, and even when Dan was home, it was typically both parenting the girls, not solely Dan. But they were going to be his responsibility, at least for part of the time, and that was going to be something Karina would have to come to grips with. This change was also going to shift her relationship with Dan. It was easier to move forward from the divorce because he wasn't there as a reminder of the life she lost and the marriage she wanted so desperately to have. Now he was going to be a part of her weekly, if not daily, life, and that would completely transform her. Yet, with all the confusion she was wrapped up in, she also felt a sense of joy he was coming back. Not for herself, but for her girls. Even if it would be a rough and bumpy transition, this would ultimately be a positive thing for both girls, but especially Kayla, who struggled so much with Dan not being there. They would now have the opportunity to build a real relationship with their father, and he would be able to go to things like school plays, and parent-teacher conferences, and take them out to the movies. He would be able to feel the true and beautiful gift of what it meant to be a parent, and that was something Karina was so glad for.

But, on the other hand, Karina had the other big thing to think about: William's proposal. Karina had no idea what to do, and it didn't make sense to her as to why. She should have seen it coming; she and William had become very serious very quickly. They had been talking off and on for years and had been in a serious relationship for the past six months. It may have felt a little fast, but they were both a bit older, and Karina already had a life and kids, and William was starting to integrate beautifully into that life. Then why was Karina so hesitant? She loved William, she knew that for sure, and she even loved the idea of him being a part of her life. But she couldn't shake the feeling something felt off. Maybe it was the idea of being married again.

A few years ago, Karina never would have seen herself considering a marriage with an entirely new person. The thought of going through another wedding, the newlywed phase, and then adjusting to living with another person again….it all sounded like so much work that she did not have the mental capacity for. But shouldn't she want to take that next step? That was the next step, wasn't it? Karina found herself frustrated she wasn't jumping for joy, and that she didn't immediately agree to the proposal. It all felt like too much for her, but she also felt terrible for leaving William in this state of confusion. Even though he was understanding, she still believed it was unfair. He had been so good and patient with her through all of it, even though some of the things he had to go through she couldn't imagine going through herself. Yet, he treated it all with a sweetness she was so grateful for.

But when Karina sat on her front porch holding a beautiful diamond ring in her hand, she knew she couldn't put it on her finger, not yet anyway. She needed more time, and now that Dan was returning to her life again, it would be wrong to put everyone through another huge change. The girls would already have to adjust to having their father in their lives. She couldn't imagine bringing another man in and changing their day-to-day worlds. It was too much.

Karina took receiving these two big pieces of information on the same day as a sign she had to pick one. Even though she had worked so hard in the past year to choose herself, it was at this time she had to choose her family and put them first. She hoped more than anything William would understand that, and perhaps one day she would be able to wear that ring on her finger, but not that day.

Chapter Twelve: Now

Kayla was not a very neat person, but she tried to tidy up her home a bit before her guest got there. Melinda had reached out to her a few days ago and asked if they could get together, and so Kayla invited her over for coffee. Kayla wasn't quite sure how to prepare for having her ex-boss in her home, especially under the circumstances. It was a strange position for her, because not only was she the messenger who told Melinda of her husband's betrayal, but she could also relate to what Melinda was going through, at least somewhat.

Melinda was right on time and greeted Kayla with a smile and a bottle of wine. "I decided we needed something a bit stronger than coffee," she explained, and they both laughed as Kayla invited her in.

Her home may have been small, but she tried to make it as welcoming as possible. Kayla did not have the interior decorating touch her mother had, so it looked a bit eccentric, but they settled at Kayla's kitchen table, and Melinda complimented her decor anyway. Kayla fished two wine glasses out of her cupboard and Melinda poured herself a glass that was twice as full as Kayla's, but she wasn't judging. She knew the failed attempts she had when she tried to drown her own sorrows in alcohol. But, as Melinda would soon realize, the only way she was going to move forward would be if she dealt with her feelings head-on.

"How have you been doing?" Kayla asked.

At first, Melinda was tempted to give her cookie-cutter "I'm hanging in there" response, but then she remembered Kayla had already seen her in a bad spot, so she decided she wasn't going to fake it. "I'm doing terrible," she responded, and Kayla nodded.

"That is completely understandable. The fact that you are even up and dressed is pretty impressive," Kayla reminded her, and Melinda smiled.

It was easier for Melinda to do things every day than lie in her bed and wallow in her sadness. At least if she was doing things, it gave her a distraction, and Melinda's focus was to constantly distract herself so she wouldn't have to think about how devastating her circumstances were.

"Have you talked to him?" Kayla asked cautiously. She didn't want to pry too much, but she also remembered Melinda had reached out to her, so maybe she trusted Kayla enough to become vulnerable.

"I have, a few times. The first time I just yelled at him and he didn't say much in response. He's taken over BlockWorks, and I'm still left spinning," she admitted and took a big sip of wine. "Our last conversation just really threw me and I don't really know what to do with it," she confessed apprehensively. Kayla nodded, and Melinda took another sip of wine and continued. "He asked to meet up again, and when we did, he acted completely different. He told me he was sorry for what he did. Then he explained why he did it."

Kayla's curiosity peaked at hearing her last sentence. Benjamin did not seem like the kind of person to own up to his poor choices, so she wondered what he could have possibly said to his wife.

"He told me he was trying to do what was best for us. He wanted to improve our lives, I guess. He said CodeX was in a much worse financial place than I knew and he wanted to save us before the company went under."

Kayla wanted to roll her eyes at his terrible excuses. There were so many reasons Kayla believed he was spewing lies to his wife, but she kept those to herself. Instead, she remained silent and just listened to Melinda.

"But it doesn't make sense. If he was trying to save our marriage, why didn't he tell me about it? Why all the sneaking around and secrets?"

"I think those are good questions to ask. He did go behind your back and blindsided you," Kayla reminded her as gently as she could with the reality of the situation.

"But he did admit he shouldn't have gone about it that way, and that he regretted what he did. He owned that he got too caught up in the power and didn't consider our marriage. I just don't know what to do with that information."

When Melinda said that last phrase, it seemed to take Kayla back to a very different point in her life when she also received information she didn't know how to handle.

Kayla got home late that night. She had gone out to the bar. After feeling tired of sitting with a bunch of miserable people, she decided to head back home. Kayla was flipping through her mail and came upon a manila envelope that had no return address. She tore upon the envelope and found a stack of legal documents inside. It took a minute for her to figure out what exactly she was looking at, but once she skimmed through a few lines of the first page and saw Peter's name on it, she realized she was looking at his divorce papers. She couldn't understand why he would send her such a thing, but after she flipped through the papers, a small note fell out. She ran her finger across his familiar handwriting.

> *Kayla,*
>
> *These papers are probably not what you were expecting in your mailbox. I just wanted you to know I was serious. Things are over between Laurie and me. If you want to talk at some point, I would love the chance to see you again. I want to give us a real shot, Kayla. I hope you do too.*
>
> *Love,*
> *Peter*

Kayla brought herself back to the present day and let go of the ghost haunting her. "You know him best, Melinda. You have to discern whether this is something you can come back from," she told her, and Melinda just nodded.

"When everything happened, you told me you had your fair share of experience with affairs. Did you ever recover from it?" Melinda asked her.

Kayla sighed. She had no desire to dive into her personal life with Melinda, but since Melinda had the courage to be open and honest with her, the least she could do was return the favor. "No, I couldn't," she admitted with a frown. Melinda looked visibly disappointed. "But I've seen other people be able to forgive and move forward, so I know it's not impossible. I just couldn't," she quickly added, not wanting to diminish Melinda's hope.

Melinda extended her hand and squeezed Kayla's arm. "I'm sorry for your loss," she first said, and Kayla's surprised face said it all. Before she could thank her, Melinda steered the conversation back to herself. "I guess I'm just struggling because I miss him so much, and while our marriage had problems, and I knew he struggled with selfishness and control, I never thought he would be capable of doing something so cruel. I don't know if I would be able to trust him again, but I also can't bear the thought of losing him."

Kayla recognized the tough position Melinda was in. "Well, the good news is you don't have to make any decision right now. The ball is in your court and you can keep it there for as long as you want. The least he can do is give you time," she reassured her newfound friend.

That was true, but Melinda wasn't sure that was really who her husband was. She was afraid he would pressure her into making a decision or make her feel guilty for leaving him. She didn't want to leave him, but she wasn't sure what would be best for her, and for him. If she stayed with someone who didn't really trust him, that wouldn't be fair to him either.

These were the things Melinda took with her when she left Kayla's house, and it would take her a while to find the forgiveness in her heart to move forward, whether that was with Ben or not.

After Melinda left, Kayla washed the glasses and then allowed herself to look at something she hadn't since she stuffed it away months ago. She opened her desk drawer filled with random documents she didn't have the energy to clean out until she found the cluster of documents and note she received in that manila envelope. Even though she never reached out to Peter after she got them, she didn't throw them away either. It had been a long time, and she already made her decision. She believed she couldn't move forward with Peter after he lied to her, but after hearing Melinda talk, she couldn't help but wonder how he was doing. So, she gave in to the temptation and pulled up his social media. She scrolled through a few posts he had made about nature, and then one food post about a restaurant where he ate, and then, there it was: a photo with him and some young, smiling blonde. The caption said: "My favorite adventure buddy."

Kayla stared at the picture for longer than she should have, and then erased her search history and tried to pretend she hadn't seen it. But she couldn't. She wanted him to be happy, and it was very clear he was. Not with his wife, not with her, but he had found someone else who brought him joy. She was too late.

"We *are* doing this," Huxley told Bethany for the third time that morning. They had planned a trip to Boston for months now, but as her dad continually got worse, Bethany was hesitant to leave him, even if it was only for the weekend. "I know you want to stay with your father, but I think it would be a good thing for us to do something together as a family."

Bethany agreed because she knew he was right, but she was terrified something was going to happen to her father and she wouldn't be there.

They wanted to take Henry to Boston to show him around a new place, plus Huxley was dying to go to the art museum to see the new Thomas Cole exhibit they had just installed. Huxley was an art history nerd (and a history nerd in general), but Bethany loved that side of him. He would get so excited about paintings and random historical facts he learned. Through living in a historical town, he knew everything there was to know about the history of Plymouth, and they had already taken Henry to all the most important monuments that they would no doubt take him to many more times until he was old enough to complain about it.

Bethany always got a little anxious about leaving town, even though Boston was only an hour away. Plymouth felt safe for her, but she wanted this for her family. She hated that almost every weekend she was either away from them and with her father, or they were stuck in the house with her. Huxley also reminded her a few times when her father was gone, she would need other things to fall back on. If she made her entire life about her father, it would make losing him that much more difficult. Even still, she reached out to each of her father's nurses and told them where she was going and reminded them to reach out to her if his condition changed. So they loaded their car with a lot more things than they probably needed, and then they made their short road trip to Boston.

After they got settled in their hotel, they took Henry to walk around the older parts of the city. Huxley loved getting to see everything again. They tried to go to Boston every year, but they hadn't been since Henry was born. He wasn't as attached to Plymouth as Bethany was, so he loved the chance to get to explore somewhere, even if they had been there a few times already.

Finally, after the sun set over the beautiful skyline, they went back to their hotel. After Henry fell asleep, Huxley and Bethany snuggled up together to watch a movie. But midway through the movie, Bethany's thoughts became consumed with her family. She thought about her dad and her sister and even her mom.

Huxley immediately noticed his wife's mood shift, and he paused the movie. "Are you thinking about your dad?" he asked and wrapped her hand in his.

"I'm thinking about all of them. I just wish I had Kayla here for all of this. I wish she could be here to be with Dad."

"I know, but you have to give her time. This situation would be difficult for anyone, but you've told me so many times how much Kayla idolized your dad. I can't imagine someone I held to such a high regard look unrecognizable."

Kayla did really look up to their father, but Bethany couldn't help but wonder if it was more than that. She felt in her gut she was missing some piece of the puzzle. But she didn't say that to Huxley. Instead, she just changed the topic and talked about her father instead.

"I think I'm just waiting for the other shoe to drop, you know?" she started, and Huxley cocked his head a bit. "He's been sick for so long, and for the first two years, nothing really seemed different. He was just forgetful. But he's gone downhill so much in the past six months… I feel like he keeps teetering between the sixth and seventh stages."

Bethany had read a lot about Alzheimer's. She already loved reading, and even though reading about the tragic disease was not her favorite pastime, she wanted to understand and prepare herself for as much of the disease as she could. The problem was that Alzheimer's varied so greatly case by case. Some people could live twenty years with Alzheimer's, and some only lived three. No matter how much she tried, there was no way to prepare for the roller coaster that was this disease.

With all the uncertainty, it was even more difficult for Bethany to grapple with Kayla not being there. Bethany knew what was in her father's future. Soon he wouldn't be able to speak more than a few intelligible words in a conversation. She had already noticed her father's ability to speak go downhill, and she was terrified Kayla was going to miss the opportunity to have a conversation with him. As terrible as the bad days were, Bethany was grateful for the good days she had with her father, even if he didn't remember who she was or who he was sometimes. She tried to soak up every chance to be with him, whoever and wherever he was at that moment. Even that fact was hard for Bethany to accept, but even though she felt like she had lost him, she reminded herself daily it was the same heartbeat she had known her whole life. The thought that someday it wouldn't beat anymore was something Bethany couldn't even imagine.

The truth was, Kayla couldn't imagine it either, mostly because she wouldn't allow herself. She had become so consumed with her work and her own troubles that she wasn't able to see the severity of her father's condition and the direction it was going. She wouldn't let herself see.

But Bethany didn't know the extent of why Kayla was in such denial. Maybe if she did, Bethany would have felt differently. But that night she couldn't help but feel a seed of resentment toward her sister.

Bethany didn't pay attention to the rest of the movie, but the next day she put all her family problems in the back of her mind so she could enjoy the day with her family. They headed to the art museum, and when they got there, Huxley was giddy with excitement. Henry may not have had any interest in the museum, but that did not dampen Huxley's spirits. When he dragged his family to the Thomas Cole exhibit and gave a long synopsis of his life and works, he was too caught up in the joy of seeing the paintings to notice his son's tired and wandering eyes.

Bethany relished in her husband's excitement. She lit up as he gushed over how beautiful and profound the works were. Being in that museum gave Huxley a kind of glow that was one of Bethany's favorite things to see.

They spent the rest of the day at the science museum. In the same way Huxley's eyes lit up over Thomas Cole, Henry's eyes were dazzling in the science museum. He squealed with joy when they walked into one room and a giant dinosaur met his gaze. The family walked through fossils, did experiments, and filled their afternoon with the wonders of science. They stayed until the museum's closing, and Henry still threw a fit about having to leave.

The next day, Bethany was relieved to be updated by Gianna that there were no changes with her father. They were able to go back home in peace, and Bethany was grateful they had taken the trip. She agreed even more with Huxley's belief that they needed that time together as a family. When she arrived home, she found a letter in her mailbox from her sister. She let herself be filled with some hope that this would be the letter Kayla told her that she was coming back to Plymouth, but that was not what Bethany would find in the letter.

> Dear Bethany,
>
> I know that things have been rough between us, but I am writing anyway because of what is going on in my life. I don't know if any news has made its way to you yet, but I wanted you to know that the company I am working for has gone under, so I'm currently looking for work. I'm not telling you this to ask you for anything, but I just wanted to update you about what was going on in my life. If you want to look up what happened, all you have to do is look up 'CodeX Scandal' and a whole host of articles will come up about the nightmare I've had to endure. I just don't feel like explaining it all in this letter.
>
> I hope you and your family are doing well. I'm trying to hang in there and figure out what the next step will be for me. I love you.
>
> Love,
>
> Kayla

After reading the letter, Bethany looked up the scandal and read through several articles about what happened. She was shocked and even a little hurt her sister had waited to reach out to her. With something this major, she thought

Kayla would have called her. But it was clear their relationship wasn't at that point anymore, and if she was being honest with herself, their relationship surely wasn't at the place where Bethany could call and talk about her issues. Much of what plagued Bethany was surrounding their father, and Kayla wouldn't hear that.

Even still, this was her younger sister, and she was heartbroken she had suffered a drastic change such as this. She wanted to call and tell her she was there if Kayla wanted to talk, but unfortunately, she realized she was not the person to comfort her sister, no matter how badly she wanted to be. She just really hoped someone could love Kayla the way she wanted to.

Chapter Thirteen: Then

The girls were overjoyed when they heard the news their father would be moving back to Massachusetts. As for going over the details of what that would look like, Karina and Dan decided it would be best for all of them to sit down as a family and discuss how life was going to change. While the girls didn't realize it at the time, Dan moving back would incur some major life changes for them both.

When their father knocked on the door that day, the girls were beyond excited to see him. After they had many warm embraces and had the chance to relish just being with their father, they eventually made their way to their dining room table to sit down and talk. Bethany may have only been eleven years and Kayla was only nine, but Dan and Karina both felt it was necessary to address things the girls may not have even been thinking about in order to begin this new chapter of their family in an open and honest way. But all the girls could think about was how excited they were to have their father there.

Dan began the conversation. "I don't know how you girls are feeling about me moving back—"

"We are SO excited for you to be back home, Daddy," Kayla interrupted with a grin.

Dan smiled. "And I am so excited to be back, but I do want to talk to you girls about some things." He cleared his throat. He may have been talking to two kids, but Dan was nervous to have this conversation with them. While they didn't understand the gravity of it, Dan knew he had to own his failures as a father, and that was terrifying. "I am sure there were a lot of times in your life when you wondered why I was in Germany instead of with you girls. I can't imagine how hard it was to see other dads at school events and not have your dad there. I want you both to know I am so, so sorry about that." Dan's eyes started to water, but he looked up at the ceiling for a moment to compose himself. "Daddy was really selfish, and I thought I was doing what was best, but I know I have missed out on a lot of really special moments with you girls."

Bethany nodded and took every word her father was saying to heart. She had felt the emptiness of not having her father many times in her life, but she trusted her parents to do the right thing. When she heard that her dad had been selfish, it opened her eyes to the fact that her parents were more flawed than she once believed. "You're not going to leave again, are you?" Bethany quietly asked.

"No, I'm not," Dan responded firmly. "I'm here to stay."

Smiles grew on both the girls' faces.

Karina had been silent so far, but the conversation did not fall on deaf ears. She was mostly just grateful she was not having another tough conversation by herself. Now she had another parent to tackle some of the more difficult questions. Karina knew, even if the girls didn't have a lot to say now, it was crucial for them to be affirmed in whatever they were feeling about their father coming back, and about his long absence from their lives.

Also, in the conversation, they went through some logistics of what this new stage of life would look like. They planned for Dan to take the girls every other weekend, and pick them up on Wednesdays to spend the night at his place and then take them to school the next morning. Dan also promised to take them shopping so they could make their new room look a little more like home. The conversation ended with a big group hug that Kayla forced, and Dan headed back to his practically empty apartment.

"Dan, stop!" Karina playfully screamed as Dan ran towards her with a hand covered in paint. She retaliated by dipping her paintbrush in the can and flicking the paintbrush at Dan. It covered his shirt and even got a little on his face.

"That is dirty fighting!" he yelled and scooped her up as she squealed with joy.

After they were done with their laughing fit, they took a step back to look at the house.

"Can you believe this is ours?" she exclaimed and gave him a kiss on the cheek.

"I can't."

They were so excited they were able to secure a loan and buy their first house. Dan still had to put in his time to serve but, at that moment, all they could think about was the future that would exist after his time in the military was done. He was set to leave in a few days, so the couple cherished this time together.

"Think of all the memories we are going to make here," she remarked.

He wrapped her in his arms and was filled with warmth.

"We are going to have such a beautiful life here, my love," he whispered in her ear and gave her a kiss.

"But we are going to have a half-painted house if we don't finish," Karina added.

The house was perfect, except for the hideous yellow color that coated the outside. When they bought it, they vowed the first thing they would do was paint the exterior. They had gone back and forth over what color to paint it, but finally settled on a light blue with which they were both happy. However, they greatly underestimated how much work it would be to paint an entire house. Karina had painted her room once in her life, but she now understood that painting a room was an entirely different affair than painting an entire house. But they were more than okay to do the work; it meant they were doing something together for their home. Karina had dreamt of a home of her own for so long, but Dan just wanted her.

"Well, we better get to work!" Karina exclaimed. "But first, I'm going to make us some lemonade."

"Yes," Dan whispered, and a big grin appeared on Karina's face.

She came out a few minutes later with a pitcher full of fresh lemonade and a couple glasses, but she didn't see Dan anywhere on the lawn. She called his name a few times, and when she still couldn't spot him, she set the pitcher on the porch and decided to walk around the house to see if he had started painting somewhere else. When she turned the corner, she was met with a shocking surprise. Dan had filled a paint tray *and surprised Karina by coating her with the remaining paint. She screamed at the sensation of the cold paint dripping down her whole body.*

"Dan! I'm going to get you for this!" she yelled and they resumed goofing off and not getting as much painting done as they probably should have. But all the silly moments were worth it in the end.

Dan held an old photograph in his hand. It was of the two of them standing outside their freshly painted house on the day Dan left to serve. He didn't know at the time he would soon receive a letter and learn his wife was pregnant. In the picture, they were a young couple eager to start their lives together. Dan reflected on those days of painting and all the memories they were so hopeful to make, and how badly Dan failed at creating them. Most of the memories made in that house were done by Karina and the girls without Dan. It broke him to carry such a burden.

Since moving into his apartment, Dan had thought a lot about when they moved into their home together. He seemed to be stuck in a state of reflective guilt but tried to hold onto the hope he could make some things better, at least through being a good father. But most of the things he wanted to make up for, he was too late; he missed so many firsts with his daughters, and it was more than too late with Karina. He had told her several times how sorry he was since he moved back, and after the last time he apologized, she told him he needed to learn to forgive himself. He just had no idea how to do that.

Dan had been talking to his counselor and examining his emotions, but one hour a week wasn't helping as much as he needed. His new counselor wasn't the same as the one he had in Germany, and he struggled to connect with her.

Dan was also at a loss for things to do. He didn't have any friends, he didn't have a social life, and he wasn't even living with his family. He also didn't maintain his previous friendships in Plymouth well enough to rely on anymore. While Dan was happy with his decision to move back, he didn't register how it would feel starting over, and it made for painful loneliness. Sometimes he found himself just wandering around his apartment, or going for runs that took a lot longer than necessary just because he wanted to fill the time.

His work was a lot of paper-pushing and being the middleman between the employees and his boss. Dan didn't hate the job, but felt he wasn't doing anything worthwhile. There was no overwhelming sense of purpose. So, that night, instead of wallowing in his own self-pity, he would do something positive and decided to write a letter to his parents.

Dan's relationship with his parents was distant, but that wasn't because he wanted it to be. His parents hadn't made the effort to connect with Dan growing up, and while they sent him letters and called him sometimes to check in, it always felt shallow. After he was kicked out, Dan stopped making as much of an effort with his parents, and when he went to Germany, he only wrote them a letter every few months. Sometimes, they never even wrote a letter back, and sometimes Dan would forget he had even sent one until six months later when a one-page letter returned in the mail. Even in the letters, Dan struggled to see the love he hoped to receive from them. It wasn't that they didn't love him, they just didn't view parenthood the same way as Dan did. It was more of a responsibility to provide for another person than it was a chance to build a relationship or pour into a child.

The distance he felt his entire life with his parents may have even been a reason why he physically remained distant from his children, even if Dan didn't connect these dots himself. But even with the disconnection with his parents, he hoped if he reached out and told them he was back in the States, perhaps they would take more interest in his life.

> Dear Dad and Mom,
> It has been a while since your last letter, so I wanted to reach out and tell you some exciting news. A few weeks ago, I moved back to Massachusetts! I've settled into my new apartment in Marshfield, and I'm doing a human resources job. If you guys are up for it, I'd love to visit with you sometime. I hope you both are doing well.
> Love,
> Dan

The letter looked a little short, so Dan tried to add a few more details about his apartment, and then Bethany and Kayla. He wanted to know more about his parents and how they were doing, but they tended to keep their lives private. While he hoped that this time he would receive a meaningful response, it would be months before his parents ever acknowledged his letter. In fact, that would be the last letter he would receive from them. Years of Christmas cards, birthday parties, and even a wedding invitation would find their way into his parents' mailbox, but he would never receive a response to any of them.

Dan ran downstairs to put the letter in the mailbox. He looked extremely tacky in his oversized stained shirt, which he probably would have changed if he knew who he would run into in the foyer. He tried to skirt by unnoticed, but when they made eye contact, he knew it was too late.

"Hey, you're new here, aren't you?" the gentle, violet-eyed woman said to Dan as he put his letter in the mail.

"Yeah, I moved here a few weeks ago. I'm Dan." He reached out his hand to shake hers.

"I'm Tina. 1D," she said and gestured to a white door. "Nice to meet you."

Even though it was Dan's first time meeting Tina, he already knew all about her. His landlord was a well-intentioned older woman who also wanted to know more about Dan's personal life. Once she learned he was single, she immediately told him all about Tina, the beautiful woman who lived in 1D. Tina was a single mom whose husband had died a year after their son was born, and while she previously lived in Boston, she moved to Marshfield to get a fresh start with her kid.

Dan did not want to know all this personal information about a stranger, but Ms. Betsy was intent on telling Dan as much as possible so he could somehow fall in love with her before even knowing her. Even still, he was self-conscious about finally meeting the infamous Tina while he was poorly dressed, but their interaction was not the "love-at-first-sight" meeting for which Ms. Betsy had probably hoped. But who knew? Maybe this wouldn't be the last that Dan saw of Tina.

Dan's newly acquired Ford Ranger was a great car (at least that was what the car salesman promised him) except for the fact the A/C was broken. While this would mean a lot of rolled-down windows in the summer, for now, it was cool enough to where it wouldn't be a problem. Dan's task today was to buy some new furniture, but first, he planned to swing by his old house to pick up a gift certificate for the local furniture store. He remembered the gift certificate was specifically in a file folder filled with a bunch of important documents Karina hadn't gotten around to giving to him, since a lot of the documents were for them both. Even still, Dan didn't want to go all the way to his ex-wife's for a gift certificate, but he wasn't doing great on cash after the big move, and so he figured it was best to save money wherever he could. Plus, he could make copies of the rest of the documents so Karina would have one less thing to deal with on her plate.

Dan decided he would swing by. Unfortunately for Dan, he had a momentary lapse in judgment to let Karina know he was stopping by. What awaited him was something for which he was not at all prepared. He knocked on the door, which still felt strange, and a man answered. He looked to be about 5'10", with strawberry blonde hair, and his smug smile was the last thing Dan expected to greet him.

"Who are you?" Dan asked in an accusatory manner.

"Um... I'm William," the man replied.

Immediately footsteps scurried towards the door. When Karina arrived, her face turned red and she gaped at the awkward situation that stood before her in the form of two territorial men.

"Dan, what are you doing here?" she asked in a calm manner, even though her insides were turned upside down.

"I, um..." he stumbled over his words, too in shock after staring at William in the flesh. He had tried so hard to forget William ever since the accidental phone call he made a few months ago. But now, here he was, standing before him, and Dan had to do everything in his power not to have a panic attack on his old doorstep. "I was going to grab those important documents left in the office, but I see that this is a bad time, so I'm just going to go," he said and excused himself from the situation.

But before Dan could get off the front porch, William, probably unwisely, decided to speak up.

"Hey, wait, Dan," he started.

Dan's anxiety spiked after being called back to the front door.

"I know this is awkward, but it doesn't have to be. This used to be your home, so you should come on in and do whatever you need to do."

William was trying to be considerate, but Dan took it as extremely offensive. He wanted to explode with something like: "Oh, so you're giving me permission to enter my old home like it's yours now?" But he bit his tongue. Instead, he politely denied William's request, and once again excused himself.

When Dan got into his car, Karina ran over before he had a chance to drive away. She tapped on his window and he cautiously rolled it down. All he wanted was to escape the hellhole Karina and William kept bringing him back into, but he couldn't ignore his anxious ex-wife's desperate attempt to make things better.

"Hey, are you okay?" she asked with her brows furrowed and eyes wrought with concern.

"Aside from having an unwanted encounter, I'm fine," he coldly replied, but then softened. "I'm sorry. I shouldn't have just shown up at your house like that. I really have to go now," he hastily told her. She nodded and he sped away as fast as he could.

Dan did not go to the furniture store that day. In fact, he drove straight home. When he got there, he couldn't help but pick William apart. He thought about the entire interaction; what he looked like, how he spoke, and how Karina interacted with him. But, after a while, he could hear his counselor telling him it was unhealthy, and so he grabbed a book and tried to focus on another world that was not his own. That worked for a little while, but even between the pages, he thought about William's over eagerness to be friends. Did he acknowledge the part he played in destroying Dan's marriage? Dan couldn't get over how naïve William was to think the two of them could function in any sort of normal way. How could he even be expected to look at the man who replaced him?

Dan was swimming in a whirlwind of pain wondering what life was supposed to look like going forward. Was he expected to welcome this man into his life? Into his family's life? It was clear now he didn't have a choice. The problem was Dan knew he would never be friends with William, but he didn't know how he was supposed to be civil with him.

Karina also struggled with the interaction. There was a part of her that was glad the two had met, but she was mostly left with an uneasy feeling in the pit of her stomach. William stayed the night since the girls were at a sleepover with a friend, but even when he wrapped his arm around her as they lay in bed, she still pulled away slightly. Seeing Dan's face was what really wrecked her and filled her with even more shame than she already grappled with every day. She had to put someone she loved through meeting the man she cheated with, and that fact gnawed at Karina's soul that night, and for a while after.

After William was asleep that night, she slipped away from the bed, threw on a robe, and sat on her back porch. She didn't sit in her usual chair to watch the sunrise, but she sat on the porch itself, and felt the cold wood under her fingertips. She listened to the silence that filled the neighborhood once it got dark outside, and closed her eyes and tried to only focus on the stillness of the night. However, Dan's face popped back in her mind, and even when she tried to push it away, she felt a tear slide down her cheek over the pain she had caused him.

William woke up shortly after Karina had left the bed. It didn't take long for him to find her sitting outside on the porch. For a few minutes, he just watched her. She looked peaceful from behind, but in his heart, he knew she was in pain. While all he wanted to do was try to make the interaction with her ex-husband a little less painful, he understood he had made it worse by not keeping his mouth shut. The truth was, William felt guilty too. He never believed himself to be a homewrecker, but it was only when he let his inner demons have a voice was when he realized that was exactly what he was. All he wanted to do was love Karina, but he was the one who fell in love with a married woman, and now he had to face her ex-husband. He didn't know when he would have to see Dan again, but the thought was terrifying, because every time he saw him, he only saw the worst version of himself.

Karina took notice of William watching her and wiped the tear off her cheek and came back inside. "I couldn't sleep," she whispered, and he grabbed her hand.

"I know today couldn't have been easy. This is so messy, but I just want you to know I love you. So much," he told her, and pulled her into a kiss. Instead, she fell into his arms and started sobbing. He didn't say anything, but he wrapped his arms around her tightly and gently combed his fingers through her hair.

Karina didn't cry for long, and when she pulled away, she grabbed his arm and pulled him back into the bedroom. When they got there, she sat up in the bed and he held her hand firmly as she stared at the wall in front of her. There were many things running through Karina's mind at that moment, but when she looked at William, some of those things melted away.

"I'm sorry for all my mess," she told him, and held back the tears that desperately wanted to come out again.

"This isn't your mess. It's *our* mess, and we are going to get through it together," he reassured her.

"I want you to move in with us," she abruptly stated.

This wasn't entirely out of the blue for Karina, although it was for William. She had thought about asking him to move in after she turned down his proposal. While she stood by the fact she wasn't ready to jump into a new marriage, she didn't want to leave William out to dry. While she wasn't entirely sure if she was ready to have someone else living in her house, and it would take a lot of adjusting for all of them, she wanted to take a next step with William. If it wasn't marriage, at least it would be something. Of course, William eagerly agreed.

For a day that turned out so badly, it was a night full of excitement for William's future. Even though Karina was left feeling terrified about the future, she also wanted more than anything for her love for William to be enough to push her past all her fears; and eventually that night, it was.

Chapter Fourteen: Now

Kayla found herself staring in the bathroom mirror for a long time that morning. After looking at Peter's social media, Kayla was left spinning into a tailspin of self-hatred. She was filled with conflicting voices in her head and caught in between two very different mentalities. The first was one of regret. She regretted not being with Peter after he sent her the papers. She let that mentality fill with happy memories of Peter, and how real and deep everything felt in such a short amount of time. She also was reminded of how willing Melinda was to even consider going back to her husband after he betrayed her so deeply. For Kayla, getting back together with Peter was never even an option in her mind.

At the very same time, Kayla's other mentality fought for the spotlight. This was the one she had held onto for the past several months. This mentality reminded her of the betrayal she felt with Peter, and how cold sitting on that park bench was. It told her all of Peter's efforts to get back together with her were very selfish. After all, she didn't want anything to do with him, and yet he continually kept disrespecting her by leaving voicemails. And then he had the audacity to send her his divorce papers. But then her first mentality would say perhaps what he did showed he was willing to fight for her, and didn't she want someone who would fight for her against all odds, even herself?

The problem with these mentalities was they both spoke so loudly, sometimes at the same time, Kayla had no idea which to listen to. Since each mentality wanted something different, it meant that, no matter what, one of them was going to be disappointed. Of course, with each mentality, her self-hatred slipped in. On the one hand, she wondered if she had sabotaged her own happiness then and given up her one shot at finding love, and on the other hand, she wondered if she was sabotaging her own happiness now by allowing herself to be drawn right back into the Peter mess she wanted to avoid. Either way, she resented herself and her own mind that couldn't even do the one thing it was supposed to do: think straight.

Aside from the self-hatred, looking at his social media also left Kayla feeling deeply incomplete. At first, she didn't understand why, but after a few days of not being able to force it out of her billowing mind, she realized it wasn't seeing Peter again that screwed her over, it was seeing him with someone other than Laurie. Part of her assumed Peter would go back to his wife, but when she saw that he didn't, she discerned he must have been telling the truth when he said it was over between them.

Kayla also felt stir crazy. She was jobless, and even after applying to several jobs, she hadn't even gotten an interview. Rejection from employers, as well as Peter, fueled her unhealthy state. When she continued to stare at herself in the mirror, she asked her reflection what was wrong with her. She couldn't get a job, she gave up the one love interest who meant something to her, and she didn't even have any friends. She had coworkers who occasionally she got lunch with or grabbed a drink with after work, but not even one of them had reached out after the company fell apart. To be fair, Kayla hadn't reached out to any of them either. The closest thing she had to a friend at that point was her ex-boss. Sometimes, even that didn't feel like a friendship, as most of their conversations involved listening to Melinda talk about Benjamin. Kayla didn't share her own burdens. In fact, Melinda didn't know anything about Kayla's past except for the vague comments she sometimes dropped in conversation. The trouble was Kayla resented herself for this too. Was it her fault no one took interest in her life? Or was it her fault for not being open and vulnerable in the first place? Maybe she was missing the cues that it was okay to tell Melinda about her own life struggles, but she also didn't want to burden her if she wasn't interested in hearing them. It was conversations and questions like these that filled Kayla's mind when she wandered aimlessly around her apartment.

After staring in the mirror, Kayla impulsively decided to get in her car and drive to the hardware store. Once she arrived, she picked out a few succulents and small plants to fill her apartment. While Kayla was not much of a gardener, she wanted her apartment to have life in it. So, there she was, driving home with seven small plants in her passenger seat, and a genuine smile grew on her face as she looked at them riding next to her.

When she got home, Kayla set up some of her plants on the windowsill: one on her nightstand, and the rest scattered about her kitchen. After that, she flopped onto her bed and was soon stuck in the same rut as when she left. She had nothing to do. Usually, when she was bored, Kayla would go out and take a walk, or go out to a bar, but she didn't have the energy to do either of those things.

Kayla's heightened impulsive state encouraged her to make the very unhealthy choice of checking Peter's social media again. He hadn't posted anything since the last time she checked. Once she had it open, there was a small part of her that feared she would turn this small action into an unhealthy habit, but the part of her mind in the driver's seat continued to scroll through the photos. He had deleted the posts with his wife.

As she was scrolling through, Kayla's hand froze when she noticed a post he had made ten months ago, shortly after she found out about Laurie. At first, it looked like a meaningless photo of his keys hanging from his ignition. To anyone else, that was the only thing they would see, but not Kayla. On his keys hung one keychain, the other half of the matching keychain they got on their first date. The caption read: "Regret is such a short word…and yet it stretches on forever." It was a quote Kayla vaguely recognized. This post made everything even more painful. It was another attempt to reach her, and it had gone completely unnoticed, until now.

Now all Kayla felt was more regret. She gave into her first mentality that yelled at her for throwing away her chance at happiness. This was the only voice she heard in her head for weeks after seeing that painful post. She was drowning in the belief she was foolish until she finally couldn't take it anymore. On a whim, she threw some clothes in a backpack, hopped in her car, and headed for Plymouth.

Music played softly in the kitchen as Huxley and Bethany swayed to the notes. It was rare they got a night in their home without Henry, but he was at a birthday party, so the couple took advantage of the quiet moment together. Huxley gently hummed to the song, and Bethany pressed closer against him and closed her eyes so her only focus was his heart beating against her chest. She didn't think about her father, who continued to sway through emotions, or her sister, whose life decisions she still struggled to understand. Bethany only thought about her wonderful husband and the beautiful family they had built.

Even though her dream was to settle down and have a family, she never thought she would actually get it. Sometimes you love too much and end up scaring it away before it even has a chance to welcome you. That was why Huxley was such a beautiful surprise; she wasn't even expecting to fall in love with him. Sometimes, as Bethany learned with him, the unexpected stories were the best ones.

"I love you," she whispered, and he squeezed her tightly.

"I love you too," he responded and grabbed her face to kiss her.

Even now, kissing him made a huge smile grow on Bethany's face and butterflies swell in her stomach.

Huxley twirled her around into the next song, and then brought her close again and hummed to a new beat.

In the middle of the song, their doorbell rang. They both looked up at each other with confusion. Huxley walked over to stop the music as Bethany headed towards the door.

Of course, our quiet moments don't get to last that long, Bethany thought as she approached their big front door. When she opened it, she thought her eyes had fooled her. "Kayla?" she questioned, even though it was undeniable that she was staring into the face of her sister. Before Kayla could respond, Bethany pulled her into a hug. "You're home," she said softly, and tears poured out of her eyes.

Showing up to her sister's house was not at all part of Kayla's plan. In fact, going to Plymouth was not in her plans until she got in the car and started driving. Over the eighteen-hour drive, a lot went through Kayla's head. She tried to put every thought of Peter out of her head, but with nothing but open road and bad radio music to distract her, Peter tended to creep into her mind.

She also thought a lot about her father, which led to a lot of sobbing at the wheel. If Kayla was being honest with herself, she had been in complete denial about her father ever since he started his steep decline. This drive was the first time she allowed herself to imagine a world without him, which was necessary. Even though she hated it, a world without him was coming up sooner than she wanted.

In her drive that consisted of mostly tears and heavy metal music to distract her, Kayla tried to come up with a plan for when she got to Plymouth. She planned to get a hotel for two nights, clear her head, say goodbye to her father, and leave. But, when she pulled over at a rest stop to get a couple hours of sleep, she checked her bank account and realized she was in no financial place to sleep anywhere except for her car. She shouldn't have even been taking this road trip in the first place, with gas and fast food stops on the way, but her impulsiveness got the better of her. Since she was already halfway there, there was no turning back. When she rolled into Plymouth with her car filled with fast food wrappers and her eyes barely able to stay open, Kayla drove to her sister's because it was her only option.

Of course, Bethany didn't know any of that. All she knew was her prayers had been answered; her sister had finally come home and they would be able to go on the last part of their father's journey together.

After the unexpected embrace from Bethany, Kayla awkwardly asked if she could stay with them for a few days. Bethany eagerly led her to the guest bedroom. Kayla set her stuff on the nicely made bed and glanced around. The room was simple; one queen bed with rustic-looking sheets, a few photos of nature around the room, and a landscape painting above the bed. The nightstand had fresh flowers in it, which affirmed Kayla's belief her sister was way more on top of her life than she would ever be.

"You are welcome to stay as long as you would like," Bethany assured her. "I'm just really glad you're back."

Kayla nodded and Bethany left the room to relish in her excitement with her husband.

Huxley was a little more cautious about his sister-in-law's sudden arrival but tried not to show it with Bethany. He hoped this would be the start of a new relationship for the two of them, but for as long as he had known them, he saw a great disconnect. They often left so many things unsaid, and he believed the only way they would really move forward would be if they dealt with the issues that kept them apart.

But that was not Bethany's focus. She just wanted to be with her sister. When she knocked on her door, she had the giddiness of a child.

Sitting on the bed, Kayla didn't even look up when her sister entered.

"Are you okay?" Bethany asked and hoped her sister would finally open up and talk to her.

"Yeah, I'm fine," Kayla brushed her off and continued to stare at the carpeted floor. "I think I'm just tired. It was a long drive."

"Oh yeah, of course. You should take a nap. I can wake you when Henry comes home. He will be so excited to see you," Bethany exclaimed, but Kayla's response was lackluster at best. Bethany backed out of the room and delicately closed the door behind her. The rejection was far greater than the actual reality of what had happened, but she didn't care. At that moment, she was a teenager being shut out by her sister time and time again. She knew why, and at the end of the day, she believed she deserved it. But that didn't change how painful it was.

It was a new day, and Bethany hoped this would be the day Kayla would be ready to see their father. Her sister had been staying with her for three days, and even though Bethany offered every day for them to see their dad, Kayla said she wasn't ready yet.

Even though Huxley was okay with Kayla staying with them, he was getting a bit frustrated that all she did was stay in their guest bedroom.

Bethany wanted to give her sister the time and space that she needed, but Kayla had barely spoken to anyone in the house, and it was getting old for all of them. A part of Bethany wanted to get back to her normal life with just her husband and her son, and it didn't help that she knew Huxley wanted that too, even if he wasn't pushing for Kayla to leave. But at the same time, she didn't want to squander the opportunity to reconnect with her sister.

Bethany was up early that morning and expected Kayla to still be asleep, but she found her sitting on the front porch with a cup of tea in her hand as the sun woke up in front of her.

"You know, you remind me of someone sitting out here," Bethany re-marked. Kayla looked up from her drink with a puzzled expression on her face. "Every morning, bright and early, Mom would get up, pour herself a cup of tea or coffee, and go on the porch to watch the sunrise. Every morning, with-out fail."

"How do you know that?" Kayla asked.

"Well, when I got older, sometimes I'd do it with her. You were never one for getting up early though. Always a night owl like Dad," Bethany told her.

Kayla sighed.

Bethany searched for another casual conversation topic, but there was only one question that pulsed in her mind. It had been gnawing at her for so long she knew there was never going to be a perfect time to ask it, so she decided now was as good a time as ever. "What happened, K? You were far closer to Dad than I was. I thought you would want to be here. What's taken you so long?"

Kayla set her tea down on the porch. "Nothing happened with Dad. I just... I can't deal with someone else dying."

"It seems like it's more than that," Bethany pushed. It had been too long, and Bethany still firmly believed her sister should have returned earlier, but she wasn't going to say it at that moment. She wanted to give Kayla a chance to explain herself, but Kayla didn't seem very willing. "I know we haven't been in the best place. Is it because of me?" Bethany asked. Kayla remained silent. "Because, if it is, I don't have to go with you when you see Dad. You don't even have to stay here. I could pay for you to stay in a hotel for a bit too."

"Not everything is about you, Bethany," Kayla replied flatly.

"That's not what I was saying. I just meant—" Bethany began.

"I was the last person to talk to Mom before she died."

Bethany was taken aback. She replayed a precious memory in her head and spoke up to correct her. "No, we were together. At lunch, remember?"

Kayla paused before she responded. She thought about the same memory. Part of her thought about pretending Bethany was right, but she was tired of her sister persecuting her for not returning to Plymouth, and it was time she knew the truth. "I know you've always thought the diner was the last time we talked to her, because I wanted you to have that good last memory of her, but I went by her house after lunch, B."

Bethany sat down next to Kayla and waited for her to continue. When she didn't, Bethany asked: "What happened?"

Kayla didn't speak at first, but after taking a deep breath, she shared something that would shift Bethany's entire perspective of her sister, and her mother. "When I went over there, we got in a fight. She didn't agree with the decisions we were making. She thought I was being too frivolous and that you had settled down too soon. I didn't agree with her, and told her she was the last person in the world who should be judging our lives; that her decisions had already screwed us up enough." Her voice cracked at the pain of having to repeat the conversation. "That was the last thing I said to her." Tears welled up in Kayla's eyes. "I marched over to the front door, slammed it behind me, and have lived to regret that conversation every single day. Now when I think about our mother, I can't help but think about that. I don't want the same thing to happen to Dad. I don't want to have a bad memory...or any more memories with him."

Bethany's eyes widened at the boldness of Kayla's statement.

"The last time we spoke was good. He knew who I was, and we laughed, and it was happy. I walked away and told myself I was going to hold onto that memory because I couldn't handle seeing him as anything else." At that moment, all Kayla wanted to do was bury her face in her hands or grab her car keys and drive somewhere far away, but she stayed sitting on that front porch. Not because she had some newfound strength, but because she didn't have the energy to run anymore, not from her sister, at least. "I know my decision has hurt you, and I'm sorry about that, but I just couldn't do it."

Bethany put her hand on Kayla's arm. "I'm so sorry, Kayla. I didn't know. I never would have asked you to come back. You don't have to see Dad. You don't have to do anything," Bethany told her. While Bethany didn't fully understand what Kayla was going through, she was in so much shock that she would have said anything to keep her sister there, even if she didn't agree with it.

Kayla pulled away from her sister. "No," she sternly responded and wiped the tears off her face. "You have made it very clear in the past several months how much you don't approve of my life. Every time you send me some letter or give me some speech, it reminds me so much of Mom." Kayla stopped and tried to compose herself before continuing, while tears streamed down Bethany's face. "I didn't want to lose you too. That's why I'm here.

And just because you've heard my sob story doesn't change the fact you fundamentally believe I have a requirement to see our father and spend time with him before he dies. I am afraid if I don't, then you'll resent me, and I can't take that risk."

"No, that won't happen. I don't resent you."

Kayla stood up at the comment. "Yes, you do. You wouldn't have pushed as hard as you did if you didn't resent me. I know you shouldn't be the only one carrying the burden of losing Dad but I didn't know what else to do. You know how to handle it. I can't. But you have made it very clear I have to, and that isn't something I can just let go of."

Bethany could feel herself becoming angry and defensive over Kayla's remarks, and after sitting in that anger for a few minutes, she let it overtake her. She completely shifted away from the kind and understanding person she was a few minutes ago. "You can't choose when Dad dies, Kayla!" she said. Her voice was louder than she intended it to be. "He is still here, and I know you want to pick and choose your last moment with him, but that isn't how life works. It isn't fair that your perfect moment comes at the cost of me," she said, her hand shaking with anger and pain. The last thing Bethany wanted was to explode at her sister after she just shared something so vulnerable, but she was so tired of Kayla making decisions that affected Bethany's life. All her pain seemed to flow out in an incredibly ill-timed moment. "I wish I could have one special memory to hold onto, but instead I have had to watch our father slowly disintegrate over the years while you've frolicked around St. Louis without a care in the world."

"You don't know anything about my life!" Kayla yelled, and with that, she stomped into the house, grabbed her car keys, and left.

Bethany's heart was racing as she stood on the porch and watched her sister drive off. She fell to her knees and buried her hands into her face as she sobbed. Bethany tried to not give in to the anger she sometimes felt, but when she sat on her porch, filled with regret, she realized what she had done. All Kayla was trying to do was share what she was going through, and Bethany had once again obliterated her because of her own feelings.

An hour later, she still sat on the porch, but instead of crying, Bethany sat against the front of the house staring blankly at the neighborhood. Huxley found her. It took all but one look into her eyes for her to break down again. Kayla drew another line in the sand by driving away, and once again, Bethany believed it was all her fault.

Chapter Fifteen: Then

"Tina!" Dan called a little too keenly when he ran into her in the foyer of their apartment complex. She was struggling to carry several bags of groceries in her hands, and he rushed over to grab a bag that was close to spilling bunches of apples and potatoes.

"My hero," she teased and unlocked her door. She gestured for him to come in and directed him to set the groceries on the counter. "Where are you off to today?" she asked as she put boxes of pasta in a cabinet.

"I'm going to pick up the girls. It's my weekend to have them. I'm going to take them to see some animated movie they are dying to watch." He fiddled with his keys unsure if he should help her unload her groceries, or continue to awkwardly lean against the counter. He chose the latter.

"Oh, that should be fun! I'm taking Cassian to the park after school today since it is so nice out. Plus, he needs time to play around before his big soccer game tomorrow." Now Tina had moved on to washing the fruits and vegetables she purchased.

Dan glanced at his watch and realized he was running late to pick up the girls. "I should get going. I hope your son scores big tomorrow. Go…" Dan hesitated, having no idea what the team mascot was for the young soccer players.

"Bengals," she helped him out.

Dan threw his fist in the air and uncomfortably eased out of her doorway before speed walking to his car to get the girls.

As he drove to their school, Dan replayed his interaction with Tina. After his horrendous meeting with William, something interesting had happened to Dan. He started to let go of Karina. It wasn't that meeting William made him fall out of love with her, but seeing him made Dan realize there was no future with her, and he couldn't keep holding onto hope they might be together, even if it was only a sliver. Once he did that, he ironically found himself running into Tina everywhere he went. Every time Dan left his apartment, she seemed to be coming home, or vice versa. He even ran into her and her son at the grocery store.

Cassian was a fourteen-year-old bundle of energy with a lot of sass, and from his small interactions with Tina, Dan knew where he got it from. While their interactions were never flirtatious, Dan did start to notice her bright eyes and her rich, dark hair more. It was the first woman he found himself genuinely attracted to since Karina, and after seeing her in a relationship with someone else, he decided to roll with what he was feeling. The only downside: he had no idea where Tina stood on the matter.

After picking up the girls, Dan took them straight to the movies. He planned to go after dinner, but they were so eager to see it that he decided to treat them. Before he knew it, they were sitting in uncomfortable, sticky chairs and the girls were already halfway through their candy before the previews were finished.

After the movie, Bethany and Kayla were tired and hungry for dinner with stomachs full of candy, but that didn't stop them from running into two familiar faces in the foyer.

"Tina!" Dan greeted her with the same eager inflection he had earlier.

Kayla shot up a look in reaction to her father's recognition of another woman.

"Dan, fancy seeing you here. These must be your girls." She looked down to face them with a kind smile. "I'm Tina. I live over in 1D. This is my son, Cassian."

Cassian gave a hormonal muddled greeting and then sauntered off to their apartment. When he got to the door, he glanced at his mother for the key, but she gave him a look that told him he would not be going inside until she was ready.

"I'm Bethany, and this is my younger sister, Kayla. Nice to meet you," Bethany responded and reached out her hand to shake Tina's.

Kayla just rolled her eyes and fidgeted with her hair.

Dan's face grew red at his youngest daughter's lack of manners, but it didn't seem to faze Tina. She asked the girls about their movie, made a few minutes of small talk with Dan, and then walked over to her apartment door where Cassian leaned against it while he played his Game Boy.

Dan and the girls walked upstairs to his apartment, and the girls rushed into their bedroom while Dan cooked dinner. The bedroom was not decorated to their liking quite yet, but it had two beds with bedding the girls had picked out themselves and a couple posters on the wall. Bethany shut the door to their room and sat on her bed excitedly.

"Kayla, did you see that boy?" Bethany asked in hushed tones. The last thing she needed was her dad hearing her girlish boasts.

"Ugh, Bethany, not another boy. I am so sick of hearing about boys," Kayla groaned.

Bethany may have been in the "obsessed with boys" phase, but Kayla was as far from it as a nine-year-old could be. She was friends with boys, and Bethany saw several of Kayla's friends she thought would make great boyfriends for her sister, but Kayla was adamantly against it. Bethany, on the other hand, looked at almost every boy with interest, and she swore each boy was different.

"This one is different. He's older and quiet. I bet he's super sweet too," she gawked and pictured him in her mind.

"He didn't look sweet. He looked stuck up and old," Kayla remarked.

Bethany threw a pillow at her. "Don't talk about him like that!" she said defensively.

Kayla threw a pillow back at her in retaliation. "Then don't be boy-crazy!" she yelled back, only partially joking.

Bethany continued to talk about the boy she hadn't spoken a word to, while Kayla half-heartedly nodded until Dan called them out for dinner.

Dinners at their dad's apartment often consisted of either pizza or spaghetti, and tonight was spaghetti night. They ate and then rushed back into their bedroom until their dad tucked them in for bed. He read them a story, because even though Karina hadn't read to them in two years, Dan still wanted the chance to experience some of the things he missed out on, and the girls didn't mind. They liked listening to their dad's voice as they dozed off to sleep. Bethany dreamt of her new love, while Kayla surely had a dream about being a pirate or a fairy.

While the girls slept, Dan sat on the couch and flipped through the channels until he found an interesting marine life documentary. As whales surfed across his small television screen, he heard a soft knock at the door. When he opened it, Tina stood on the other side, hiding something behind her back.

"I would have brought wine, but we Cubans like rum," she said, and pulled out a bottle from behind her.

His face lit up and he welcomed her inside. She walked in and immediately grabbed two glasses from the cabinet and filled them with the dark-colored liquid inside the beautifully decorated bottle. She slid a glass across the island towards him and made her way over to his couch as if she had been there a hundred times. Her boldness was exhilarating and somewhat terrifying for Dan. He had just come to terms with being attracted to Tina, but he certainly never imagined her showing up to his door before he even had the chance to express his interest.

"I figured the girls would be asleep and you would be in need of a drink," she told him, almost seeming to read his mind as he sat down.

"Ah yes, this is exactly what I needed," Dan replied and held up his drink for them to toast surviving the day. After he took a sip, he relaxed slightly into the couch. "Cassian must either really like that Game Boy or really not like the small talk," he commented.

"He's just a hormonal teenage boy who wants to sit in his room all day and play video games. You remember what that's like, don't you? Or are your teenage days too far in the past?" she teased.

"Well, I certainly didn't have video games to glue my eyes to. I mostly just rode my bike and tried to keep myself entertained."

"No siblings?" she asked and took another sip of rum.

"Not any who lived with me. I have a half-brother, but I've never met him. He was on my dad's side, previous marriage."

She nodded and twirled the already curly strands of hair that hung down and framed her face. "My wager was three weeks, but Betsy said two," she randomly started. Dan looked at her with an utterly confused face. "How long it would take for you to ask me out."

Dan choked on his drink and it burned his throat.

Tina burst out laughing and had to set her drink down on his coffee table. "You had to know Betsy was pushing, or more like barreling, you towards me, right?"

Dan took a deep breath to process what she had just said. He had never met someone so blunt, and he had no idea what to do with it. "Well, I knew she was definitely gunning for us to get together, but I definitely did not know there was a bet going that was probably not going to work out in my favor," he responded. Tina looked caught off guard. "Not that I wasn't planning on asking you out...I'm just new to all of this," he shyly responded.

Tina reached out her hand for him to grab. He did, and she squeezed it tightly. "My husband has been gone a long time now, but I still struggle with the whole 'dating' thing." She looked down at her necklace with a locket. "I still carry his picture with me because it feels wrong not to. I don't want him to think I've forgotten him." She paused and opened the locket to glance inside. She closed it a moment later and looked back up to make eye contact with Dan. "I know it's stupid."

This time, Dan grabbed her hand. "It's not stupid at all," he assured her. "I've been divorced for two years now, and I still have no idea what I'm doing. She's the mother of my children and I still must see her all the time...this whole thing is hard to navigate. I can't imagine what you've gone through," he lamented.

Tina let out a slight snicker when she heard those words. "No one can," she whispered. "But hey, you can ask me out whenever you would like. You know where I live," she teased.

Dan couldn't help but smile at her wit. "How about next weekend?" he asked, and she agreed. Even if he had no idea what he was doing, he was thankful to be navigating this new reality with someone exceedingly kind and very bold.

They sat on his couch and chatted until Tina yawned and looked at her watch. Startled by how late it had gotten, she decided it was time to head back downstairs.

After she left, Dan continued to swirl what was left in his glass and then made his way to bed. For the first night in a while, he was going to bed with a bit of hope for the future, and that made going to sleep alone a lot easier.

"What if this turns out terrible?" Karina asked herself in the mirror one morning. William was supposed to move some of his stuff into the house that day, and Karina's stomach had been in knots about it the entire night before. It wasn't that she didn't want him to move in, because she loved the idea of waking up next to him every morning. It was the girls who scared her. The last thing she wanted was for him to move in and then move out for some reason. She didn't want to put her girls through another big change, especially if it would all be for nothing. She didn't believe it was for nothing though. She wanted so badly to see a future with William, but all her fears clouded it. Perhaps it was too soon after Dan to be able to see success with someone else, or perhaps it was all in her own head, but she tried to swallow the fears and move forward.

When she told the girls William would be living with them, their reactions were not what she expected. It was Bethany who seemed to really struggle with the idea.

Karina told herself the problem was that she and William were moving too fast, but that wasn't it for Bethany. Sure, William was not her favorite person, but all she wanted was for her mom to be happy. The problem was she had gotten used to it just being the three of them, and the thought of anyone changing that was terrifying. After her mom told her, Bethany cried in her room that night and didn't tell anybody. She didn't want to burden anyone with her feelings, especially when she felt she was being childish. She wanted to grow up and adjust to the change but couldn't help but fear losing her mom. Bethany counted on her mom, and while her being with William was different, not a lot changed in Bethany's life. Aside from him coming over sometimes, everything else in their lives stayed relatively the same, but this change was going to mean an entirely new chapter for her mom, one where her kids were not the main thing in her life.

Kayla, on the other hand, reacted better than anyone was expecting, including herself. For the past two years, she had been so convinced her parents would get back together, so Karina feared telling her about William moving in. However, the news wasn't that surprising to her. After having her dad move back, all she really cared about was spending as much time with him as possible. Kayla already asked her mom once if she could move in with her dad and she was quickly denied, but somewhere inside of her, Kayla hoped William moving in would give Karina another push to let her leave. Kayla still loved living with her mom and sister, but she felt like her dad understood her in a way that neither of them did. Bethany and their mom were very similar, and so often Kayla felt like the outsider, but she never felt that way with her dad. Even though she didn't get to spend as much time as she wanted with him, the move back to the States was a positive change in many ways. She finally felt as though she had her family back, even if they weren't together. William moving in seemed like another reason for Kayla to leave, and she made sure her mother knew it.

It was these reactions that fueled some of Karina's panic. The last thing she wanted was for her older daughter to be upset, and her younger daughter wanting to move out, but she also knew if she allowed them to dictate her decision now, she would never choose herself in the future. This was healthy for her, even if the fear said it wasn't.

William arrived a few hours later with a car full of stuff. He still had three more months on his lease and no desire to break it, so he decided to leave some things there, at least at first. Karina also thought it was best if he didn't move everything in at once, but slowly phase himself into their home instead.

William showed up with a few boxes of clothes and another box of small knick-knacks that he couldn't bear to live without. After he put his things in Karina's (or perhaps his?) room, they settled down to eat their first dinner together. For William, sitting with the woman he loved and two kids he adored, filled him with peace. Even if he didn't recognize it until then, this was the life he always wanted.

Kayla and Bethany did not hold the dinner to such a weight. For them, it was just like any other time William came to dinner: a little quieter than normal, a few surface-level questions (How was your day? What did you learn in school?), and then off to their bedroom.

For Karina, dinner was not everything she had dreamed of. She already had her dream. Her dream was to have a family. When she first loved William, she believed through him, she could have her chance at happiness. Now, as she sat at the dinner table next to a man she loved, and near her two beautiful daughters, she wondered if she could finally allow *that* to be enough.

She couldn't.

Chapter Sixteen: Now

After Kayla drove off that day, she ended up getting a motel for the night. She did not have the money to do so, but there was no way she could give her sister the satisfaction of crawling back to her. When Kayla got to her motel room, which was the cheapest one she could find in Plymouth, she ended up sitting on her bed and sobbing for a while. Being back in Plymouth brought up a lot of feelings, mostly about her mom, and about how she left things. When she moved out after high school, it wasn't a happy time for the family. She left in anger, and wanted to escape Plymouth, but if she was being honest with herself, she really wanted to escape her family. Being back in that small town brought up years of negative emotions: the desperation she felt for so many years about leaving Plymouth, the isolation when she believed she was the outsider in the town, the betrayal by those closest to her…the feelings compounded on top of each other the longer she sat in that dank, dark room.

Kayla left her room and decided to drive down the same streets she had driven down countless times before. She drove by her old high school, the park she liked to go to, and, of course, her old house. Her drive took her outside of Plymouth and into Marshfield where she found herself driving to her dad's old apartment building. Even when she got there, she was not planning on going inside, yet she unconsciously unbuckled her seatbelt, got out of the car, and walked up to the remarkably familiar exterior.

When Kayla walked into the foyer of the building, an eerie familiarity followed her. She hadn't been to the building since her dad lived there, and it hadn't changed a bit, but that was typically true of anything in a small town. She slowly crossed the foyer towards 1D and thought about all the memories she had in that apartment. Kayla climbed the creaky staircase and stood at the door of her dad's old apartment. Part of her was tempted to knock on the door and ask if she could come in, but she didn't. Instead, she slid against the wall until she was sitting with her legs crossed on the floor and let memories of her father fill her.

"You have no idea how much I needed this," Kayla told her father as they walked up to his apartment. Kayla had been dying to do a weekend with just her and her father, and after much convincing and scheduling, they were able to pick out a weekend. Kayla counted down for weeks and had already planned the entire weekend. The first step was for her dad to rent a horror movie from Blockbuster. Karina and Bethany hated horror films, but Dan tolerated them enough to watch them with his daughter. Kayla wasn't even that big of a horror film fan, but she liked the idea of doing something with her father that the two of them enjoyed together.

Once they got into the apartment, they settled in to watch the film. Unfortunately, it was a lot scarier than either of them anticipated. Even though Dan refused to admit it, he, just like Kayla, had nightmares about it that night.

The next day, to get their minds off all the blood and gore, they went to the grocery store and bought everything necessary for the best ice cream sundae Kayla could dream of. They also went to the park and had races down the street to see who was faster. Even though Kayla viewed her dad as old, he was still able to beat her, and it made her competitive side roll over and die.

When they returned to the apartment, they stacked two mugs full of ice cream, chocolate sauce, whipped cream, a whole bunch of sprinkles, and then ate them on the floor while they played card games. Dan was currently in the process of teaching his young daughter poker, something he had become quite skilled at in Germany. After she was tired of losing, they sprayed whipped cream in each other's mouths until their stomachs hurt, and then sprayed each other some more.

That weekend, and so many moments in that apartment, were filled with a lot of laughs Kayla shared with her father. He always knew how to make her laugh so easily, and for how much pain she was in that day, the thing she wanted most in the whole world was for him to make her laugh like that again.

When she was tired of crying outside a stranger's door, Kayla got up and hopped back in her car. Instead of returning to her sad motel room, she drove to the nearest bar to be around strangers, which somehow sounded a lot better than being by herself.

When Kayla got there, the bar was quiet. After all, it was a workday, and since Marshfield was a small town, just like Plymouth, there wasn't a lot happening any day. The bartender was quick to serve her a beer and eager to make conversation with a face he didn't recognize.

"Are you from around here?" he asked as he wiped off some glasses that looked still warm from the dishwasher.

"No, well, yes. Not anymore." She rolled her eyes at her own aloofness, and he took notice.

"Sounds complicated," he quipped. She nodded without making eye contact. "Well, whatever it is, I think you might need something a bit stronger, on the house." He pulled out a finely decorated bottle of vodka and made a martini. He plopped a twist of lemon in the glass and gently sat it in front of Kayla.

She wasn't sure if she should smile at the sweet gesture, or cautiously accept it for fear of him wanting more. But he didn't press her further. He continued to wipe down glasses and then moved onto cleaning other areas of the bar. When he started stacking chairs on top of tables, Kayla suddenly became aware she was the only person left in the bar.

"Wait, is the bar closed?"

The man grabbed two more chairs to flip onto a table. "Oh yeah, it's been closed for about half an hour now," he replied nonchalantly.

Kayla's face grew red. "Ohmygosh, I'm so sorry. I had no idea. I hope I didn't cause you to stay too late." She started to gather her things as he moved to the next table.

"No, the owner might be a little annoyed, but it's fine." He flashed a toothy smile and moved back behind the counter.

"Let me guess, you're the owner?" she asked even though she already knew the answer.

The grin on his face grew. "For two years now. Last owner died and gave the place to me."

"Well, that is really great. Thanks for letting me stay late. I needed to be around people." Now that Kayla's things were in her hand, she scooted off the stool and prepared to leave, but something in his eyes made her hesitate.

"You know, I still have a bit of cleaning up to do if you want to stay a little longer," he offered.

Kayla smiled and set her stuff back down on the bar. The two made light conversation, but she avoided anything to do with her family. Finally, once everything had been cleaned in the bar (and recleaned, since they both enjoyed each other's company) he called it a night. She didn't invite him back to her hotel room, and he didn't invite her back to his house. Instead, he walked Kayla to her car, and they stood outside in the cold for a minute making conversation.

"I hope things start looking up for you," he told her, and decided to screw it and give her a hug.

Even though he had no idea what was going on in Kayla's life, and she normally did not welcome random physical affection, this time, it felt genuine. She didn't know it until it happened, but she really needed it.

"Thank you. I really appreciate it." She got in her car and watched him walk to his. On a whim, she started her car and drove over to his parked car. She rolled down her window, and after a moment of confusion, he did the same. "It's my dad...he's...dying," she painfully admitted.

"I'm sorry," he replied with a frown. "I lost my dad too." The only sound was the soft hum of the two engines humming. "If you ever want to talk, you know where to find me."

Kayla smiled and rolled up her window. She may have been going back to the same lonely motel room, but at least she felt a little less alone.

Kayla walked up to the house apprehensively with a bouquet of yellow carnations in her hands. She wasn't sure what to bring her dying father, who might not even remember who she was, but Kayla thought some bright flowers could be a start. Before she knocked on the door a second time, a young woman answered.

"You must be Kayla." She greeted her with a warm smile and welcomed her into her father's home. "Your sister told me you might be coming by at some point."

Kayla rolled her eyes slightly, but tried to swallow her animosity. She couldn't imagine what Bethany must have said to these nurses. She was sure all of them judged her harshly for not seeing her father sooner. At that moment, she tried to put that out of her mind and focus on the daunting task ahead.

"How is he?" she asked. Even in saying those words, Kayla felt like she was saying all the wrong things. *How was he? Well, he was a dying man living alone and couldn't remember who he was half the time, so probably not great.* She ridiculed herself and her stupid question, but Gianna merely told her he was doing alright, but was very quiet that day, which wasn't that unusual these days.

Kayla found him staring blankly at the television screen in front of him. He was never much of a television person; the only thing he was ever interested in was documentaries, so she was surprised to see a poorly made crime show and yellow tape flashing on and off the screen.

"Dad?" she stammered. Her heart was beating out of her chest, and all she could think about was him looking at her with no recognition of who she was. That was her greatest fear in all of this, that her last memories of him would be ones in which he didn't even know about their life together.

He cocked his head for a moment, then a flash of recognition crossed his face. "Kayla!" he pleasantly greeted his daughter and motioned for her to come to sit on the couch.

Her heart leaped a beat at hearing her name from her father's mouth. Kayla wanted to apologize to him, but she wasn't even sure how. How could she give him her reasons for not coming sooner? When she realized she couldn't, she just sat with him in silence. The silence dragged on and was only interrupted by Gianna shuffling in with a small cup of pills and a cup of water. That was when things took a turn for the worse.

At first, Dan was unresponsive to Gianna's attempts to take his medication on his own, but then when she got a little more forceful, he turned violent. He grabbed the plastic cup of water that sat on the television tray and chucked it at the TV. Since it was plastic, it did not make much of an impact, but water splashed across the room.

Kayla stood up out of fear and took a few steps back. "Dad?" she stuttered. She was at a loss of what to say or do.

He didn't acknowledge her. Instead, he yelled unintelligible words to his nurse. Even still, she was gentle and patient with him. But her gentleness did not faze his outrage.

Kayla started to shake. This was not how she wanted to see her father. She couldn't take it. This wasn't him; he would never do something like this. Yet, there he was, yelling words no one could possibly understand, and flipping the TV tray over so it hit with a *thud* against the carpet. Then, it was with three words Kayla's world completely flipped on its head. He turned to her, slowly, gently, and looked at her with two eyes that she did not recognize.

"Who are you?" he asked in an accusatory manner.

Those three words cut Kayla's insides to pieces. Suddenly, the shaking turned to sobbing and she ran out of his home before Gianna could even offer her a word of comfort.

"No, no, no," Kayla kept repeating in the car as she yanked the gear knob into reverse and jammed her foot on the gas pedal. She heard the rev of her car as she sped out of the driveway and onto the street as fast as she possibly could. She waved her hands as she drove and tried to erase the memories out of her head. She touched her face to make the unknowing eyes that stared into her soul go away. But she couldn't. There they were, clear as day, staring at her with absolutely no remembrance of who she was.

That was not her father, Kayla reminded herself. It may have looked like him, it may have even sounded like him for a moment, but he was gone. Then the sobbing turned to anger, a fit of vicious anger, not at her father, but at her sister. How dare she expect Kayla to come back and face this? Bethany could handle this stuff; Kayla couldn't. Her father meant everything to her, how could she fill her head with such awful memories? The answer was: she couldn't.

His soul was a giant rock, one that stood near the shore in the ocean, like something that could be seen at a beach on the Oregon coast. His mind was the water that surrounded the majestic rock. Sometimes, the waves were still, gently caressed by the breeze, and only coating the rock with a blanket of its cool embrace. But sometimes, the waves were aggressive. They churned against the rock, and whipped it with an unholy amount of force. The sad reality of this rock, and anything else exposed to the toils of the ocean was this: it eroded. Sometimes it took a long time, and when the waves were still, it appeared nothing could break the immovable rock that stoically stood in the middle of the water. But, other days, when the rain was coming down, and the waves went high enough to completely envelop the rock in their bloody tyranny, it looked like the rock couldn't stand a chance, and eventually, it wouldn't. It would crumble.

Some moments, Dan could look at the world and see something recognizable. He could get a whiff of cinnamon and be taken back to his favorite bar in Germany, or looking at his daughter could spark a memory from when she only came up to his waist. But, at other times, he would have the same experience and feel absolutely nothing, as if the color had been drained out of the world only moments ago he had recognized. No one could understand it, including him.

Against his own will, Dan had taken everyone left in his life in a boat on those unpredictable waves. As much as he regretted it, he had booked them a one-way trip. They were stranded in the middle of the ocean and there was no way to escape, not even for him.

He didn't remember his angry outburst an hour ago. He had moved to a new page in the book, and now he heard her voice as clear as day, humming a Beatles song in the kitchen. "Karina!" he called for her and stretched his head to try to see into the kitchen. He tried to get up, but for some reason he couldn't tell his legs to do so. Instead, he called for her a few more times. Soon, she walked out to greet him.

"Dan, is everything okay?" she softly asked.

He smiled to look at her beauty again. She hadn't aged a bit since the day he met her all those years ago.

"I heard you humming one of my favorite songs," he remarked and smiled. He closed his eyes for a moment, but when he opened them again, he did not recognize the woman standing in front of him. "Karina?" he questioned.

The woman smiled and said something that couldn't understand because his mind was still trying to take in the world around him.

"Where's Karina?" he asked frantically, and his eyes darted across the room to see where she had gone. *She was just standing here a minute ago,* he thought in his mind, and yet she appeared to have gone completely out of sight. But here was this woman he didn't recognize, wearing the clothes he had just seen Karina in. None of it made sense. "Where is she?" he asked, perhaps in his mind, perhaps out loud. Panic started to flood his insides as he couldn't understand where she had gone. *She was just here a minute ago. Where was she?*

Immediately, his mind jumped from one worst-case scenario to another. Something must have happened. Where was he? Soon the recognition of his own home slipped from his consciousness. Had someone taken him from her? Then, his own thoughts seemed to mesh to a point where he couldn't untangle them anymore. He was in a dazed state trying to fit together puzzle pieces that weren't even part of the same puzzle. He clawed at his face to try to pull him back to the reality he thought he knew, but he felt something pull his hands away. Before he could yell for the force to let go, his world went quiet.

Gianna tossed the empty needle she had used to sedate Dan in the trash and moved Dan from the couch to the hospital bed that had been recently moved to the living room. None of this was unusual for Gianna. She had been a live-in nurse for several years, but watching her patients slip away never got any easier. The hardest part was watching the families suffer. Her heart broke for what happened with Kayla that day. Dan was her third patient as a nurse, so she had started to become familiar with how family members responded to the disease, and the reactions varied.

The way his two daughters were handling this loss represented two distinct archetypes of someone dying, and her heart went out to them. She knew each daughter would tackle her own challenges because of the path she found herself on, even if both paths looked different. Bethany would be forced to confront a life without her father, and as he continued to become a greater part of her life, the new reality that awaited her would seem even more daunting. Plus, seeing her father in such a deformed state would alter the way she looked at death, and how she remembered her father for the rest of her life.

Kayla's pain would come in a much different state. She would probably feel a lot of regret and guilt, and while the loss of her father would fit a little cleaner into her world because she was already separated from him, it would not make the loss any easier. If Gianna had learned one thing as a nurse, it was that death was not only a part of life, but was one of the ways that made life the most difficult to continue to live.

For the two girls, this would be a rude awakening they would both have to face.

"How did you even find me here?" Kayla asked as Bethany stood in the doorway of her motel room.

"You forget, I've lived here my whole life. I know everyone in this town, and when my sister who hasn't been back in over a year shows up, someone will say something about it. You know Plymouth, everyone has a big mouth."

Kayla scoffed at what was most definitely the truth about most small towns in America.

"I don't know why you are here," Kayla sighed.

"I know you saw Dad, and I know it wasn't easy. Whether you like it or not, I do understand what it is like to experience him in those states."

Even though their relationship was broken, there was a part of Kayla's soul that wanted to cry out to her sister. But she resisted that part. Instead, she gestured for Bethany to come inside. They stood uncomfortably in her small motel room. There was an awkward silence. While Bethany wanted to tell her sister stories of when their father didn't remember her, or when his angry outbursts led her to tears, she didn't think that was best for now. Instead, she wanted to listen.

Kayla did not take that opportunity to share anything. Instead, she asked a simple question: "Is it really worth it for you?"

Bethany looked up with compassion and confusion, but Kayla's expressionless face remained unchanged.

"Wouldn't it just be easier for him to be in a home and let people who know what they are doing take care of him? Is anyone really qualified to be there for someone when they are like this?"

At first, Bethany was put off by her sister's ease to throw their father in a strange place, but she took a step back and tried to look at where her sister was coming from and respond from there. "I'm not doing it for me, Kayla. I'm doing this for him. I don't know what's going on in his mind, but I do know that on the days he does remember something, I want to be there. I don't want him to die alone."

While Bethany now knew some of the guilt Kayla harbored over their mother's death, Kayla had no idea of the guilt that Bethany carried. Bethany lived so close to their mom, and yet she often failed to see her. She avoided phone calls because she didn't want to be berated, and she even canceled them getting together a few times shortly before they lost her. She wanted so desperately to make it up with her father, even if Kayla didn't understand it.

"But he wouldn't be alone. He would be around people who are trained to take care of people in his condition. I'm not."

"And neither am I," Bethany responded. "But sometimes God puts us in positions to do things that we are not qualified for. That is what sacrifice means."

Anger boiled up inside of Kayla because of her sister's saintly responses, but she took another breath of composure. "That isn't sacrifice, Bethany, it's self-preservation! Are you really keeping Dad at home because of a sacrifice? Or are you doing it for yourself?" Kayla paused to let the words sink in, but it didn't take long for her to continue. "Do I not get a say over what happens to our father? Because I think it would be better for him to be in a home than destroying his own and surrounded by nothing but empty reminders and a few nurses. At least if he was somewhere else, they'd have activities and other people to be around. Maybe it would make things a little easier on him."

"Kayla, when you stopped being involved with Dad, you lost your say. Why would we put him in a home when there is someone willing to make sure he gets to stay in his?"

"Because it comes at the cost of me! You constantly make me feel guilty for not moving back here, and thinking of yourself as righteous because you are sacrificing your life when you don't have to!" Kayla wailed.

Bethany's heart ached in fury. She was tired of hearing the same complaints from her sister when she refused to acknowledge the truth.

"I didn't have a choice!" Bethany screamed and her mouth suddenly felt dry. When she spoke again, it was much softer, and more broken. "When Dad started to get worse, the only person the decision fell on was me. And if you don't agree with it, then fine. But things are staying the way they are until I say differently."

"Then I don't see any reason to stay here anymore."

When Kayla said this, Bethany froze. This was the exact thing she was trying to avoid, and yet they seemed to find themselves there anyway.

"I think you should go," Kayla whispered with her head down.

Bethany raised her hand to touch her sister's shoulder, but then pulled back before Kayla even noticed. She let her arm fall softly to her side and took a breath of composure. "I don't want you to leave, but if you do decide to go back to St. Louis, can you at least come with me to see Dad one more time?" Kayla opened her mouth to speak but Bethany raised her hand to stop her. "I think it would go a long way for him to see both of us together one more time."

Kayla wanted to fight the request, but instead, she begrudgingly agreed. They made plans to see him together the next day, and then Kayla would start driving back tomorrow afternoon. She didn't imagine she would be making plans to leave Plymouth so soon, but she also couldn't be surprised considering the broken state of the only family relationship she had left.

So, Bethany left the motel. She was glad the conversation didn't end with either of them storming out or screaming at each other (although she couldn't forget the screaming that did occur), but she lamented the way it ended. Bethany was consumed with the guilt and blamed herself for pushing her sister away after she had barely been in Plymouth. Perhaps it was because of their broken relationship that she had ripped away her sister's last chance to get to spend time with their father.

When Bethany got home that night, Huxley assured her she was not to blame. He was honest with her, as he always was, that things could have been handled better, but he also reassured her numerous times of the truth: the two women were in completely different places in coming to terms with their father's condition. If she was ever going to come to a place of forgiving her sister, Bethany would need to accept Kayla for exactly where she was and what she believed, even if she didn't agree with it.

Bethany lay in bed that night long after Huxley had dozed off, and she still found herself thinking about the conversation with Kayla. Perhaps Bethany should have given Kayla more of a say when it came to deciding what happened with her father, but, as with most decisions Bethany made in her life, she felt a justification for not involving her sister more. After all, it was Kayla who stopped visiting her father after things became too difficult. It was Kayla who isolated herself from her family. It was Kayla who left Plymouth in the first place.

But that part of the conversation was not what was keeping Bethany up that night. What haunted her was Kayla's question. She always believed what she was doing was for the good of her father, but if Bethany looked deep down inside of herself, she knew some part of what Kayla said was true, even though Kayla didn't fully understand why. The guilt Bethany had over her mother was deep, and it was possible Bethany held onto her dad so tightly because she was desperately trying to preserve her image of herself: that of a good and loving daughter. Maybe this was her atonement.

On the other side of town, Kayla was feeling justified in everything she said to her sister. It didn't take long for her to realize she had no desire to sit in her motel room, and would have preferred sitting at a bar talking to a certain someone. It was odd for Kayla, who was not typically a person to pursue someone else. Especially since she was leaving tomorrow, she had no idea why she was going back. At the same time, she wanted someone to listen and validate how she felt.

When she got to the bar and explained her side of the story, Kayla got the exact justification she wanted.

"I think it is completely valid to want your dad to be in a nursing home," he affirmed as he pulled a seat next to Kayla at a table. The bar was completely empty, so he felt comfortable sitting down next to her instead of standing on the other side of the bulky bar. "I get that your sister wanted to take care of your dad, but maybe it is selfish of her to be keeping him in a place he doesn't recognize. Maybe he'd receive better treatment if he were at a care facility."

Kayla nodded and relished in the vindication he was giving her. "I don't really tell a lot of people my dad is sick because I feel like a lot of people will judge me for not moving back here, but he's not even there, you know? And if there are people taking care of him, why do I need to put myself through more pain than I am already going through?"

He nodded and pondered her statement. "I think it's pretty clear you are trying to protect yourself from more pain, and I do understand that, but maybe sometimes we don't get a choice on pain. Sometimes pain chooses us, and we can't do anything to stop it. Maybe part of not staying here is actually avoiding that truth."

Kayla groaned loudly. "Well, that's what you and everyone else says," she grumbled and cracked open a pistachio sitting in a dish on the table.

"Don't you think if everyone is saying the same thing, that maybe there is some truth to it?" he hesitantly suggested. Kayla shot a look of complete and utter annoyance his way. "I'm not saying that you are wrong. I'm just trying to offer you another perspective."

Kayla's typical response to "another perspective" would have been one of defense. She did not like her decisions questioned. However, there was a kindness with him that caused her to give it a second thought. "Maybe you are right. But I think, right now, avoidance is the best I can do."

"And if that's the case, then that's okay too," he assured her with a grin.

The conversation shifted into a more casual tone. They talked about what they had done with their lives and things they wanted to do in the future, but there was one point in the conversation where something dawned on Kayla.

"Wait," she interrupted as he was in the middle of telling her a funny story about how he got his keys locked in his car. "I've never asked you your name," she remarked, and he laughed.

"I guess I haven't asked you yours either. Well, better late than never." He reached out his hand for her to shake. "I'm Cass."

She smiled and met her hand with his. "Kayla."

He gave her a probing look, and then in an instant his eyes widened to twice their original size. "Kayla Fitzpatrick?" he hesitantly asked her.

She looked at him with complete and utter confusion. "Yeah?" she cautiously replied.

"Oh my gosh. It makes so much sense now." Cass stood up and paced the floor in front of them.

Kayla studied him and was even more caught off guard with his peculiar reaction.

"You don't recognize me, but we know each other," he snickered, and the ignorance on her face was apparent. "Cass is short for Cassian. My name is Cassian."

Kayla burst out laughing, and soon Cassian joined her. She should have known that even in the next town over, she couldn't escape the small-town syndrome of somehow always running into people that she already had a history with. Should she really be surprised? And yet, she looked at him with astonishment.

They talked for half an hour about the mere fact they hadn't put the pieces of their true identities together earlier.

"I just can't believe it. You don't even look the same!" She laughed.

Cass nodded. "Well, same to you! I guess we aren't kids anymore," he scoffed. Kayla smiled, but then her face grew red. "Did you know my sister had the biggest crush on you?" Kayla asked.

Cassian nervously laughed and looked at her with a knowing glance. "I think all eleven-year-old crushes are pretty obvious. Hey, maybe if she was a little older, I would have gone for her too, but my teenage self just couldn't get past the My Little Ponies," he teased and they burst out laughing again.

For the next hour, they took a dive into the past and reflected on memories they had shared with each other and lamented the way that things ended.

"They did really love each other," he said quietly.

"I know. Life really has a way of throwing you a plot twist when you least expect it," she added.

Cassian wholeheartedly agreed with her. As they continued to catch up, Kayla realized a lot had changed for Cassian since they last saw each other.

After going to college and realizing a degree in philosophy was worthless, Cassian didn't initially find his way back to Marshfield. He settled in Boston for a while, and after a string of heartbreaks, he learned he was terrible at holding onto a relationship. Finally, one of his best friends from high school moved back to Marshfield and was in need of a roommate. So, Cassian decided he would rather be in a town he semi-tolerated instead of alone in a town that reminded him of all his shortcomings. So, he went back to Marshfield, and started working at the bar. The owner grew to love him enough to give him the place when he passed, and Cassian found himself cemented in Marshfield once again.

All this he was comfortable sharing with Kayla. This was the surface-level view of his life. What he did not mention was what was most prevalent in his life at that time. Cassian was going through the process of becoming a foster parent. It was something he had wanted to do for a while, and at first, imagined doing it with a life partner, but when he saw that absent in his life, he decided he would rather be a father and not a husband than be nothing at all. He had started the process eight months ago and was still waiting for the system to take him in as a serious candidate. There were not a lot of single men looking to foster children, and so the system was rightfully suspicious of Cassian's intentions. But it was still heartbreaking for Cassian. All he wanted to do was be a father, even though the thought of doing so was incredibly intimidating. He didn't have any father figures to come to for wisdom. He gleaned a bit from stories of his dad, and even from Dan, but he still didn't feel like he was adequately prepared for fatherhood himself. Yet that didn't change how much he wanted it.

Part of Cassian considered sharing all this with Kayla, but it was clear she was too caught up in her own family problems to have the emotional capacity to listen to his. Perhaps that was an unfair judgment on his part but, as Kayla would probably be able to relate if she knew, Cassian struggled with opening up to people, especially since he had been burned in the past.

It didn't help that Cassian had his own baggage with Kayla's family. Once he put the pieces together that the person dying was a man he had previously looked up to, it made Cassian's feelings even more complicated. After things fell apart, Cassian thought Dan would keep in touch with him. After all, they had bonded. But he desperately failed to do so. This rejection was devastating. Luckily, he was able to put aside the feelings in his heart and be there for someone he never imagined coming into his life again.

At the end of the night, the two exchanged numbers, and Cassian encouraged Kayla, if she ever needed to talk about things, he would be there.

Surprisingly enough, Kayla viewed his offer as something genuine she considered following. She was not one for reaching out to people, but perhaps it would be good for her to talk to someone who knew her father but didn't have the emotional baggage her sister brought with her. Maybe this would be a good thing.

But Kayla couldn't focus on the potential of a new friendship at that point. What she had to focus on during her drive back to the motel and when she got to her room was what tomorrow would entail. Even if they didn't know it, one thing both Bethany and Kayla could agree on was they did not want to fight in front of their father. Not while he was like this. Therefore, they would both have to do everything in their power to not do that.

Bethany had waited a long time for the moment she would get to walk up to her father's door with her sister by her side. But this wasn't exactly how she imagined that moment. She envisioned many times sharing meals and memories with their father, but none of that was the case.

Before Bethany got in the car that morning, Huxley reminded her that she needed to focus on reality, not the fantasy of what she wanted to be. So, she rejoiced in the fact she would get to be with Kayla to see their father while he was still cognizant enough to hold onto this day.

When they walked up to the house, Sarah Beth greeted them. "Well, it is a delight to have both of you here," she spoke in her charming Southern accent. Sarah Beth was originally from South Carolina but had moved to Massachusetts to be close to her own dying mother ten years ago. After losing her mother, she became a nurse for Alzheimer's patients.

Dan hadn't been moved from his bed that morning because he wasn't feeling well, but he was awake and sitting up, drinking a strawberry banana smoothie Sarah Beth made for him.

"Dan, you have quite the treat here! Both your girls are here to see you!" she told him, but he didn't make eye contact with her or his daughters. Instead, he continued to drink his smoothie and stare at the ceiling.

Bethany continued her normal routine with her father, which was to make light conversation and tell him updates about her life. She told him how Henry had lost a tooth, and she was continuing the family tradition of having the tooth fairy be an old man like the girls had grown up with. Yes, it was something Karina and Dan had started first as a joke when they decided they wanted the tooth fairy to be an old, decrepit, grumpy man who sometimes brought the girls money (if he was feeling up to it), and sometimes he wrote a note and complained about how their room was not clean enough to fly through. It didn't take long for the girls to realize "Sir. Tooth," aptly named, was a creation of their parents' imaginations. However, when Bethany told Huxley about Sir. Tooth, he believed it was too hysterical not to keep up with their family.

It pained Kayla more than Bethany to see her father's lack of reaction and response to Bethany's stories. It didn't faze Bethany to see her father being unresponsive. She did it so, perhaps somewhere in his mind, he would remember the things she shared with him, and hold onto them. It was probably wishful thinking on Bethany's part, but, after reading many books, she knew the best thing she could do was to treat him as normal as she could, given the circumstances.

Bethany rarely brought up the ice cream shop, as it was still a sore spot for Dan, but she briefly mentioned that business was starting to pick up again. She looked to Kayla and waited for her to start talking about her life, but the thought of doing so made Kayla extremely uncomfortable.

Bethany leaned over and whispered to her anyway. "I know it feels weird at first, but once you start talking, you start to forget all of the weirdness," she assured her.

For more her sister's sake than her own, Kayla decided to give it a try. "Hey, Dad," Kayla awkwardly started, "I'm going to be leaving tomorrow."

Bethany shot a disapproving glance at her and then looked back at her father. She hoped her sister's news would not catch her father off guard, but luckily, he didn't seem to take much notice.

Kayla's face grew hot at her sister's watchful stare. "Well, that doesn't really matter right now…" Kayla was unsure of where to begin. Her life wasn't anything worth sharing right now. "I'm still looking for a new job. I have an interview next week for an administrative assistant job, but I don't know if I'll get it." Kayla wasn't all too thrilled about the idea of having to work as an administrative assistant. For her, it was not only a step down in pay, but it was a step down in her career path. She wanted to do something that mattered, and being an administrative assistant at a diagnostics company was not what she had in mind.

"It looks like my friend is going to try to patch things up in her marriage," she added. Melinda had called Kayla late the night before to tell her she missed her in St. Louis and wanted to know when she was coming back. They planned to get together next week. In their phone call, she also told Kayla she had been talking to Ben and they were starting couples counseling together. Of course, Kayla was cautious, but Melinda sounded hopeful, so all Kayla could do was support her.

"I think I'm going to try reading when I get home. Before you say anything, I know I haven't been much of an avid reader, but I figured, with all the extra time on my hands, maybe I could pick up a new hobby...." Kayla searched for other things to say as her sister quietly listened next to her. "Oh! I asked my neighbor to water my plants, so I'm hoping they aren't all dead when I get back. I bought them just before I left. I think they really add life to my apartment." Kayla continued to avoid eye contact with her sister, but instead tried to focus on her father's expressionless face. She felt uncomfortable sharing any of this with her sister sitting right next to her, especially since everything Kayla said, Bethany was hearing for the first time.

It was far more painful to listen to her sister than Bethany realized it would be. It made her realize just how far they had fallen.

"You'll never guess who I ran into the other day," Kayla started again, and Bethany's ears perked up at her sister's sentence. "Cassian."

Although Dan didn't react, Bethany certainly did. "You ran into Cassian?" she questioned.

Kayla looked harshly at her sister. "Yeah," she replied in a snarky tone and turned back to her father. "He owns a bar in Marshfield, ironically enough. He seems to be doing pretty well."

"Can I see him?" Dan croaked, and both the girls looked up in shock that their father spoke at all.

"Cassian?" Kayla questioned, to make sure she understood her father correctly. Dan nodded in response, and Kayla looked to her sister for guidance.

Bethany shrugged. She was just as unsure of how to respond as Kayla. Her father hadn't asked to see anyone for the past couple months, and certainly not someone he hadn't spoken to in years. Perhaps hearing a name he hadn't heard in so long triggered some remembrance in her father. No matter what the reason, Bethany was just grateful that her father engaged with Kayla at all.

"I could call him and see if you guys can talk on the phone?" she suggested apprehensively, and her father just nodded again. She dialed Cassian's number and, for some reason, her heart trembled at the rings.

Cassian picked up after three rings. "Hey, I didn't expect to hear from you so soon," Cassian answered awkwardly.

"Hey..." Kayla began, then only silence filled the line. She wasn't sure how to bring up that her dying father wanted to speak to someone she had just reconnected with two days ago, but she gave it her best shot. "Do you remember when I told you I was seeing my dad today?" He replied in affirmation, and she continued to explain the strange turn of events her father had created. "Well, I brought up that I had been talking to you—"

"Ooh, you talked about me?" Cassian teased.

Kayla nervously laughed. "Yes, well...he asked if he could see you." She waited for a response, but there was just silence. "I don't really know where his head is right now, but if you want to maybe talk on the phone, he's here."

Cassian was completely taken aback by the call. Not only did he never expect to hear from Kayla again, but he certainly never expected to hear from Dan, and he was feeling mixed emotions about the entire thing. But he agreed to talk on the phone.

Kayla walked back into the living room and put the phone on speaker. "Hey, Dad, Cassian is on the phone right now for you."

Dan was silent for a minute, and Bethany quickly grew worried Dan had forgotten about his entire request, but he soon spoke up in his old and raspy voice.

"Cassian," he started, "I've missed you."

On the other end of the line, Cassian's eyes began to water. "It's really good to hear from you," he responded. "I've missed you too. How are you doing?" he asked, and Dan chuckled.

"Well, I've been better, son."

Bethany and Kayla were both at a loss at that moment of their father sounding so...normal.

After neither man knew what to say next, Kayla spoke up.

"Dad, Cassian is the owner of a bar in Marshfield, remember?" she told him.

Dan smiled. "That's good for you, my boy," he said slowly, as if speaking at all was painful for him. Perhaps it was.

"Thank you," Cassian softly responded. He wasn't sure what to say to the man who, for so many years, he felt so wronged by. But, at that moment, all he felt was love from him.

"Cassian," Dan rasped into the phone, "I wanted to tell you I'm sorry." Dan took a deep and shallow breath before continuing. "Your mother and I… we thought we made the right call for me not to reach out to you anymore, but now I'm not so sure," he said.

Bethany took notice of the tear that rolled down her father's old, wrinkled face. She was reminded again of the moment she had a few months ago with Henry and her father, and hoped that, even though the moment they were witnessing wasn't with them directly, Kayla would cherish it anyways.

And Kayla would.

Cassian was sobbing on the other line. "It's okay. I forgive you," he assured him.

Tired from all the emotion, Dan batted his eyes a few times and then dozed off.

Kayla took the phone off the speaker and walked into the kitchen. "Are you okay?" she asked him gently.

"I just…" his voice was soft and still filled with emotion. "I never could have seen something like that coming. Especially from the state you told me your father was in."

"I don't think anyone saw that coming," she spoke under her breath. "Thank you for answering. I think it was good for him," she told him and sighed. "I guess I didn't understand the extent of your relationship. I didn't even know he felt guilty about anything."

Cassian sniffled on the other end of the line. "It was hard after everything happened not to hear from him…or you guys…again." He paused and tried to compose himself.

"I'm so sorry. I had no idea," she replied, and her heart ached for Cassian. She didn't have any idea how much the brief words Cassian got to share with Dan would provide so much closure for him in his life, but it would. He would cherish those words, and in a year from that day, when he would finally get the call that he was going to get to foster a little boy, he would feel a little more prepared to be a father because of that very phone conversation.

The rest of the time Kayla and Bethany were with their father, he was quiet. He seemed to have fallen into a state of being lost within himself, but they were both okay with that. They cherished the moments they did have with him. Perhaps Kayla was wrong, perhaps there was more of her father left in this man than she thought.

They drove back to drop Kayla off at her motel. When they got there, Bethany walked Kayla to the door and gave her an awkward hug. "I love you, Kayla. If you decide to come back, you always have a place to stay with me, and if you don't decide to come back, that's okay too," she added.

Even though Kayla didn't believe what her sister said, she accepted it at that moment. And so, she packed up what little she had with her in her car, and started the long drive back to St. Louis. Unfortunately for Kayla, she would be back in Plymouth much sooner than she anticipated.

Chapter Seventeen: Then

The truth haunted Karina everywhere she went. When she picked the girls up from school, when she went grocery shopping, when she saw the framed picture that had just been placed on the fireplace mantel...she couldn't escape it. The guilt she felt was overwhelming at best and suffocating at worst. Yet, she felt paralyzed to do anything. How could she be so cruel? She felt like she was all the terrible things she so desperately wanted to avoid. She felt like her parents, who had lied about who they really were for most of her childhood. She felt like Dan, who had kept her in a marriage for years that he neglected.

Every morning that she woke up, she found herself vomiting into the toilet before William was awake. She was a fraud.

It had been three weeks since William moved in, and the girls had already started to adjust to him living there. This was difficult at times. There were moments he had to parent them, and they struggled with a new adult telling them what to do, but he handled it in much better stride than the ice cream fiasco from so long ago. It would have been easier if he didn't fit into their home well. One of the most devastating problems was that he did. William made the girls laugh, they played board games together, and sometimes even snuggled up to watch movies.

It was the life that Karina always wanted, so why couldn't she just be happy with it? But the truth, the evil, tormenting truth, was that she was miserable.

153

Ever since William had moved in, she felt more unhappy than she had in years. It was heartbreaking because it had nothing to do with who William was. He treated her so well. He made her coffee every morning, and sometimes he joined her to watch the sunrise. He kept the girls entertained when she needed a moment to herself, he surprised her with little gifts, and he even stepped up to clean and take care of the house before she came home from work. He was doing everything she could have dreamed of (and then some), and yet, she had no desire to lay next to him at night. She didn't enjoy the life she had built for herself, and the happiness she was so desperate to create wasn't making her happy.

It was impossible to say whether someone could fall out of love, but if they could, that was what Karina felt. She was deeply haunted by the ghosts of her past marriage. There were a few moments (and they were only moments) when she looked at William lying in her bed and imagined Dan there instead. She hated those moments and resented them even crossing her mind. When William moved in, it was a constant reminder of the life she could have had with the father of her children if they had just made different decisions.

Even though the ghosts told her they weren't harmful, they were the most harmful to Karina's self-image. She looked at herself and was disgusted with the person who met her eyes in the mirror. She was deeply struggling to live with herself because of how terrible she felt, and that day, she had enough. A small part of Karina told her she could push all these feelings down deep enough that she could still have a happy life with William, but she realized that was a fantasy. There would never be a good moment to break William's heart, but since Dan had the girls that day, she would have the heavy obligation to do just that.

When William got home from work, he greeted her with the same sweet smile and kiss he did every day he lived there. Without fail, he told her every night how happy he was, and how much he loved her, but that would not be happening that night. Karina led him to the dining room table and shared a glossy version of the truth. She didn't tell him how deeply depressed she was, but she did tell him she still had a lot to work through and he deserved to be with someone who could love him well, because she could not.

Karina didn't know it at that time, but this would be the most heartbreaking thing William had encountered in his life at that point.

After she told him her truth, which completely blindsided him, William packed up his stuff and left. Just like that, the life he always wanted was gone. Perhaps the sickest part, the part that would haunt him for months after, was that he woke up next to the woman he loved and had no idea it would be his last. He hated himself for not cherishing it more. Then he looked at every minor mistake he made in their relationship and resented himself for ever making them in the first place. He played a series of "would haves," "could haves," and "should haves" in his mind until his mind became too cluttered to take anymore.

Maybe if he had loved her better, she would have stayed.

Maybe if he had loved her more, she would have stayed.

Maybe if he would have connected with the kids more, gone along with more of her plans, not moved too fast, never proposed….

These were the thoughts haunting William, not just the day he moved back to the apartment he couldn't stand the sight of, but would torment him for weeks and months to come.

Perhaps Karina and William could have found their way back to each other, but that could only happen if both parties wanted it, and the truth was, Karina didn't. She wanted to want it, but her heart wasn't where her head thought it should be. She was too broken to love him well, but all he could do was blame the brokenness on himself.

A few weeks after Karina left him, a friend would remind William he was worthy of love. He would deny it, and then give a list of all the reasons he wasn't. His friend would tell him that, yes, some of the mistakes he made were bad, but nothing he had done made him unworthy of the love he thought he had with Karina. In fact, he deserved a greater love than even that.

But, for William, all he saw was Karina. He couldn't see anything greater, and didn't believe anything greater existed. For a long time, William only saw darkness; his future was this unformed, unshaped mess he had no interest entering, because the farther he walked into the darkness, the farther away his life was from Karina. But, one day, he would see a light, and would even say that walking through the darkness was worth it. But not that day. That day, living didn't even feel worth it.

After William left that day, the house felt emptier than usual, as Karina imagined it would. After Dan would leave to go back to Germany, the house always carried a sad tone with it for a while. This was a different kind of sadness, for it was one Karina caused. What Karina appreciated as she sat in her bedroom and cried from the overwhelming guilt was that she was not ready to commit to somebody else. She had taken all the pain and heartache she felt over losing her marriage and turned it into love for somebody else. But since it wasn't the true love necessary for a relationship, it was bound to sour. William moving in was the final step in coming to that realization. Unfortunately, for Karina, she learned this too late. Somebody else was already obliterated in her process, and now? She would have to learn to live with that.

As soon as they parked the car, the girls bolted towards the ticket booth as fast as they could so they could buy as many tickets as their allowance allowed. Dan and Tina were excited about taking their kids to the county fair. It was both of their first times at the Marshfield County Fair, and even though it was a small town, the fair was a classic reminder of both of their childhoods. Sugary foods, the thick stench of manure, and questionable rides they probably shouldn't have gone on, but went on anyways brought back happy memories for them both.

While the girls were overjoyed to be at the fair, Cassian was not as much. It wasn't that he didn't like fairs; in fact, he really enjoyed them, but he wanted to go with his friends, not his mom and her new boyfriend's daughters. However, Tina was adamant this would be a good bonding experience.

When Dan and Tina got out of the car, they themselves raced to see who could get to the ticket booth the fastest, and then made themselves belly laugh for how ridiculous the other one looked. There was a pure, childlike joy captured in many moments that day, and their laughter at the ticket booth was just one of them.

While Dan and Tina rode the Ferris wheel and kept an eye on their kids from afar, Kayla was busy begging her sister to go on the Super Spin ride with her, but Bethany refused. She could do roller coasters, she could do the Ferris wheel, but she could not do the "spinny" rides. So, she looked to Cassian who conceded and went on the ride with her. They ended up going on it three times in a row until they got woozy and decided to take a break. They ran back over to their parents and got a plethora of cotton candy and funnel cakes for all of them.

After they all ate the classic carnival food, the kids left again to go on more rides, and Dan dragged Tina to play the carnival games.

"Now, I must warn you, I am a pro at this dart game," Dan told her. The game was simple: all Dan had to do was throw a few darts and pop the balloons. The first dart he threw narrowly missed the balloon, and Tina burst out laughing.

"A pro, huh?" she teased, and his face grew red.

"That was the practice shot," he responded and threw another one that popped a balloon.

"If you pay another dollar, I'll give you two more darts and you can try to win your woman this big teddy bear," the carnie jeered at him.

Dan shoved another dollar in his direction.

"Why don't you let me get my own teddy bear?" she asked him, and he handed her a dart.

They both held a dart and prepared to throw it.

"Whoever makes it owes the other one a kiss," he told her, and she grinned.

They both threw their darts, but only one landed. It was Tina's. The carnie handed her the teddy bear, and she handed it to Dan as his prize. He groaned at his defeat. She gave him a kiss and he wrapped her up in his arm. Then they walked over to a bench to watch their kids hopping from ride to ride.

Tina leaned her head on his shoulder and closed her eyes for a moment. "I didn't think I was going to get this again," she admitted. Dan looked down at her. She opened her eyes and met his. "A family, I mean. After Cassian's father died, I thought it was just going to be the two of us, but you've given me hope."

Dan felt his insides warm after Tina's remark. At that moment, he wanted to tell Tina the truth: he was falling in love with her. But he was too scared to admit such a thing, and so instead he just squeezed her tighter and laughed as Kayla drug Cassian and Bethany behind her to go on another ride.

When Dan dropped the girls off, they immediately ran into their rooms to play, still filled with energy from the previous night's excursions, but Karina lingered in the doorway even after the girls were gone. Dan, still knowing Karina enough to know something was up, asked if everything was okay.

Karina wasn't sure how to approach this needed conversation, but she knew she had to say something. "I know this is really awkward, and I don't even know why I'm telling you this, but I guess I just wanted to give you a heads up that William and I broke up." Karina lingered in the door, clearly not wanting to finish the conversation, and so Dan hesitated to leave. She invited him in for a drink and they sat down on her couch in the quiet.

"So, what happened with you guys?" Dan casually asked. He was hesitant to ask too much about his ex-wife's personal relationship, but he wasn't sure if she had anybody else to talk to, so he wanted to be there for her. After all, he still cared about her, even if it was just as a friend.

"It was a lot of things," she said vaguely. Her eyes met his and felt a comfort within her that said she could continue. "I wanted to make that next step with him, which is why after I turned down his proposal, I still asked him to move in."

Dan choked on his drink when the word "proposal" came out of Karina's mouth.

Karina tried not to be fazed by his reaction. She didn't want to make things a bigger deal than they needed to be. "I just don't think I'm ready to get married again. I know he is a great guy, but it always felt like there was something holding me back. I don't know what's wrong with me." Her words carried on in the room long after she spoke them.

Dan's immediate thought was to jump in and tell her there was nothing wrong with her, but he held himself back from doing so. That wasn't his place anymore. Instead, he nodded and continued to be a listening ear.

But Karina took the conversation in a different direction. "So, are you seeing anybody?" she nonchalantly asked him.

Dan was hesitant to tell her about Tina. This wasn't because he didn't care about Tina; he was terrified of Karina and Tina meeting. Over the past few weeks, as he got to know Tina and enjoy his time with her, he realized how opposite she was from Karina. Tina was a very blunt, straightforward, and not extremely emotional person, at least not about trivial things. She was also easygoing, which Dan loved. It made for a lot of spontaneous adventures, like when she randomly asked if he wanted to grab donuts in the middle of the night, or when they did laser tag with Cassian and the girls and ended up having more fun than the kids did. It was things like that that really made Dan start to fall for Tina. Karina, on the other hand, was not that way. She was a very emotional person, and while she said she liked adventures, she struggled to do anything out of the norm or spontaneous. She wasn't necessarily organized, she still had an uptight aura around her, and while Dan appreciated it, he knew Tina was not the type of person she would get along with.

"Yeah, I've started seeing someone. It's pretty new," he clucked haphazardly.

"Oh, that's good," Karina responded in an almost melancholy tone. Karina was taken aback that Dan was seeing someone and hadn't mentioned it to her. Even though he said it was new, she assumed she would have heard something, if not from Dan, then surely from her girls, but she hadn't heard a single word. She made a note in the back of her head to casually ask them about it later.

"I think I've struggled so much in the past because all my 'relationships' lacked in depth," he remarked, entirely unaware of what was going on in Karina's head.

When he said this, it made Karina think about her relationship with William again. It wasn't that it lacked in depth, they often had very deep conversations about whatever crossed their minds, but it was that he lacked in struggle. She never imagined she would need someone who had gone through tragedy in their life, but after being with William, she started to wonder if that was part of why she never felt fully secure in their relationship. She now knew what a lot of people who had deep pain in their lives knew: struggle was drawn to struggle.

"Have you told the girls yet?"

"Well, it won't take a rocket scientist for them to figure out he doesn't live here anymore. I'm sure they won't really care," she scoffed, and Dan brushed it off.

When he finished his drink, Dan stood to leave. When he did, Karina gave him a look he hadn't seen from her in a long time: a look of longing. It was as if she didn't want him to leave. He had to fight himself for a moment. That familiar look tempted him to crumble and stay, even if he told himself it was just as a friend. However, he had grown too much for that. If he gave in now, it would destroy everything they had built, not just in an acquaintanceship with each other, but the relationship he was beginning to build with his girls. He was just starting to learn the ropes of fatherhood, and there was nothing that was going to stand in his way of that, especially not a fleeting moment of desire to comfort someone for whom he still cared about.

After she closed the door behind Dan, Karina sauntered over to the girls' room. The girls were busy playing a board game when their mom awkwardly knocked on the door. "Hey girls!" she gushed in a tone neither of the girls recognized. "How was your time with your dad?" Karina walked over to sit down on Bethany's bed and the girls followed her with their eyes.

They were a bit caught off guard by their mom asking how it went with their dad. Karina did not typically ask the girls these types of questions. It wasn't because she didn't care, but it was difficult for her to hear about all the ways Dan stepped up as a father many years too late. Of course, the girls didn't understand this reason, and so they obliged their mom with a brief summary of how much fun the fair was. They couldn't shut up about the big cotton candy machine they saw, and Bethany couldn't help but mention that Cassian shared his funnel cake with her.

Karina's interest peaked at hearing a name she didn't recognize. "Who's Cassian?" she questioned.

Kayla groaned at her mother's engagement with the boy she could not stand.

Bethany's face grew red, and even though her sister expected her to fully divulge about her new crush, she was hesitant to share all the details with her mother. "Oh, that's just Tina's son," she replied to brush her mother off her trail.

"Who's Tina?" she asked.

The girls glanced at each other with a look that asked: *Should we really be talking about Tina with Mom?* With just their eyes, they were able to determine they should not go into details about their dad's new girlfriend, so Kayla piped in.

"Oh, she's just someone who lives in Dad's apartment building. We go out with them sometimes," Kayla said nonchalantly.

Karina responded cheerfully, but she knew by her girls' reactions she had hit the jackpot. Whoever this Tina was, she was exactly the woman their dad was seeing. "Do you like Tina?" she pressed, and once again, the girls were put in a precarious spot.

This was their first time having to deal with the divorced-parent-interrogation-of-the-other-parent's-love-life, because Dan never asked about William. But this was because Dan had absolutely no desire to learn anything about William more than he was required to by proxy. The truth was, the girls liked Tina.

Bethany liked her mostly because she was the mother of the boy she liked, but Kayla liked her too. While it took some time for Tina to grow on her, Kayla realized Tina was a lot of fun to be around. Most of all, it was the first time since her father had been back that Kayla saw him look truly happy. This was good for Kayla. It was perhaps the first time she was coming to terms with her parents being separated, and her being okay with them moving on.

So, instead of giving their mother what she wanted, the girls ended up doing the mature, adult thing two kids should not have even been thinking about doing. They gave Karina a vague version of the truth, telling her while they didn't know Tina very well, she seemed nice.

Karina wasn't very happy with that answer, and she went to bed feeling something she fully denied: a bit of jealousy.

Bethany was busy with homework when Kayla randomly hopped onto her bed and looked at her expectantly. "Can I help you?" Bethany asked her.

"I don't understand," Kayla started, and Bethany gestured for her to continue. "Mom and Dad got divorced, right?"

"Yeah, that happened a couple years ago. I thought we got through this by now," Bethany teased, and Kayla rolled her eyes.

"No, I get it. So, Mom and Dad get divorced, and then Mom gets together with William, and then he moves in, and then he moves out a few weeks later. Now, Dad's in a relationship, and we've spent the past six months with Mom moping around and being miserable. Why didn't Mom just stay with William?" she asked. "If Mom was so unhappy with Dad, and he is happy without her, why can't she be?"

Bethany took a moment to process her sister's question. It was one she had thought a lot about herself. For a while, she saw her mom quite happy with William. When he moved in, it seemed he was there to stay. But when he moved out six months ago with no explanation other than Karina merely telling the girls it didn't work out, the girls didn't know what to make of it.

Karina had spent the past several months struggling deeply with depression, and while she tried her best to hide it from the girls, she couldn't. They all knew she was miserable, but they also knew there was nothing they could do about it. Bethany considered reaching out to William and asking him what happened, but she was also trying to be less nosey, so she fought her instincts and did not reach out.

Instead, it was the unfortunate reality that Bethany and Kayla had to watch their mother struggle. Even though they were happy their father was so happy, they imagined his joy couldn't have been easy on their mother. Bethany often reflected on the day she found her father crying in the hotel room and imagined her mother was probably suffering in the same way.

In those months, Karina continued to struggle with self-hatred and guilt. She had written several letters to William that still sat unsent in her bedroom because no words could sum up how terrible she felt.

William wasn't doing much better. Where Karina and William fell in common was that neither was able to throw themselves back into the dating scene and search for a rebound. Instead, they each spent many nights alone in their own sadness and misery, and in their own ways, attempting to heal amid all the sadness. But they were both struggling to do that healing for very different reasons. William continued to fight the demons telling him to blame himself, and Karina fought the demons telling her to hate herself. Neither was easy to ignore.

"Bethany!" Kayla snapped and pulled Bethany out of the deep thoughts she found herself waist-deep in.

"Sorry," she responded and straightened her back. "I don't know, K. I think she's trying to be happy. Maybe she just doesn't know how." Bethany wished she could give her sister a better answer, but she was just as clueless as

Kayla. Although, she did suspect things with William were a bit more complicated than their mother led them to believe. After all, who moves in and disappears three weeks later?

"You should ask Mom," Kayla suggested.

"I don't think that's a good idea. Besides, why don't you ask her?" Bethany said to throw the responsibility onto her sister.

"She listens to you more than she listens to me," Kayla admitted, but Bethany denied it.

"That's not true, Kayla. You know she loves us the same," Bethany assured her.

"Even if that were true, which it isn't," Kayla started, "she still looks at you as the 'wise one.' How many times has she called you an 'old soul'? She never says that stuff about me."

Bethany put her hand on her sister's shoulder. "She loves you, K, just as much as she loves me. Probably more," she added.

Kayla looked up at her. "I doubt it," Kayla scoffed.

"Well, you know what they say. Younger siblings are usually the favorite," she teased.

Kayla just shrugged and let her sister go back to her homework.

Dan had no intention of mentioning what he had planned for that day to the girls. He didn't want to lie to them, but he also knew Kayla would get jealous and he didn't want to cause any problems. In fact, his only intention that day was to bond with his girlfriend's son.

Dan was taking Cassian to his first baseball game, and Cassian was extremely excited. He was not a huge baseball person, but he had never been to a live sports game before. All his friends always talked about how fun they were, and he was excited he would finally get the chance to be part of the conversation. That day, they were going to watch the Red Sox and the Cubs play.

Dan told Cassian he was obligated to root for the Red Sox, and Cassian was okay with that. He didn't have an attachment to any of them, so he just told Dan he was going to be on the side of whoever won the game, which Dan laughed at.

Once they found their seats, Dan left Cassian so he could get all the baseball essentials. He got a couple hotdogs and two boxes of cracker jacks. When Dan got back to their seats, Cassian was hunched forward, intensely staring at the game. His eyes were glued to the players. He didn't even notice Dan was back until he said his name and shoved a hot dog in his direction. Without making eye contact, Cassian unwrapped the hot dog and continued to intently watch the game.

The entire game, Dan found himself grinning from ear-to-ear. Not because of the game itself (in which the Red Sox were dreadfully losing), but because of how happy Cassian was. When they all stood up to sing "Take Me Out to the Ballgame," Cassian's face lit up more than Dan had experienced before.

This day was also important to Cassian. Since his father died when he was so young, he never had the opportunity to do the classic father-son activities, and this was the first time he felt like he was getting something back from his lost childhood.

The boys found themselves talking about the game, even days after they went. Cassian proudly displayed his Roger Clemens bobblehead on his nightstand and would look to it and be reminded of a happy memory. It was also not the last baseball game Cassian would go to with Dan. The next game Dan brought the girls along as well, but it wasn't quite as special as their first game together. That would be one Cassian would cherish.

Dan and Tina were both dreading the evening awaiting them. To be fair, neither of them asked for this, and yet there they were, driving their kids over to Karina's house for dinner. If Tina had been with Dan when Karina jumped him, she never would have allowed this to happen. The last thing she wanted to do was share a meal with her boyfriend's ex-wife at her house, but Dan was more easily swayed.

After Dan had dropped off the kids one day, Karina randomly asked if Dan, Tina, and Cassian wanted to come over for dinner next week. For Karina, this was not random. Dan had been dating Tina for a year, and Karina was becoming upset she still hadn't met this woman. After all, Dan saw William several times when they were together, and so she felt that it was only fair to get to meet the woman who was spending time with her daughters (and her ex-husband).

However, Dan tried to keep his life private from Karina. Whenever Karina shared how she was doing after the breakup, he tried to keep his own interest at a minimum. He didn't want to cross any lines with Karina because of how much he cared for Tina. Perhaps he should have been the one to let them meet at some point, but it was too late. Now he had to accept this dinner, because if he didn't, there would be hell to pay. So, Dan agreed and informed Tina that night her Friday plans would consist of going to Karina's house so they could all eat dinner together.

If Tina had her way, she would have preferred to meet Karina in a neutral area, like at the girls' choir performance, or even at the park. Going over to her house was the last place Tina wanted to be. However, she agreed to go because sometimes you had to accept the reality, and whether Tina liked it or not, this was her reality.

When they got to Karina's house, she instantly felt underdressed. Karina was wearing a tight-fitting dress and heels, while Tina found herself wearing black jeans, a nice blouse, and a worn-out pair of boots. Dan was also caught off-guard by Karina's attire, as she wasn't one to typically dress up. Karina figured, if she was going to meet Tina, she was sure as hell going to look her best.

Bethany and Kayla ran out after they heard the door open to greet their father and Tina with big hugs. But when Bethany saw Cassian, her face instantly grew red, as it was often in the habit of doing. Even after a year, she still could not get over her crush on him. He had broken up with his girlfriend two months ago, and Bethany may or may not have bought a cupcake to personally celebrate his newfound singleness.

Kayla had reached the point where nothing in her sister's obsession could surprise her. Even still, Kayla had grown to tolerate Cassian's company a bit more once he started teaching her how to play guitar. They only had a few lessons, but Kayla loved it. She never imagined herself to be someone who enjoyed playing an instrument, but Cassian told her she was a natural. It even gave her the confidence to ask her mom if she could have a guitar for her birthday that was coming up soon. Luckily for Kayla, her mom obliged and a gently-loved acoustic guitar was sitting in Karina's closet.

Dinner consisted of a new curry dish Karina had tried out a few times on the girls. It was a dish William taught her how to make, but she loved it so much she tried to forget where it came from.

When the girls were at the table, the conversation was lively. Tina asked the girls a few questions about their school projects, and the girls and Dan talked to Cassian about sports.

Karina had been quiet during this time, just observing how everyone else at the table interacted with each other. She watched Tina keep a steady interest in what her girls would say, complete with nodding and asking follow-up questions. She looked at the way Dan looked at Cassian, with a similar love he had for their girls. Most of all, she watched how Dan and Tina interacted with each other. Their love was subtle: side glances, spurts of laughter when they would catch the other one staring, things that weren't necessarily noticeable if you weren't looking for them. But Karina was.

After dinner, the girls went into their room, and Cassian asked if he could play his Game Boy on Karina's couch. She agreed, and suddenly it was just the three adults sitting at the table.

"So, Tina. What do you do for work?"

Ah yes, the first awkward question Tina would have to answer.

"I'm a criminal investigator. At least, that's what my degree says. The crimes here surely don't compare to what I dealt with in Boston." She glanced over at Dan, who gave her a warm smile and squeezed her hand in encouragement.

He thought back to how terrible every conversation he had with William was, and squeezed Tina's hand another time to assure her he was right there.

Karina noticed.

While she may have been observing Dan and Tina, Tina was watching Karina too. And she did not like what she saw.

"Wow, that is impressive," Karina replied.

The three of them continued to have polite conversation for a half hour before Dan finally decided it was getting late. The three of them loaded up in the car, and Cassian made a snarky remark about how awkward the whole thing was. Dan expected Tina to retort back, but she remained silent. It wasn't until they got back to his apartment that he learned the truth.

"Well, that was not as terrible as it could have been," Dan added as he slumped his coat on the couch and waited for Tina to come and sit next to him. But she didn't. She stood awkwardly at the kitchen island with her head down as she anxiously twiddled with her necklace. Dan walked over to her and touched her hand pressed firmly on the counter. "What's wrong?" he gently asked her. He watched as a tear streamed down on Tina's face and landed delicately on the wood of the countertop.

"I saw the way she looked at you, Dan," Tina muttered in a quiet and pained voice.

"Who?" Dan questioned, even though he suspected what the answer would be.

"Your ex-wife. She's still in love with you," Tina lamented.

Dan took a step away from the counter. "What? No, she's not," he countered. "She cheated on me. She was in a long-term relationship right after me. It's been years. Trust me, there is nothing between Karina and me," he assured her. Tears continued to stream down Tina's face and she was quiet. "Tina, you don't have anything to worry about," he assured her once again, but the words did not stick with Tina.

"Dan, I saw the way that she looked at you, and that is not the way someone who has moved on looks at someone else. Maybe she thought she had moved on, but it's pretty obvious she hasn't."

Dan felt anger boil up inside of him. "Tina, she doesn't have feelings for me. And even if she did, what does it matter? I love you."

"And I love you too. But, Dan, I can't risk this," she sobbed. "Cassian is already attached. I can't put him through any more of this if there is even a chance you could get back together with her." Tears were streaming down her face and her heart trembled. "Is there a chance?"

Dan's silence only lasted about five seconds, but that felt like an eternity for Tina. "No, I love you, Tina," he assured her, but it was too late.

"We have to end things," she sternly replied as emotion poured out of her. "You can't talk to Cassian anymore. It is going to be hard enough on him, but if you keep talking to him, he is never going to move forward," she cried.

Tears were streaming down Dan's face as well. He felt powerless to stop what had been set in motion by feelings outside of his control. He didn't want to be with Karina. He wanted to be with Tina. Why couldn't she see that?

"But I'm committed to you. You don't have to do this," he reminded her, but she just huffed in disagreement.

"You don't understand," she started, "when I lost my husband, I didn't think I was ever going to recover. I can't take the risk that one day down the road, you will realize you have feelings for her too. I know you still love her, and you are always going to be connected to her. It is too much of a risk. I don't want to be abandoned again. I can't allow my son to be abandoned again."

"I don't want to abandon you!" Dan cried.

"I know. I know right now you don't. But it's clear now there is a possibility that you could, one day—"

"How? How is it clear?" Dan interjected.

"You hesitated, Dan! When I asked you if there was a chance, you hesitated."

Dan spun around in a circle and lifted his hands in frustration. "Tina, I want to be with you! I love you! I just—"

This time Tina interrupted him. "If there is a possibility of you and Karina getting back together again and having a whole family for your girls, I don't want to stand in the way of that," she told him and wiped away the tears staining her face. "I'm going to go now," she said, but before she got to the door, Dan grabbed her hand.

"Please don't do this. I don't want to lose you," he pleaded and grabbed her hand so tightly it started to pulse.

"That's exactly why I'm doing this. Because I can't lose you. I have to leave before I do."

He shook his head in denial, but it was clear he couldn't stop it. Before he knew it, she was gone. The relationship he had been so incredibly happy in for the past year had dissipated in an instant, all because of Karina. Although it wasn't really her, it was because of him. He loved Karina too much. Even if he had no romantic feelings for her, and no intention of pursuing her ever again, the love he had for her was too much for Tina to bear. She deserved someone who was fully devoted to her. One day, several years down the road, after Cassian was long moved out of the house, she would find that again. But no matter what, Dan would always have some devotion to the mother of his children. That was why he hesitated.

Perhaps it was unfair of Dan to have such devotion. Perhaps it was unfair of Tina to resent and leave him for it. But, either way, it was the end of their story.

Chapter Eighteen: Now

Melinda opened her laptop and shoved it in Kayla's direction. "Read it," she commanded.

Kayla inquisitively looked at her, but she obeyed.

CodeX Founder, Benjamin Weedle, Repents for His Technology Sins

Kayla looked up at Melinda with a puzzled face, but she gestured for her to keep reading. The article included a personal confession from Ben in which he admitted everything he did was for his own personal gain, and included an apology to every employee of CodeX. He not only owned that what he did was selfish, but the article revealed how terrible he felt for letting his employees down. Because of this, the article also announced Ben would officially step down as CEO of BlockWorks as soon as the contract was up, which in this case was one year. Even still, he promised to put his all into growing the company during his time as CEO, for the sake of the hard-working coders there.

As she continued to read, Kayla noticed another interesting piece of information in the last paragraph:

Weedle not only took the vow of unemployment next year, but he is also using his salary to make up for some of the damage he did to his CodeX employees. Weedle promised to send every CodeX employee some sort of financial compensation for the trouble he caused. It looks like some people can have a change of heart after all.

"Wait, so he's giving us money?" Kayla questioned after reading the last paragraph a second time.

Melinda nodded. "Half of his salary is going towards you. Split so many ways, it won't be worth a lot, but he figured it was the least he could do to try to make up for the pain he has caused."

Kayla couldn't believe it, and Melinda couldn't either. However, in couples counseling, Benjamin admitted the way he wanted to work through his guilt was to give up his position at BlockWorks and make his betrayal public. Kayla couldn't help but suspect that part of this was to heal his own public image, but she also couldn't ignore the fact that he turned down leading one of the major tech conglomerates just because he felt bad. No one cared about their image that much, not in St. Louis anyway.

Melinda surely seemed to believe Ben had changed for the better. While she had gone back and forth on whether to give them another shot, she ultimately realized their love was too valuable to give up on just yet. So, she was giving him another chance, however, she made it abundantly clear that if he did anything like what he did to her once, he would never get another chance again. This was his one chance to be different, and change. Kayla sincerely hoped that for Melinda's sake, he would take it.

After Melinda shared a bit more about the revelations they made in counseling, she finally asked the question Kayla had been dreading: "How did the trip go?"

At first, Kayla thought about brushing her off and being vague, as she typically did. But then she decided to take a different approach: honesty. Or as much honesty Kayla could muster, being a vulnerability newbie and all. "It was hard, a lot harder than I thought it would be. All my sister and I seemed to do was fight, and it was terrible seeing my dad," she admitted, and even felt guilty saying it out loud. She looked to Melinda and feared judgement, but

Melinda just nodded understandingly. "There were a few good moments, but they were fleeting. I just wish he was *him*."

Melinda nodded reassuringly. "I lost my aunt to breast cancer a few years ago, and I remember thinking the same thing. I didn't even want to see her after she lost all her hair. She just didn't look the same, and she didn't act the same either. I wish I could say she was resilient through all of it, but she struggled a lot with depression during her final stages. No one in my family really talked about it, though. They all remember her as the happy and bubbly person that she was for most of my life. But I remember. I witnessed her go through some dark moments, and those are memories I will never get out of my head."

Kayla thanked Melinda for sharing about her aunt. She had no idea about her, or anyone in Melinda's family, really. They mostly talked about the present, which was usually Ben. "Do you wish you never saw her during those times?"

Melinda paused to think about the question. "Sometimes I do. But then I think about the alternative. If I never saw her at her worst, then I never would have seen all of her. For better or for worse, when she died, I felt like I really knew her. After all, even after seeing all the ugly, she was still so good. It gave me hope, in a strange way."

Kayla took what Melinda said to heart. After talking to her and re-meeting Cassian, she wondered if she was making the wrong choice by staying away from her father. Perhaps they were all onto something. Maybe she was the one missing out after all.

Kayla was lying in bed reading one evening when her phone rang out of the blue. She picked it up and her phone displayed a name still unusual to see: Cassian. She hadn't spoken to him since he spoke to her father, so she was surprised to hear from him. But she picked up anyway. After some polite chitchat and catching each other up about the past few weeks, Cassian suddenly became quiet.

"Is everything okay?" Kayla asked the strangely quiet line.

"Yeah, I just remembered the real reason I called," he stated awkwardly. Kayla remained quiet to let him continue. "I talked to my mom the other day and told her about my call with your father. I told her he apologized, and she admitted she was the one who asked your dad not to reach out to me anymore."

"Oh?" Kayla responded with surprise.

"She gave me some stock answers about how she thought it was what was best for me, so that I wouldn't get too attached to someone she had no future with, but really, she was doing what was best for her. She wanted to be able to move forward and didn't think she would be able to do that if she still had a tie to her ex-boyfriend. So, she didn't let him reach out to me."

"I'm sorry," was all Kayla could say. "How are you doing after learning that?" Through developing her friendship with Melinda, Kayla had grown a lot in her abilities to be there for people, and through relying on Cassian a bit with her father, she also felt like she had grown in letting other people be there for her too.

"I'm feeling a lot of things," he admitted. The silence on the other line gave Cassian permission to elaborate. "I feel a lot of guilt for being so angry at your dad for so many years when it wasn't even his fault. I'm angry at my mom for taking away my one other chance of having a father figure in my life," he stated.

Hearing the word "father" in regards to her dad caught Kayla off guard. Cassian had only been in their lives for a year, and so it came as a surprise that someone else had looked to her dad as a dad without her even knowing it. She had no idea how she could have been so blind, and was even more heartbroken for what Cassian had been deprived.

"I just wish I could go back and do things differently, you know?" he confessed.

"That I do know," Kayla sighed.

Through coming back to St. Louis, Kayla was filled with a bit of regret about how things went down with her sister. Even though she didn't imagine going back to Plymouth and repairing their entire relationship, she also didn't anticipate making things worse like she did.

But, in the long, exhausting drive back to St. Louis, Kayla realized another thing: her father was dying. She knew this in a surface-level understanding, but she saw things in a whole new light when she saw him in person. This meant the only family she would have left would be her sister. This also meant when her father did die, her sister would be the person who would understand what she was feeling the best. A part of Kayla hoped the two sisters could become closer now they had gotten some things off their chests, but if Kayla was being honest with herself, there were a lot of other things that still weighed heavy on her regarding her sister. Conflicts that were years old, and yet still never fully resolved.

She and Cassian found themselves talking for an hour more. She heard stories about her father she had never heard before, and in a way, it made her feel closer to her dad. Perhaps in learning a new perspective, she was able to get closer to how Melinda described her aunt. Maybe she was closer to fully knowing her father. Besides, there weren't that many people left who could tell stories about him, so it was comforting to hear about the baseball games, and the way he and Tina would burst out laughing in her living room over bad jokes. Happy moments both she and Cassian could hold onto. Kayla also found herself sharing some special moments with her father. While it was emotional to share them, it was also refreshing. She had put in so much effort to compartmentalize feelings about her father because she knew how much pain it would cause her, but now she allowed herself to remember the good moments and let them be separate from the sad reality. That was something good for them both.

"He just keeps getting worse," Bethany remarked as she zipped up her boot.

"I know," Huxley replied and put his hand on her shoulder.

She looked up and saw his sympathetic face looking back at her. "I just thought I had a little more time with him, you know…" her voice faded off.

Dan had taken a turn for the worst in the past couple months. His physical body stayed about the same, but his mind was more convoluted. The biggest loss was his ability to speak, which was almost completely gone. He mumbled a lot of words no one could understand, and it had gotten to the point where he only spoke a few words or one sentence a day that included intelligible words.

While Bethany was aware her ability to communicate with her father was something that would eventually dissipate, she didn't imagine it would happen so quickly. While in the past six months there hadn't been many of them, there had been a few good moments in which Bethany fooled herself into thinking she had a few good years left with her father. But his quick downhill spiral made it evident he didn't have as much time left as she had hoped.

Bethany gave her husband's hand a squeeze and then grabbed her coat. She planned to spend some time with her father before going to her doctor. She hadn't been feeling the best lately, and was due for a physical exam anyway, so she figured now was as good of a time as any to go in.

When she got to her father's house, Sarah Beth answered the door with a frown on her face.

"Rough day?" Bethany questioned, and she just nodded. When she walked into the living room, her father was lying in his bed. He had been given a sedative because of an angry outburst from that morning. She pulled up a chair, sat down next to him, and reached under the sheet so she could hold his hand. She was silent, and merely listened to his breathing. "I miss you, Dad," she whispered. In the past few months, Bethany tried even harder to remember what her dad was like before he got sick. It was something that all the Alzheimer's support websites recommended doing to help cultivate compassion for the family member you stopped being able to recognize. But it became harder for Bethany to remember good moments as he continued to become less recognizable. Still, she closed her eyes, took a deep breath, and tried to think of a happy memory anyway.

"Dad, he's just my prom date. It's not a big deal," Bethany assured him.

"Ha!" Dan chuckled. "'It's not a big deal,'" he mimicked his daughter and rolled his eyes. "You may think it's not a big deal, but I remember what was going on in my head during my prom, so I WILL be speaking to this man before he takes out any daughter of mine."

Even though Bethany's hormonal self was frustrated with her father's protection, another part of her found it endearing.

"Now go grab your mother so she can pull out the big JVS and capture everything."

Bethany did as he asked, and Karina came out a few minutes later with her camcorder glued to her hand.

"Look at you! You look so beautiful. Now do a twirl for the camera."

Bethany's face grew red as she did a lackluster spin and her light blue dress spar-kled on her. Before she knew it, there was a knock at the door.

"Is that him?" Karina asked. She was filled with the giddiness of a girl living vicariously through her daughter since she didn't get to have a prom herself.

On the other side of the door stood a tall, stocky boy with bright red hair, freckles, and a very nervous smile. He fiddled uncomfortably with the tux one size too big for him, and held a clear corsage box in his sweaty hands.

"Hi," he stammered. "I'm here to pick up—"

"Bethany!" Karina interrupted before he even got a chance to finish his sentence.

Bethany knew Ethan from biology class. He was extremely nerdy, but also very funny, and knew how to make Bethany laugh. Both their friend groups had been push-ing them to go to prom together, and finally they conceded with him nervously asking her one day after biology. Bethany had missed her prom last year because she didn't have a date and had no desire to go. Now it was her senior year, and she could make one last classic high school memory before she graduated.

While senior prom was a special memory in Bethany's heart, she didn't care to relive the details of the prom itself. What she wanted to remember was what her dad whispered to her before she walked out the door.

He gave her a squeeze before she was on her way to the cheaply decorated high school gym and leaned over to tell her something. "Please do not forget that you are wonderful, and beautiful, and worthy of so many good things," he whispered to her. As he pulled away, he added one more thing. "And make good choices. I do not want to be picking you up with the police," he said, and Bethany laughed.

Bethany now knew her father probably only said that to dissuade her from making stupid choices on her prom night, but she let the words fill her anyway. She looked at her father's wrinkled and fragile hand now and tried to re-member what his strong and sturdy hands used to feel like. It seemed like a different person. Unfortunately, he was becoming more and more like a stranger every day. Bethany left her dad without him saying anything, which was the new normal. Then, she went to her doctor's appointment.

"So, what's new in your life, Bethany?" Dr. Kaur politely asked her as she pulled the blood pressure cuff off her arm.

"Oh, the usual. Dad dying, sister's not here, and of course dealing with the typical dramas of a young child," she teased. "But I've been feeling a lot more fatigued and light-headed lately. It's probably just stress, but I wanted to make sure."

"Well, we will run some tests to make sure you are in tip-top shape."

After Dr. Kaur did all the necessary tests, Bethany was left in the doctor's office on her own. Instead of just sitting and staring at the ceiling, she got up and stood in front of the posters that hung on the wall. The first was a poster about mental health, and the second was a 3D poster that showcased the human skeleton. Bethany lightly traced her finger along the skeleton, and then found herself looking around at all the various tools and instruments that hung in the room. Bethany thought about the brief period in her life when she considered becoming a doctor, but then she reminded herself of what changed. It was her sister. After she almost lost her on the beach that day, it made her realize she never wanted to go through the trauma of watching someone die. Who would have known she would have to go through that anyway, doctor or not?

Dr. Kaur returned a while later with an expression Bethany couldn't quite place.

"Well," she started, "you are definitely healthy."

Bethany grew concerned with how vague her doctor was being. "Am I dying?" she questioned, only half kidding.

"No, no, no. I just said you were healthy. Remember?" she assured her. "But," she looked down again at her clipboard, "I'm assuming that, given the fact you didn't say anything to me, and judging by your reaction now, I do have a bit of news. You're pregnant."

Chapter Nineteen: Then

This was not an impromptu meeting with his ex-wife. This was planned. They even got a babysitter so they could meet at Karina's house without the kids listening in. Dan had been tormented in the past few months after losing Tina. He tried to reach out to her multiple times, but she didn't respond. This was Tina's way: a complete cut-off.

Of course, she wanted to answer all the times her phone rang, but she believed it would be best for her to not engage with him any further. She did write him a letter and apologized for not answering his calls. She reaffirmed all the things she had already told him in person, and answered some of the questions he left on her voicemail. But Tina believed there was nothing more she could do for him without hurting herself, or Dan.

While Dan said he wanted answers, what he really wanted was Tina back, but it seemed she was not willing to give him anything more, and he would have to learn to accept that.

Dan not only resented himself (and the ridiculous, stupid, five-second hesitation) but spent several hours figuring out why he hesitated in the first place. The only conclusion he could come to was that, for a moment, he imagined having his family back. But what Tina didn't understand was it was only for a moment, and after that moment he was able to rejoice in the family he already had, and the one he was stitching together with Tina.

But she didn't see that. All she could see was the hesitation.

After that night, he quit engaging with Karina other than what was necessary. He even quit coming to the door to drop the girls off. The only conversations they had were regarding the girls. That is, until he reached out and asked if he could meet with her one-on-one to discuss some "important matters." He was purposely vague, because he didn't want to give her any ideas, but he also didn't want to get into any arguments over the phone.

When he came over, Karina was cold to him. She was frustrated with how rude she thought him to be in the past few months. From the girls, she had gathered things had ended with Tina, but he didn't even have the decency to tell her. After all, she told him immediately after things ended with William.

Dan didn't think it was necessary. She didn't need to know anything about his life, and the only thing he needed to know was whether what Tina said was true. He needed to know if Karina still had feelings for him. If she did, he wanted to shut them down as quickly as possible. He was so angry at her, that her existence was part of what destroyed the most important relationship in his life, that he didn't even want to look at her. Dan didn't even want to have this conversation at all, but he needed answers.

Karina sat down on the couch, and Dan positioned himself across the living room in what used to be his favorite chair.

"So, what did you want to talk about?" she callously asked him.

Dan's heart thumped in his chest and he realized asking this question caused him a lot more anxiety than he expected. As angry as he felt with Karina, he still wasn't sure how he would feel if she admitted to having feelings for him. He certainly didn't have feelings for her, but would he feel angrier to know she was in love with him? Would he feel sad? Bitter? Resentful that it took her so long to figure it out? Would he see the life they could have had as lost because now he was too far from her to come back? The uncertainty of it all was what racked him with anxiety. In order to build his courage to speak, he thought about what Tina would want. Perhaps she wouldn't want this conversation at all, but if she was in his shoes, she would be blunt. So that was exactly what he was going to be.

"Are you still in love with me?" he flatly asked.

Her eyes seemed to bulge out of her skull. "What? Where did you get that idea?" she growled.

"Answer. The. Question. Are you still in love with me? Yes or no," he insisted.

Karina stood up from the couch. "What the hell is this, Dan?" she yelled, but he remained quiet and poised with his hands folded in his lap.

"Just answer the question," he said again, refusing to engage with her antics.

She scoffed at his presumptions. "How dare you? You make me pay for a babysitter for you to accuse me of still being in love with you? No, I'm not. Are you happy?" she questioned and continued to stand over him with her arms crossed.

"Do you still have feelings for me then?" he asked, this time a bit more cautiously.

This question made Karina march to her bedroom, yelling as she had her back turned to him. "I can't do this. You are unbelievable!" she hissed as she walked into her bedroom and slammed the door hard behind her.

Dan continued to sit in the chair and wondered what to do next. If she wasn't in love with him, then did he lose Tina for nothing? Or maybe Karina was just denying it. The only thing he did know was he didn't know anything anymore.

There was a part of him tempted to go and knock on her bedroom door and apologize for being so forward. But when he thought about it again, he decided against it. *If she wants to throw a fit, then let her throw a fit,* he thought. He would sit there until she was ready to talk again, instead of chasing after her like he used to do.

Soon Karina did indeed find her way out of her bedroom, and sat back down on the couch.

"I'm sorry for catching you off guard," he said when she made eye contact with him. "I'm sure you've heard that my life has fallen apart in the last three months. I'm just trying to get some clarity," he added.

"Yes, I did hear, which is exactly why I wish you would talk to me about it," Karina commented.

Dan paused for a moment to take in Karina's response, but then something clicked in his mind. "I don't think you are the person I should be talking about it to," he responded and then shifted his glance from the floor towards her.

Her eyes shot up at his response. "What's that supposed to mean?" she questioned. She looked as if she was ready to stand up and walk away again, but instead she waited for his answer.

"I don't know what kind of relationship you think we should have, but you're my ex-wife. Do you really think we should be talking about those kinds of things? Or is that crossing a line?"

At that moment, Karina's emotions completely broke down, and she sobbed. Dan was unprepared for the extreme emotional reaction his simple statement caused. While his initial instinct was to comfort her, he tried to take a mental step back and let her comfort herself.

"I'm sorry," she sniffled. She took a few shallow breaths and rubbed her eyes. "I just don't have anyone else to talk to. About anything."

This was the truth. In all the years Karina had lived in Plymouth, she never made any friendships beyond her coworkers at the school, and the acquaintanceships with other parents. It wasn't that she didn't want friends, but her childhood trauma put her in an isolating position. When her dad went to jail, most of the friends she did have weren't interested in being involved when her life became so messy. So, she had to carry all those burdens on her own. Then, she met Dan, and of course her life only continued to get messier. When she was married and had children, she didn't seem to fit in with any group. She couldn't have any couple friends, because her spouse was always gone, but she also couldn't fit in with the single parents because she was still in a committed relationship. She found herself to be the outsider of every group, and eventually, she stopped trying.

Ironically enough, Dan's counselor had prepared him for a moment such as this. He had spent a lot of time in his counseling trying to understand why Karina left him for William in the first place, and now he had a deeper understanding of some of the possibilities. But Karina's statement made everything clearer. While his counselor recommended not to say any revelations he made about Karina to her, as she may not be ready to hear them (or he may not be the person to say them) he felt like it was too much of a coincidence for him to keep his mouth closed. Instead of asserting his own thoughts, he merely asked a question.

"Isn't that why you started talking to William?"

Such a simple question, and yet it made Karina's mind go haywire. Her immediate response was to be defensive and object to Dan's assumptions, but a voice in the back of her mind told her he was right. She started emotionally relying on William because she felt like she couldn't talk to Dan. Even though she wasn't with William anymore, she still believed she needed someone she could rely on. She needed someone safe. Back then, safe meant William. Now, safe meant Dan. He was familiar, he knew her, he loved her, and no matter what, he would always be a part of their life because of their children.

As for their conversation, Karina didn't say anything else. Nothing more needed to be said. For Dan, at least he walked away with a better understanding of where Karina stood. Maybe she did have romantic feelings for him, but the most prominent thing for her at that point was that she just needed someone to lean on, and he looked like the safest option for that. But this was a healthy revelation for them both.

Dan got up to leave, but before he got to the door, he swiveled on his heels to turn and say one more thing before he left her. "I don't want to assume anything about you, but one thing I have learned in the past two years is I needed to start leaning on myself more than I leaned on other people. I had to learn how to rely on myself, because sometimes, that is the only person I have." Again, she didn't say anything, but Dan could leave knowing she didn't have to.

When he got to his apartment that night, Dan thought about Tina again. Some part of him wanted to tell her about the revelations he made with Karina, but then he realized how selfish that would be, especially given the circumstances of their parting. Even harder for Dan, was he thought about Cassian frequently. He missed that kid so much, and he had finally felt they had gotten to a solid place in their relationship. It was devastating not to talk to him about everything that had happened. He had no idea what Tina said to her son about him, but he assumed because of how hurt she was about the situation, none of it would be good. Dan had to continually remind himself of something his counselor told him about their breakup: he was not the only one at fault. Some of the reasons Tina left were because of her own insecurities, and he couldn't take ownership of those. What he could do was set boundaries with his ex-wife so she wouldn't be a problem in the next relationship he entered. What Dan didn't know was the next serious relationship he entered would present a whole other set of complications.

It had been a few years since Dan was in Germany, and while he occasionally sent and received postcards from the other guys on his team, the only person he kept consistent contact with was Emerson. Luckily, technology had progressed enough where the long-distance calling was a bit cheaper and they were able to schedule a phone call around every six months. It wasn't much, but it was enough to keep informed about each other's lives.

"Dan!" Emerson exclaimed when he picked up the phone. "It's been too long. Tell me: what's new in your world?"

Dan gave him an update about Tina, which was as painful as ever. The last thing he wanted to do was talk about how terribly his last relationship ended. "I'm still pretty angry at Karina, and I'm not sure how to move past it," Dan admitted.

"Karina? Why are you angry at her?" Emerson asked.

Dan wondered if something had gotten lost in translation.

"Didn't you hear anything I just said? She's one of the reasons why my last relationship fell apart." There was silence on the other line. "Did I lose you?"

"*Nien*, I'm still here. I'm just thinking."

Dan could picture Emerson's thinking face clearly. He always knew something wise and important was coming after he would make that face. "Do you think that maybe you aren't mad at Karina, but are actually mad at yourself and are just letting it out on her?"

Hearing this made Dan's defenses immediately go up. Before he got a chance to respond, Emerson stepped in.

"Could it be possible you still have feelings for Karina?"

"Of course I don't," Dan instinctively replied.

"Okay," Emerson hesitantly accepted Dan's answer. "Listen, I'm just speaking from my own experience with you, Dan. Even after you split up, you loved her hard. In fact, I've never seen anybody love another human being as much as you loved her," with that statement, Emerson let out a big sigh. "I know the guys tried to push you into a new relationship, but even when you left, it was pretty obvious you hadn't moved on. Now that she isn't with the scumbag she cheated on you with, it would make sense if those feelings came up again."

Dan huffed, and for a moment, he considered hanging up altogether. But he stayed on the call. Instead, he quickly changed the subject to Emerson's life.

After they bid their farewells and hung up, Dan slouched into his couch in dismay. *How could he think that?* Dan wondered. *I was happy with Tina. Where would he get the idea I was still hung up on Karina?* But then, when he thought about it for longer, he allowed himself to remember some of the happier memories with Karina. He couldn't help but feel a twang of desire to have that again. Maybe it was because he made the reality into more of a fantasy in his head, but he couldn't hide the fact that he was truly happy with her at one point in his life, especially before he moved to Germany. Those were good days. So maybe, just maybe, amid losing Tina, some residual feelings for his ex-wife had popped back up. And maybe Karina had them too.

He thought back to what Tina had said the day they broke up. *"I saw the way she looked at you, and that is not the way someone who has moved on looks at someone else."*

Maybe she was closer to the truth than he originally allowed himself to believe. But what did it matter? They had been divorced for four years. Were they just going to pick up where they left off? Not to mention their friendship was in dire straits now. Ever since Dan accused Karina of being in love with him, their friendship almost completely dissipated. Karina had no desire to talk to him more than what was required, and until that day, Dan didn't either. Now, all his emotions were completely out of sync and he was left spinning.

Instead of trying to figure out everything that night, Dan focused on the logical next step: repairing his friendship with Karina. No matter what, she was the mother of their children; he wanted to be on good terms with her. So, he called her and apologized. After a bit of yelling on her end, she forgave him. Things wouldn't go back to normal right away, but it was a start, and for that day, it was all Dan could do.

While spring cleaning was the bane of most of the Fitzpatrick family's existence, Bethany was the only one who could tolerate it. Both Karina and Kayla were terrible about holding onto things they didn't need, and so Bethany volunteered, usually for a few dollars, to go through their stuff and organize it. This year was no different. She started with Kayla's room and went through an entire year's worth of schoolwork, notebooks, folders, clothes—a whole bunch of things Kayla did not need. After she went through everything, she made a pile of things she planned to throw away, and a pile of things she would drop off at the thrift store, and left them in Kayla's room for her to go through and make both of those piles smaller.

While Kayla hated getting rid of clothes, seeing clothes she didn't even recognize in the piles Bethany made often encouraged her to at least get rid of some things.

Even though Bethany was exhausted from a full Saturday filled with organizing Kayla's life, she decided she could at least get started on the home office before giving up for the day. The home office was often filled with piles of receipts and unnecessary documents Karina kept because she didn't have the energy to organize or throw them away. While Bethany would have loved to tackle her mother's bedroom as well, Karina refused to allow her daughter to go through her personal stuff. But Karina had to admit it was nice to come home to an office that was completely organized.

Bethany started with the desk and began to rummage through crumpled up papers Karina was too stressed, or too lazy, as Bethany believed, to get rid of them. She stifled through some of the drawers stuffed with paper, but then Bethany noticed one of the desk drawers was jammed and she couldn't open it. After a quick peek in their toolbox, Bethany was able to jimmy open the stubborn drawer with a screwdriver. When she opened it, she found a box labeled "keepsakes."

Now, Bethany should not have gone through this box. She should have just set it aside for her mom to look through later. Bethany would later say it was her cleaning-driven mind that forced her to go through the box, but if she was being honest with herself, she only went through the box to find out what was inside. She would later deeply regret that decision. But, at that moment, she opened the box and started to flip through her mother's personal things. She found a few older photos of her parents, and a cluster of cards her dad had given her mom, but then she came upon an envelope with a W on it. She assumed this stood for William and tore open the envelope to see what was inside. In it she found several photos of the two of them together, notes he had written to her, and at the very bottom, a receipt.

186

2 Scoops (Cone) 4.99
2 Scoops (Cup) 4.99

Tax: 0.62
Total: 10.60

I'm here if you want to vent. Anytime.
(508)-555-0131

-William

It didn't take long for Bethany to do the math in her head. The receipt dated back five months before her parents even got divorced, and perhaps if Bethany didn't already suspect something, this wouldn't have been a big deal, but too many red flags were shooting up all around this offensive piece of paper. A still, small voice whispered in Bethany's mind as she held this receipt, containing a truth of which she was nearing the cusp: her mother was involved with William while her parents were still together.

Of course, Bethany had no idea to what extent, but her mind feared the worst. Before she could think, she stuffed the receipt back into the box and slammed the desk drawer shut to deny the reality she was facing. She ran into the bathroom and sat on the teal shower mat while questions swirled in her mind. *How long were they together? Were they sleeping together? Did Dad know? Is that the real reason why they got a divorce?*

While these questions all burned in Bethany's hormonal and already confused mind, she grappled with an even greater question: should she confront her mom about it?

Bethany paced in her room when her sister walked through the door.

"Ugh. Mom still won't clean out the home office." Kayla had been trying for months to get her mom to clean out the home office so Kayla could make it into her bedroom. This seemed like a valid request since Karina rarely used the home office and the girls had been living in the same bedroom their entire lives.

Since Bethany was a teenager and Kayla was closely falling behind, it seemed time for them to each have their own space. But Karina's procrastination prolonged this process. She was still struggling off and on with depressive bouts, but recent revelations had contributed to the bouts happening less frequently. In part because of Dan, she was working even harder to forgive herself, and rely on herself more than she ever had before. This was not an easy feat for Karina, and she had a long way to go, but the progress was there. However, menial tasks never failed to overwhelm her, and cleaning out the home office was no exception.

"What's up with you?" Kayla questioned after she noticed her sister's anxious pacing.

"What?" Bethany asked as cluelessly as possible. "Oh, nothing. I just have a lot on my mind." Bethany brushed off her sister. It had been a few days since Bethany found the receipt she wasn't supposed to know about and discovered the secret Karina had spent the past several years trying to hide. She still hadn't confronted her mom about it, and was at war with herself over what the best course of action would be. On the one hand, it seemed logical to confront her mom with the facts and get the truth from her. On the other hand, Bethany didn't want to deal with the repercussions of snooping, but even deeper, she didn't really want to know the truth. It was a secret she was not ready to harbor.

The worst part was Bethany hadn't said anything to her sister. At first, she wanted to share with Kayla what she had found, but then she decided it would cause her a lot more harm than good. If Kayla found out her mother had been cheating on her father, the person she idolized most in the world, it would destroy her and her relationship with their mom. The last thing Bethany wanted to do was be the pin that set off the grenade.

Kayla had finally come to a point in her life when she was getting closer to her mom. Their entire lives, Bethany was closer to their mom and Kayla was closer to their dad. This wasn't intentional, but the girls found a lot of similarities in their respective parent. Now it seemed like they were finally getting to the point where Kayla and her mom were able to bond and find things to laugh about together. That was a miracle itself considering how much they butted heads after the divorce, and Bethany couldn't bring herself to risk destroying that.

"Really, Bethany? There is clearly something wrong. What aren't you telling me?" Kayla asked with her hands now firmly placed on her hips.

Bethany racked her mind in search of something she could say to her sister. "I just got a bad test grade, that's all," she lied. It was a weak excuse, but her sister bought it, for now anyway. Bethany tried to think of a way to change the subject, and she knew the only way she could quickly end the conversation was to talk about the one thing her sister could not stand discussing: boys. "So, there's this cute kid in my math class."

"Ugh," Kayla groaned and slumped down on her bed. "Please spare me," she begged, and Bethany laughed with relief.

"Fine, I won't bore you with another crush."

"Thank you. Consider me indebted to you," Kayla dramatically responded and hopped on the computer.

Bethany reached over to the boombox and turned it on. Popular hits filled the room, and for the rest of the night, the girls found themselves doing their own thing. For now, Bethany was in the clear, but she couldn't stay that way forever.

Okay. You can do this. It is only a big deal if you make it a big deal.

Karina had been giving herself a pep talk ever since she dropped the girls off at their respective middle and high schools. Surprisingly enough, Karina enjoyed taking the girls to schools other than her own because it meant she had a few minutes of quiet time between dropping them off and getting to work.

Karina walked into the school with her head held high, her shoulders back, and her back a little straighter than usual. She continued her internal pep talk as she casually walked into the faculty lounge and approached one of the tables. "Hey, ladies!" Karina cheerily greeted the three women sitting at the table chatting. Karla Robinson, Angela Cardenas, and Georgina Castillo were the three other teachers at the school around Karina's age. Karla and Angela had both been married for several years, but Georgina was single and had never been married.

When Karina first started at Franklin Elementary School, a couple of the teachers made efforts for Karina to join them for drinks, but since she had two young children at the time, and was terrible at making new friends, Karina always came up with an excuse to turn them down.

But not anymore. Karina was turning over a new leaf, and that started with making some friends. Who would have known a woman in her forties would have to learn the basics in human connections, but here she was, awkwardly hovering over a table of women she had worked with for years with whom she had never made an effort to connect. "Would you ladies like to get some drinks after work today?"

The ladies glanced at each other with surprised and confused faces.

"I'm busy tonight," Karla replied. "My son has a piano recital."

"Oh, okay," Karina replied in a dejected tone. She started to walk away, but Karla stopped her.

"But I'm free on Friday!"

A smile grew on Karina's face. The ladies all exchanged numbers and planned to get drinks at a dive bar on Friday night. While Karina was anxious about the idea of going out with three women who were practically strangers, there was also a giddy excitement that followed making plans. She felt like she was doing something to better herself, and that was something she could be proud of.

She had also finally gotten past the anger she had been harboring for Dan, and they had evened out to a normal friendship again. Karina was grateful for this. They had known each other for so long it seemed ludicrous not to be speaking to each other at that point, especially after they both had suffered tough losses.

When Karina was done at the school that day, William popped into her mind, as he sometimes liked to do. Even though it had been a year and a half since they broke up, she still found herself thinking about him occasionally and wondered how he was doing.

Finally, William was doing better in his life. He had gone to counseling and was able to parse through some of the residual emotions he had because of his breakup with Karina. Now, he was dating someone he really cared about and was in a healthy place in his life. But, since William was an extremely compassionate person, he still thought about Karina from time to time. He hoped she was doing better and, ironically enough, when William was thinking about her that night, the phone rang, and she was on the other line.

"Hi, William," Karina gently spoke to someone she was extremely nervous about calling in the first place.

"Karina. It's a surprise to hear from you," he admitted. "Is everything okay?"

The line was silent for a moment, but then she spoke up. "Yeah, everything's okay. You were just on my mind today and…" her voice faded. The nerves she tried to deny started to bubble up in her throat. "I just wanted to tell you how sorry I am for the way everything went down. I know it is way too late and I've let too much time pass. I'm sorry about that too, but I just wanted you to know I really screwed up with how I handled everything. I know I blindsided you, and I hurt you, so I am really sorry." Karina took a breath after all those words fell out of her mouth.

William was quick to respond. "Well, oddly enough, I was thinking about you today too. I want you to know I forgave you a long time ago. I'm sorry too. I moved hastily, and probably pushed you to do things a lot quicker than you were comfortable with. I think I just wanted something you weren't quite ready to give, and I wasn't ready to accept that."

While they didn't know it, they both nodded at the same time.

"I don't think you have anything to apologize for, but I certainly forgive you," Karina told him.

The past Karina would have been tempted to find out about William's life and how he was doing, but instead, she decided to let him go. After all, she didn't want to start slipping into old habits. Besides, now she could finally let go of the guilt she felt with William, and she did.

After that call, Karina found herself feeling a bit lighter than she had in a long time.

It had been three weeks since Dan acknowledged he had feelings for his ex-wife again, and he still had no idea what to do with them. What he did know was the way he interacted with Karina had shifted once he became self-aware of said feelings.

Karina took notice. She wasn't sure why Dan was acting so strange around her lately, but she just wrote it off as him going through something she didn't need to concern herself with. She was too caught up in the new friendships she had built.

Karina fit in well with the group of teachers at her school. They went out at least once every week, either to the bar, or someone's house, or even once to Karina's house when they sat on the porch with wine and laughed together. It was refreshing for Karina to finally find out what female friendship looked like, because it was the first time she had a group of friends to hang out with.

The thing she loved most about these women was they could have a good time, but also talk about real struggles they were going through. Georgina had just gotten out of a long-term relationship because she found out her partner was cheating on her.

At first, Karina felt very uncomfortable when she learned this information, overwhelmed with the guilt of her own mistakes. But she ultimately confessed her choices with William to the three women. Even though it was painful to talk about, she felt a weight released from her afterwards like she wasn't walking around with some big secret anymore.

That day, Karina was getting comfortable on the couch to enjoy a time of quiet before the girls came home from their friend's house when she heard a knock. She begrudgingly got back up and walked to the door. When she answered, a familiar face greeted her. "Dan?" She gawked at his presence standing in her doorway unannounced.

"Hey, I was just in the area, and thought I'd drop by and say hello," Dan awkwardly told her.

"In the area? Really, Dan? You couldn't have come up with a better excuse than that?" Karina scoffed and walked back into the house with the door open for Dan to follow. Without asking, Karina grabbed the tea kettle from the top shelf of the cupboard and filled it with water. Once she flicked on the stove, she grabbed two mugs and gently placed a packet of peppermint tea in each. "How are you doing?" she casually asked as she leaned into the kitchen counter.

Dan just shrugged in response. "Can I talk to you about something?" he asked her, and she looked at him with a concerned face.

"Is everything okay?" she questioned, and sat down on the kitchen stool next to his.

"I've done a lot of reflecting in the past several months and I..." his voice drifted off and he redirected his eyes away from Karina and onto the countertop.

The room was silent except for the hiss of the kettle as it filled the open space. The stool screeched as Karina slid off it and pulled the hot water off the stove and into the two mugs. She set a mug in front of him, sat back down, and waited for him to continue (or say anything at all).

Dan's heart was racing. He knew exactly what he wanted to say, but he didn't have the courage to say it. He wanted to tell her he was still in love with her. The problem was he wasn't sure if that was completely true. He knew he loved Karina, that never stopped, and he also knew recently, especially once she started to break out of her shell and find herself again, he found himself liking who she was becoming as a person more and more. He realized the highlight of many of his days was the doorway conversations they had when they were picking up or dropping the girls off. But they had been divorced for several years. How was he ever supposed to tell her he had grown feelings for her again? Instead, he awkwardly sifted the tea bag back and forth in its mug and let the silence speak for itself.

Karina noticed the shift in Dan and how a sadness seemed to fall over him. She bent down to meet his eyes glued to the teabag. When she was in his peripheral vision, he looked at her. She laid her hand on his and squeezed it. "Dan, what's going on?" she asked him softly.

Dan didn't respond with words. Instead, he leaned forward to place his hand on Karina's face. He stroked her cheek and looked deeply into her eyes. He knew in that moment there was only one thing he wanted to do, so he did it.

He pulled her closer and kissed her with all the passion she remembered it to feel like. Karina was completely shocked by what was happening, but instead of pulling away, she pushed herself closer to him. She wrapped her hands around his waist and gently slipped her hands under his shirt so she could feel his warm skin.

There was no measurement of time that could capture how long the kiss lasted; both were so wrapped up in each other that time became irrelevant. It would have lasted longer, that is, if they hadn't heard the lock click on the front door. They quickly pulled away with both hearts still racing and heard their daughters walk through the door.

The girls casually came into the kitchen and were surprised to see their dad sitting there.

"Dad? What are you doing here?" Bethany questioned and threw her bag on the counter.

Dan scrambled for an excuse he could give them. "I just had to pick something up I forgot here the other day," he hastily said.

Even though it took them off guard to see their father sitting there, it didn't catch their attention enough to give it any extra thought. After grabbing a snack, they went into their rooms silently.

"Finish your homework!" Karina yelled as she heard two doors slam in synchronicity.

Once the doors were shut, Karina and Dan were silent; they both had no idea of what to say.

Karina's face was hot and she couldn't begin to process what had just occurred.

While Dan wanted to tell her the truth then, he made a remark that he should get going, and then left in a hurry.

Dan was flustered during his entire drive home to his apartment. For one thing, he couldn't believe he had the guts to kiss Karina but, for another thing, he couldn't believe Karina didn't stop it. He wasn't sure whether to be happy or terrified or both, so instead he was filled with panic, the great emotion that encapsulated all the other emotions.

And Karina? Well, she was just as lost.

Chapter Twenty: Now

"I'm sorry. Can you just say that one more time for me?"

"You're pregnant. Not too far along, but definitely pregnant."

Bethany tried to process what simple and life-changing words her doctor was saying to her. She pointed at Dr. Kaur and looked like she was going to speak, but then dropped her hand in silence. She looked down at her stomach and then pointed it at. Her mouth gaped open and yet no words came out. She covered her mouth and squealed with a combination of shock, excitement, and fear.

"Pregnant," she said in an exhale when she got in the car. She was still in complete shock and had no idea what she was going to say to her husband. They were not trying for a child, and since this was happening during one of the most traumatic seasons of her life, she couldn't figure out if it was irony, fate, God, or all three.

Regardless of what it was, she rushed home and found her husband playing on the floor with their son. He looked up at her with a kind smile, and then noticed her face.

"Hi, honey. Is everything okay? You look like you've seen a ghost." He chuckled, but Bethany silently gestured for him to join her in the kitchen. He walked in apprehensively, unsure of what his wife was going to say. "Did everything go okay at the doctor? Is something wrong?" Immediately, terrible scenarios ran through his mind, but before he could start thinking grim thoughts, Bethany grabbed both his hands and looked up at him with tear-filled eyes.

"We're pregnant," she said in a soft voice.

Huxley's eyes were so big they looked like saucers. "We're....pregnant?" he confirmed, and then a huge smile grew on his face. "Oh my gosh!" he yelled, and picked her up and twirled her around. "We're pregnant!" he exclaimed.

She couldn't help but rejoice with her husband, even though her mind was still trying to come to grips with this huge piece of unexpected news.

"I can't believe it," he said. "We're going to have another baby!"

The joy on Huxley's face was incredibly contagious, and in that time with him, Bethany was able to put aside all the pain she was feeling with her father, and her sister, and everything else. She was able to focus on *their* family and the new addition to their family, and that was a cause for celebration.

However, the celebration lasted a lot longer in Huxley's mind than it did in Bethany's. Eventually, the reality of Bethany's life started to creep back in. Her dad was dying. Her sister was halfway across the country. They now had a new baby on the way and they were going to become a lot more committed to a budget and saving money. With all her father's medical bills, there wasn't a lot of extra money floating around anyways, and a new baby was going to strip them of all that. Huxley would have to pick up extra hours, Bethany had to hope the ice cream shop had a successful summer season, and they would have to pray they would have enough money for an extra mouth to feed.

These weren't things Bethany wanted to think about. She wanted to be where Huxley was, excited and fantasizing about what their new baby would be like, but there was just too much on her plate to do that. So, she went into the bathroom to hide the panic finding its way onto her face. She splashed some cold water on her face and looked at herself in the mirror. She placed her hand on her belly. "This is really happening," she whispered to herself. Then she took a deep breath, tried to suppress all the emotions she was feeling, and walked back out so she could live in her husband's joy for a little bit longer.

Kayla dropped the spoon in her hand and leapt out of her chair when she saw the email. "I got it!" she yelled to her empty apartment. Even though two months ago Kayla was offered the administrative assistant job she applied for, she turned it down. Many outsiders looking in would classify that as a terrible and irresponsible idea (Kayla also considered that possibility), however, she couldn't accept a job where she would be miserable.

So, she continued to apply for jobs, but there was one job in particular that stuck out to her. It was an entry-level coding position she was gunning for. She spent twice as long on that application than all the other ones, and when she submitted it, she said a little prayer and hoped this would be her chance. Now, she had received an email saying they were interested in an interview. When she read the email further, she realized they were interested in meeting as soon as possible. She quickly responded that she was available that day. They replied within ten minutes and asked her to come down to their office at noon.

Kayla scarfed down the rest of her cereal and ran into her closet to find the perfect "I am smart and capable enough to work at your company" outfit. After taking too long to put on Spanx, she yanked on a pencil skirt, slipped on a red sweater, and ran out the door barefoot. It only took a few seconds for her to realize her mistake and run back in to put on her nicest (and only) pair of high heels.

Kayla's heart was viciously thumping when she got to the office. She gripped the portfolio that held her resume and cover letter tightly. When she walked up to the receptionist, her voice shook when she gave the woman her name. Kayla was directed to a small hallway where she sat next to a polished man who looked to be in his late thirties.

"Are you here for the interview?" she asked cautiously, hoping he wasn't.

"No," he responded. "I'm one of their clients."

Kayla breathed a sigh of relief. The company was small; Kayla had never heard of it before her job hunt. She hoped, because of its size, there wouldn't be as much competition as other coding positions at bigger companies.

A young woman in a soft, floral, pencil dress came out of an office and asked Kayla to follow her to her office. After making brief introductions and polite small talk, the woman had no problem diving into the interview.

"So, Ms. Fitzpatrick," the woman started when she picked up Kayla's freshly-printed resume, "I see you are a past employee of CodeX. We have interviewed a few of your coworkers, and what I want to know is: what makes you different from them?"

The question caught Kayla off guard. She spent a moment thinking about her answer when something popped into her mind. It would be a risk, and it could be received poorly, but if she wanted to stand out, it was a risk she was willing to take. "The reason I am different from those other employees is I don't have a master's degree." She stopped for a moment for dramatic effect, and it worked. The woman's eyes widened and she looked intrigued to hear what Kayla had to say next. "Every person you interview from CodeX is going to have a master's, or even a PhD, in computer science, and while that is impressive, it isn't what you need here. I was hired at CodeX because of my skills. I think outside of the box and push the envelope beyond the restrictions a classical education gives. What I have is experience. I quickly became a major contender within CodeX amongst people with degrees far greater than my own because of my ideas." Kayla paused for another moment. "I am definitely not the best coder out there, but I am not afraid to try things other people would dismiss. I'm a good leader, a great team member, but I am the best at thinking of solutions that don't cross others' minds."

The woman sat back in her chair and folded her arms. "Those are some bold claims, Ms. Fitzpatrick. Tell me more about that 'out-of-the-box thinking' of yours."

In Kayla's opinion, the rest of the interview went well. She went home feeling excited about the prospects of finally doing something she would enjoy. She had picked up a few dollars dog walking the various pets in her apartment complex, but she was desperate for a steady income again. She had almost completely depleted her savings, and she was worried if she didn't get a job soon, she would be crossing into dangerously low funds.

She opened her freezer to fish out a tub of ice cream she knew she had hidden in the back. It may have been presumptuous, but Kayla decided she was going to treat herself to some celebration dessert. She had high hopes she would get the job, and if she didn't, that would be a bridge she would cross at another time.

After she ate her ice cream and watered her plants, Kayla settled onto the couch to do some reading. She had sailed through some books, and her latest one was a thriller based off Cassian's recommendation. They found themselves talking more frequently, and Kayla wasn't sure what to make of it. Even still, putting her attention to another friendship had diverted her from the obsessive track she was heading towards with checking Peter's social media. But she still found herself extremely cautious when talking to Cassian. Her friendship with him was complicated, to say the least.

Cassian had finally discussed the fostering process he had been going through the past several months.

That changed things for Kayla. Before, she may have entertained the idea of pursuing a relationship with Cassian, but once she found out how serious he was about fostering a child, she realized they were on completely different paths of life. There was no way a long-distance relationship could work if both parties were committed to where they lived. While Kayla was less committed to St. Louis, she was committed to staying away from small towns in Massachusetts, even if they weren't Plymouth. She had come way too far to do what she would consider going backwards.

In the middle of her reading, Kayla got a phone call from a number that she didn't recognize.

When she answered it, she didn't recognize the voice either.

"Hi, is this Kayla?" the emotional woman on the other line asked.

"Yes, this is she. Who is this?"

"This is Gianna, one of your father's nurses. I know this call is unexpected, but your sister is highly emotional and thought it might be best for me to reach out to you."

"Is everything okay?" she immediately responded, and her mind raced to the worst conclusions.

There was a deep sigh on the other line. "Kayla, I hate to be the one to tell you this, but your father has taken a turn for the worst. Unfortunately, he only has a few days left; a week at most. It may be difficult to imagine coming back here but, speaking from experience, I would recommend returning as soon as possible to be with him during his final days. I'm so sorry."

Kayla hung up the phone as a wave of emotion hit her like a ton of bricks. She went through waves of disbelief and devastation and didn't know which was better. What she did know was that every other menial thing in her life slipped away in her mind. The only thing that mattered now was her father, and come hell or high water, she was going to be there with him.

The day after Kayla received the call from Gianna, she found herself on a plane from St. Louis to Boston. She spoke briefly with her sister to get an update that morning, but Bethany was highly emotional and a little frantic. Instead of staying at her sister's house, Kayla asked Cassian if she could stay with him. It wasn't the ideal situation for Kayla, but she didn't have the money for a hotel and felt uncomfortable staying with her sister considering how bad the last time went. She also knew their emotions would be high, and she didn't think it would be the healthiest thing for them to be around each other for twenty-four hours a day. She also didn't want Bethany to have to feel responsible for her and whatever she was feeling, and Kayla was feeling a lot of emotions.

Melinda drove her to the airport. She asked Kayla some questions about her dad and tried to give some advice, and then gave her a tearful hug goodbye "I'll be thinking about you. I love you, Kayla," Melinda said.

She had grown so close to Melinda, and even considered her one of the closest friends she had in a long time, but Melinda had never told her she loved her before. Kayla hugged her tightly and felt grateful for the unexpected love she felt for her friend.

By the time Kayla was on the plane, she found herself deep in thought about her father and what this next stage of her life would look like. It all appeared to be moving so fast. Suddenly, there were questions about his will, funeral preparations, and what his last days would look like. It was all overwhelming, and that was just what Kayla had to deal with.

Bethany was the one truly in the heat of the situation. She was staying at her father's house and Huxley was coming by twice a day to bring her food, check in on her, and love her in the best way he knew how. Bethany was also overwhelmed with planning, and at the same time, trying to cope with her father's deteriorating condition.

Dan rarely woke up anymore. When he did, he didn't speak except for nonsensical sounds. Bethany felt like the relationship she had built with her father during the late stage of his life had been severed, and now all she could do was watch as he slowly died. It was a burden no one should have to carry.

The past forty-eight hours had been brutal for Bethany. It felt like they had gone by at triple speed, and at the same time, slow motion. The quick slip in her father's state came when he was struggling to swallow food, and last night it was clear he could no longer swallow food at all. A feeding tube was not a viable option, and so the nurses believed he only had a few days left. Bethany wanted to be the one to tell her sister, but she was so afraid Kayla wouldn't believe her, or that it would cause more harm than good, and so she reluctantly let Gianna do it.

Kayla wasn't upset over the fact it was not her sister who reached out to her. She was too wrapped up in memories of her father and the emotions that came with losing him, *really* losing him, to care about anything minor.

Once the plane landed and she saw the familiar cityscape, Kayla felt like her insides were tearing themselves apart. She got off the plane and rushed to the airport bathroom to throw up what little food sat in her stomach. She bought a bottle of water at the vending machine, and then slowly walked to the arrivals gate to find Cassian idling in his car. The drive to his house was quiet. He didn't ask her any questions except how she was doing, in which she muttered a token response along the lines of: "Not great, but I'm here," and he just nodded.

Cassian was also taken aback that Kayla asked to stay with him. He was just as lost as Kayla regarding what their relationship was. They had become close friends very quickly, and Cassian realized he was starting to have feelings for her. But, just as Kayla realized, they had a slim chance of a successful relationship if they were both committed to living in different parts of the country. Things would have been different if Cassian wasn't pursuing foster care in Massachusetts, but he was way too far into the process to risk not getting to foster a child. He was rooted in Massachusetts, and as far as he could tell, Kayla was determined to stay rooted anywhere but there, which left him at a loss of what to be for Kayla during this highly emotional time. It was emotional for

Cassian too, especially after Dan reached out to him. In a way, he felt like he was losing the only father figure he had, even though he only had him for a year of his life. When Tina remarried after Cassian had moved out of the house, he never really got to know her husband. Since Cassian was already an adult, there wasn't any parenting involved. Instead, Cassian's stepdad remained a father in title only. They were polite when they saw each other during holidays and visits, but they never really connected. Besides, Cassian wasn't interested in a father figure at that point in his life. The time had already passed. But now, losing Dan proved to be a loss for everybody involved.

Once Kayla dropped her stuff off at Cassian's, Huxley picked her up. It was another awkward car ride for Kayla. Given where Bethany and Kayla stood throughout Bethany's marriage, Huxley and Kayla never had the opportunity to get close or even become acquaintances. The only things they knew about each other were what they heard from Bethany, so as in-laws, the relationship was weak at best. Once she got to her father's house and saw her sister, Kayla's eyes were opened to how deeply her sister was struggling. Bethany had dark circles under her eyes and she looked pale, like she hadn't eaten or slept in days. For the first time in a long time, Kayla felt an overwhelming sense of sympathy for her sister. Upon seeing her, Kayla ran over and hugged her tightly.

This caught Bethany off guard in the best way. She let herself sink into her sister's embrace and felt comfort from Kayla she hadn't in too long.

When they sat with their father, the two women were quiet. Bethany held her father's hand, and Kayla had her hand resting on his knee. Tears fell from both their eyes at different points, but the other one wasn't fazed by it. They were both in states of emotional numbness and exhaustion. But the worst part of it was that this was only the beginning.

There was a knock on the guest room door. Kayla looked up from her laptop to see Cassian standing in the doorway.

"How are you holding up?" he asked with a frown. He was still unsure how to be there for Kayla in this situation. Even though he knew what it was like to live without a father, he didn't know what it was like to watch one dying.

Kayla sighed and then shrugged. "I'm just trying and failing to wrap my mind around everything."

Cassian came and sat in a soft chair in the corner of the room. "How are things going with your sister?"

In truth, things with Bethany had been better than they had been in a while. This was because they barely spoke to each other. Occasionally, Kayla put her hand on Bethany's shoulder when she cried, or Bethany gave Kayla a hug when she did the same, but there wasn't a lot to say. Besides logistical things, the room they sat in for a large proportion of the day was typically quiet.

Kayla also had no idea her sister was pregnant. It wasn't that Bethany was hiding it, she just had no idea when a good time would be to tell her. The only time they spent together was sitting next to their dying father. Was she supposed to interrupt the sobs to randomly announce she was expecting another child? It seemed absurd for Bethany to say anything, but Huxley was pushing for her to tell her. He was terrible at keeping secrets and was paranoid he would slip up and accidentally say something to Kayla. But no such slip had occurred, and until Bethany could find the right moment, or even a decent moment, she wasn't going to say anything.

That day, Huxley had a different idea. He showed up at Cassian's house unexpectedly and asked Kayla to join him. She expected he would drop her off at her dad's, but once they arrived, he got out of the car and grabbed Henry as well. When they walked inside, he called Bethany and Kayla into the kitchen. "Alright, ladies. This is what is happening today," he started and then turned to Bethany. "Honey, you have been here all day, every day, for too many days. Whether you like it or not, you need a break. Both of you do. I want you guys to leave and go to the ice cream shop, or go to a park, or do anything other than sit in this house. I also want you to promise me you won't talk about your dad. Just allow yourself a couple hours to focus on something other than him. Okay?" Bethany tried to argue, but her husband was determined. He saw his wife looking worse and worse every time he saw her, and he couldn't stay quiet anymore.

Kayla was too uncomfortable to object, so she went along with her brother-in-law's plans and hopped in the passenger's seat of Bethany's car. Bethany begrudgingly got in the driver's seat, and drove to a park that the two women enjoyed as children.

When they got out, they walked over to a bench. They were quiet for longer than Kayla was comfortable with, so she decided to speak up.

"How have things been going at the ice cream shop?" she awkwardly asked.

"They've been going alright," Bethany absentmindedly responded. She looked down at the bench and noticed a carving of two names in the wood. She traced her finger on the letters as she continued. "I haven't had a chance to stop by there lately, but I have good employees and they seem to be doing okay without me."

Kayla nodded but didn't say anything else. It was clear her sister wasn't in the mood to talk anyway.

In Bethany's head, all she could think about was the neon sign flashing in her head that said this was the best moment to tell her sister the news. "I'm pregnant," she blurted out, and Kayla's head spun to face her in shock.

"Congratulations," she told her, and tried to fake a smile.

But Bethany saw right through it. "I know it's hard to celebrate right now. I'm struggling too," Bethany admitted.

"I can't imagine how hard it is to feel excitement with everything on your plate." Kayla awkwardly reached out to grab her sister's hand.

Bethany squeezed it. She felt tears form in her eyes, but she pushed them down. She didn't have the energy to cry again. "Tell me what's new with you. What's going on with Cassian? Are you guys..." her voice faded but the suggestive nature remained.

"I don't know what we are," Kayla remarked and slouched on the bench. "In my heart, I know I still have feelings for Peter, and I don't know what to do with that, because I think I'm starting to like Cassian too."

"Peter...that was your last serious relationship, right?" Bethany questioned and Kayla nodded. "You never told me what happened with you guys."

Kayla let out a deep sigh. "I didn't tell anybody what happened," she admitted and avoided her sister's eyes. Instead, she looked out at the park in front of her and tried to think of all the memories that hid in between the tall trees and blades of grass.

"You don't have to tell me if you don't want to," Bethany assured her.

Kayla looked at her sister again and saw empathy in her eyes. Kayla decided it was time she owned the truth. She told Bethany everything about her relationship with Peter. She talked about the beautiful highs and the devastating lows, and even admitted to checking his social media two months ago. When she was done, no tears stained her face, but she was highly emotional after recounting everything.

"If you wouldn't have seen those pictures, do you think you would have reached out to him?"

"Well, that's the question of the day, isn't it?" Kayla quipped and let out a slight chuckle. "Maybe?" she questioned. She wasn't even sure of that answer.

"What's holding you back?" Bethany cautiously pressed. She was extremely grateful her sister had shared anything at all and was afraid if she asked the wrong question, things could turn badly. She still found herself at a loss for how to best communicate with Kayla.

After Bethany asked that question, tears suddenly appeared to roll down Kayla's cheek as she finally admitted to herself the true reason why she was so afraid of pursuing Peter. "I think I was afraid of being William."

Bethany cocked her head and looked over at her sister. "William?" she asked.

Kayla nodded. "There was some part of me that wondered: 'What if Peter and Laurie were really meant to be together, and I was the one who got in the way of that?'" she exhaled and another tear crept down her cheek. "But once I saw those pictures and that he had moved on with someone else, it sent me on this tailspin of realizing I had taken away my own happiness because I was too caught up in our damn parents' mistakes."

Bethany was surprised by her sister's emotions and vulnerability. If she was being honest, she had no idea how to respond. She was terrified of saying the wrong thing, but she also didn't want to stay silent, so she searched for a response. The best she could do was a couple honest sentences. "For a while, I was terrified I was going to turn out like Mom," Bethany confessed. "That I was going to live here and miss out on the world you were so intent on seeing. But I realized if I lived like that, that was exactly how I would turn out to be. I think every person faces a crossroads where they decide if they are going to claim their parents' decisions, or claim their choices as their own. But I almost guarantee you that whatever Peter and Laurie had, it can't be compared to Mom and Dad. I know it's a lot easier said than done, but try not to let their mistakes haunt you anymore."

Bethany was right. It was a lot easier said than done. Until that moment, Kayla didn't even recognize how much her mom's decisions had affected her, but they had. Even though what she needed to do was overwhelming, Kayla hoped since she now had a name and a face to her ghosts, she could finally start to let them go. But it would take a lot more than realization for Kayla to get rid of the biggest ghost that haunted her: the betrayal of her sister.

Bethany gently held her father's aging hands and hummed to him while he slept. She did this when she had a quiet moment with him. As much as she loved Kayla being there, she didn't anticipate how little time she would have with just him. Still, she cherished every moment her sister was by her side, even if they were both going through excruciating pain.

Now that she had told Kayla about her pregnancy, she allowed herself to think about it more. She had to take everything in small doses, but that day, as she sat next to her dying father, she understood for the first time he would never meet his second grandchild. Tears immediately welled up in her eyes.

When Kayla came back into the room, she noticed. She had grown used to seeing her sister cry, but she looked more shaken than usual, and so she spoke up. "What happened?" Her instinct was to ask if she was okay, but then Kayla reminded herself of what a stupid question that was and tried to find something better.

Bethany looked up at her sister with bloodshot and broken eyes. "I just realized Dad is never going to meet this baby," she told her and put her hand on her stomach. Once she said it out loud, she knew another tragic truth: Dan would never meet any of Kayla's children. She thought about speaking up and apologizing to Kayla for this fact, but then thought it better to keep quiet.

Unfortunately, Kayla had already come to these conclusions. Bethany got to introduce their father to Huxley, he got to walk her down the aisle at her wedding, and he got to meet her first child; all gifts Kayla would never receive. She didn't want to resent her sister for something she couldn't change, but she couldn't help but feel a wave of jealousy. But, instead of letting it fester, she pushed it out of her mind. She didn't say anything for a few minutes, but then she silently grabbed their father's hand and placed it on Bethany's stomach. "Dad, meet your newest grandchild," Kayla said, and then put Bethany's hand on top of their father's.

This touched Bethany in a way that couldn't be expressed in words. Instead, she just cried, grabbed her sister's arm with her other hand, and squeezed it.

"Thank you," she whispered amid the tears. Bethany would cherish this sweet gesture from her sister for a long time to come, and when she held that beautiful baby girl in her arms, she would remember it then too.

There wasn't much of Dan left as he lay unconscious in a room he wouldn't have recognized even if he was conscious. He found himself in a dark room, and whispers of memories seemed to float around him. He reached out to grab them, but they disintegrated at his touch. All he could do was watch them float by and catch a few glimpses at the wonderfully complicated life that he lived.

While Bethany and Kayla sat close to their father and watch his labored breathing, they both knew he didn't have much time left, even if they denied it. But if Dan were there, and if he could recount one memory to his little girls who had grown up to be beautiful women, it would have been this one:

The girls giggled as their dad tickled them on the couch. It was getting late, but since Karina was sick in bed, she couldn't fight them running around the house and jumping on the couch. As the girls goofed around, Dan grabbed a blanket that was not supposed to be brought outside, and laid it neatly on the grass. He called for his daughters, and after a few times yelling their names, they finally listened. The girls chased each other into the backyard, and the cold breeze sent goosebumps down their spines.

"What are we doing out here, Daddy?" Kayla questioned once she felt how cold it was.

"Come over here. I want to tell you something." Dan beckoned for them to come over, and he lay down on the grass. They both followed suit. "Do you see those stars up there?" The girls both nodded and silently looked up at all the twinkling stars. "If you look closely, you can spot the Daddy Dipper. It looks like a square shovel," he told them and pointed towards the cluster of stars. "Then that down there is the Daughter

Dipper," he told them and they giggled. He pointed out a few more constellations for the girls to learn about, but then he narrowed in on his main point. "Even though they look close, these stars are actually trillions of miles away," he told them, and Bethany's eyes widened in wonderment. Still looking up at the stars, Dan continued. "I have always told you girls I want you to dream big, right?" They nodded. "Well, you are going to have some dreams that seem really far out of reach, farther away than these stars, even. But I don't want you to stop until you see the stars."

The lesson Dan was trying to impart on his daughters would inevitably go over their young heads. But even if it went over their heads then, one day they would learn the true meaning behind what their father said.

On that day, all they did was hold their father's dying hand. In the living room, there were hospice nurses and Dan's personal nurses scattered around, and Bethany and Kayla continued to stay glued to their father's side. Huxley, Henry, and Cassian remained in the kitchen to give Kayla and Bethany all the space they needed.

Cassian wasn't planning on coming, but Kayla reached out and asked if he would be there for moral support. For Dan, it was peaceful. The memories that he watched past by were fewer and farther apart. Slowly, there were no more memories at all, just a brightness that seemed to call to him. He walked towards it, closer and closer, until it enveloped him with warmth and goodness.

In the living room, Kayla squeezed her dad's hand tightly. "I love you, Dad," she told him in between tears.

"We are going to miss you so much," Bethany gently told her father as she brushed some of his hair from his eyes.

Then Dan took his last, staggered breath.

No one talked about what it was like after Dan took his final breath. The room was completely silent and the person who was filled with life moments ago suddenly looked less like himself.

Still holding her father's hand, Kayla and Bethany hugged each other as tightly as they did when they were two kids scared of the dark. Tighter, maybe.

Kayla held onto her father's hand long after he was gone. She couldn't let go because once she let go, it would be the last time she would hold her father. It would mark the end of seeing his kind face, his old and tired hands, and his full head of greying hair. How could she prepare for something like that? How could she possibly pull away when she knew she was never going to see her father again? Even though his soul was gone, his body was the last evidence that existed of him. How could someone let go of that?

Eventually, Bethany was able to pull her sister away, and Kayla collapsed into her. Gianna played with Henry in the kitchen so Huxley and Cassian could be there for the women they cared about. The sisters were glued to each other, and so Huxley and Cassian sat on the outside and enveloped them. The tears kept flowing out of everyone's eyes, and they didn't seem to stop.

But that wasn't the hardest part. No, that came while their eyes burned and their face was rubbed raw, when Kayla saw her father being wheeled towards the door out of the corner of her eye. Cassian tried to stop her from seeing it, but that was an image Kayla would never be able to unsee. She would play it in her head repeatedly many times, and it would become one of the most painful moments of her life. Watching the man who carried her, played with her, made her laugh until her stomach hurt, the man she looked up to the most in her life being wheeled away lifelessly on a bed.

"I don't know how to live without him," Kayla wailed.

"I know," Bethany said. "But we are going to figure it out together," she assured her.

But there was no assurance. There was just pain, so much pain. And every time Kayla thought the pain was going to stop, that no more tears could force their way out of her body, the image of his body being rolled away flashed in her mind again, and then the wave of tears came all over again. There reached a point where she was so tired of crying and hurting that the pain felt like it was too much to bear, but it didn't stop then. No matter how many times she desperately begged God to please take away the pain, it continued to fester within her, and it would. Her life was never going to be the same after this, and there was nothing, not a single word anybody could say, that could make it better. He was gone and he wasn't coming back. The only thing Kayla would have left of her father was memories, and those memories were bound to fade, some would even be forgotten, no matter how hard she fought it.

The void formed for Bethany almost instantaneously. Her routine would change because her father wouldn't be part of it anymore. He was missing from every piece of her life, and now it looked completely fractured. But she was nowhere near the end. She had to figure out what to do with his home, his belongings, as well as finish planning his funeral. Her to-do list was long and she had convinced herself she was the only one who could do it, but now that he was gone, she had no desire to do anything.

Kayla ended up staying over at Bethany's house that night. By the time they drove home, the stars were scattered across the night sky. While the girls didn't remember the day they laid on a blanket in the cold with their father and he tried to teach them a lesson about something far greater than the stars, what they knew then was the only star they wanted to reach for that night, and many nights to come, had just burned out.

Bethany believed funerals were meant for rainy days, but the day of Dan's funeral was as sunny as could be. While Bethany was frustrated the sky was not as upset as she, she also believed her father would have enjoyed the sunny day a lot better. They went to the small church where all that was left of their father sat in a decorative jar. Not every seat was filled in the church, but the most important people were there. Some of Dan's friends were there, including an old friend from Germany that the girls met only once when he visited so long ago. There were also coworkers, nurses, and, of course, the only family he had left.

Bethany and Kayla both gave eulogies, but neither of them believed they were worth remembering. In truth, they didn't have any interest in recounting memories of their father to a room full of acquaintances at best. The only thing they wanted was to have him back, and if not, then to forget this was their life. The last thing they wanted to do was remember.

Instead, they each had very different approaches to their grief. Kayla's was to drag Cassian to a shooting range and shoot at the paper targets until they were torn to shreds. It was her way of channeling all the anger that coursed through her into something socially acceptable.

Bethany, on the other hand, spent many nights with her husband holding her as she cried. She didn't feel angry, she was just deeply depressed. Somewhere amid their vastly different coping mechanisms, they were able to lean on each other, at least somewhat. They both found themselves being honest with each other about how they were doing, because every day, it wasn't good. There was a uniting factor that grief brought, especially such a deep loss as this.

After the funeral, Kayla wanted some time to be alone. Nobody thought it was a good idea, but after watching her father's dust fly in the wind at the beach, she had no interest in looking at anybody. However, as she found herself driving around with no destination, reminders of her father popped in her head. All this did was make her even angrier. Suddenly, she found herself pulled over on the side of the road, researching a person she had no interest in seeing. Once she had their address plugged into her phone, there was no stopping her. Before she knew it, she was at their door.

Kayla knocked hard three times on the door. After hearing some shuffling on the other side, a familiar face answered. He had aged a bit since she last saw him. "William?" she asked, even though she knew it was him.

"Yes, and who are you?" he asked, but after looking into her eyes, he knew them. "Kayla?"

She nodded.

"What are you doing here?"

Even though William wasn't the one to blame, all Kayla wanted to do was channel her anger into something, and she chose him. She did not drill into him lightly. "My dad is dead, my mom is gone, and they didn't get more time together. And it is all because you came in and ripped my family apart. You're a homewrecker." Kayla's face was red. A fireball of anger tightened in her chest. Even if yelling at him made her feel better, his lack of a reaction took any relief away.

"Do you want to come in?" William asked without addressing the accusations.

Kayla sat on his plaid couch with a cup of water in her hands as he settled in the armchair across from her.

There was silence, so Kayla decided to speak up. "I'm sorry," she whispered. Once she was sitting on the couch, her rational mind came back and she realized how unfair it had been to show up at William's door just to chew him out. "I don't just blame you, you know. I blame her too," Kayla admitted. She took another deep breath to calm the anger that boiled up inside of her again. "I've been angry at her for a long time. It was both of you that screwed up. But she's gone so I can't be angry at her anymore and I just..."

"You have to be angry at me," William finished. "I have to admit, I never imagined you or Bethany showing up at my door, but you are right. I own my wrongs in your family."

Tears danced across Kayla's face as she searched for what to say. "The worst part is that you knew," she said, and then had to take a deep breath to continue. "You knew she was married, and you pursued her anyway. If I would have known..." she started, but couldn't finish.

"I did. But, Kayla, sooner or later you are going to have to realize it was not just her and me. Your dad is partly to blame here. She was miserable. She felt unheard in her marriage. It was broken long before I came into the picture and I—"

"Stop!" Kayla yelled. The last thing she wanted to hear was something bad about her father, not after the day she had.

But William had no idea this was the day of her father's funeral. It was a small town, so he heard of Dan's passing, but that didn't stop him from pushing back against Kayla's objections. "No, Kayla. You are going to have to hear this one day, and if it is going to be today, then so be it." He put his cup on the coffee table with slight aggression and then leaned back into his chair. "But even though all three of us played a part in this, you are going to need to forgive all of us. It will destroy you if you don't. And it won't just destroy you, it will destroy the memories you have of your parents, because once they are gone, you can't make new ones. The only thing you have left of your mother is what you make of her. Karina was a good woman, one of the best I've ever met. But all this anger you are holding onto will tarnish her in your heart. And you may idolize your father, but he was human. He had his fair share of sins too. There has to be some balance with your feelings towards your parents, or you are going to be miserable for the rest of your life."

Kayla continued to cry into her arms. When she looked up at William, she noticed a few tears had fallen down his face as well. "But how is she ever going to know I've forgiven her?" she asked, desperately needing an answer.

"Well, I don't think it's about her, I think it's about you. The moment you can let go of all this anger is the moment you will be free. You will be free to think of your mother and remember the good moments for exactly what they were, not with anger and resentment attached. And maybe you don't agree with the decisions your parents made, but all that is in the past now. If you wanted to dredge it up, you don't have anyone to hold accountable to it anymore, so there is no point. You may not be able to forget, but you have to learn to let things go and forgive them."

In between the tears and staring aimlessly at the carpeted floor, Kayla didn't even think to ask about William's life or notice the framed pictures around his home. If she would have asked, she would have learned that William had fallen in love, got married, and had three beautiful children who were all grown up now. In their own ways, Karina and William had gotten exactly what they needed out of life, just not from each other, and Kayla did too, by seeing him.

While she felt terrible for barging into his home and yelling at him, at the same time he gave her the truth she needed to hear, even if she didn't know it when she was knocking on his door.

After that day, Kayla walked away with the duty to forgive her parents for their past decisions. Even though she had no idea how she was going to do that, she had made the first step. Now all she had to do was get through the hell that mourning her father consisted of. Kayla knew it would never truly be over, but she at least needed to get past the first storm.

Chapter Twenty-One: Then

Even though she was still in middle school, through her sister, Kayla had accrued several connections to people at the high school. Therefore, she was renowned at her school as being one of the cooler kids in her class. Occasionally, when Bethany was busy or would rather do homework than hang out with her friends, Kayla found herself to be the one hanging out at Bethany's friends' houses. One wouldn't typically assume a group of fifteen-year-olds would want to hang out with a thirteen-year-old, but Kayla knew how to be sociable, and she was very funny. It also helped she threw out a few embarrassing stories about her sister her friends loved hearing. The truth was, Bethany made friends that welcomed Kayla with open arms, and treated her with much kindness.

During one of these hangouts Bethany skipped, Kayla heard whispers about a party happening at a friend of a friend's house later that week. Somehow, through Kayla's own finesse, she was able to convince one of their friends to drive her to said party. Of course, her parents couldn't know she was going to a high school party (or any party, for that matter), so Kayla had no problem making up a story that she was studying at a friend's house and would be dropped off later that night.

Instead, Kayla found herself at one of the bigger houses in Plymouth. Before she even walked through the door, she heard pulsing music and saw a cluster of irresponsible high school students drinking on the front lawn. Kayla's naïve mind thought that even if there was alcohol, not everyone would be drinking, but she was sorely mistaken. There were several cases of beer scattered across the house, and by the time she had gotten there, several people she didn't recognize had already gotten completely wasted. She was offered beer several times, and after being teased by a few high school boys for not drinking, she finally decided to grab a red solo cup and try some. She was not impressed and ended up dumping the rest of the beer in a houseplant when no one was looking.

Kayla was having fun at first; dancing to the music, laughing at some of the drunk people making stupid decisions, but things took a quick turn. A few guys she didn't know started to get a bit reckless. In their shenanigans, a vase was shattered onto the ground. Then, they ran over to turn the music up so loud it made Kayla's head ache. But it was when she heard someone else remark if they kept playing the music so loud, the police would be called, that Kayla started to panic.

Bethany had no idea Kayla had gone to the party she quickly rejected attending until Kayla called her in hysterics that night.

"I need you to pick me up. I think the police are going to get called and I don't want to get in trouble," Kayla told her with concern.

"Kayla, I only have my permit. I'm not supposed to drive without an adult in the car." This response made tears stream down Kayla's face. She had worked herself into a panic attack, and all she wanted to do was leave.

"No, please. You can't tell Mom and Dad. They'll never let me hear the end of it. I made a mistake. Please, B," she begged as she tried to steady her own breathing.

"Okay, okay. I'll be there soon."

This not only was Bethany's first time driving by herself, but it was also her first time sneaking out of the house to drive illegally to pick her sister up from a party she had no business being at. It was not Bethany's ideal night. When she got to the house, she found her sister shivering with her face buried in her hands.

Kayla looked up with hopeful eyes, as she had with every car that passed by, but this time it was her sister coming to save her. Before Bethany had made a complete stop, Kayla was jumping into the passenger's seat as fast as she could.

"Thank you," Kayla whispered in shame.

"I don't want to lecture you," Bethany started, "but what the hell were you thinking?' Bethany asked in a sterner tone than she originally anticipated.

"I don't know…" Kayla admitted. "I guess I just wanted to be cool and go to a high school party." After a minute of silence, Kayla changed her answer to something closer to the truth. "I just wanted your friends to take me seriously. I want them to like me."

Bethany chucked. "They do like you!" she exclaimed. "But even if some of our friends choose to go to parties, that doesn't mean they won't like you if you make a different choice. And, as you saw tonight, some of our friends, me included, had no interest in going to this kind of party, and everyone is okay with that." Bethany turned to glance at her younger sister who seemed to be getting older by the minute. "Believe me, you want to be friends with people who accept you for exactly who you are."

Later, Kayla would take her sister's words to heart, but on that day, all she wanted to do was curl up in a ball and never speak about that night again. Luckily for her, she wouldn't have to.

"We need to talk about what happened the other night," Karina informed Dan. This time it was Karina showing up at Dan's apartment unannounced.

"You're right, we do," he said and welcomed her into his apartment.

When Karina sat down, everything that had gone through her mind in the past days came flooding back. She didn't hesitate to tell her friends about what had happened the other night, and suffice to say, they were just as shocked as she. Karina herself was unsure of what to feel. In the past few days, she had felt the full spectrum of emotions: anger, shock, confusion, joy… all of them were jumbled together in her head. But even with the jumbled feelings in her mind, she felt the pressing need to say something to Dan about it. After all, they couldn't pretend it didn't happen. Even deeper than that, she needed to know if this was a spur-of-the-moment action, or if there was something deeper. But Karina also had to decide for herself which answer she preferred. The problem was that this had come so far out of left field.

Until he kissed her, being with Dan was not even an option in her mind. Even though she enjoyed his friendship, the last time she found herself in a place of desiring more was after she broke up with William. She thought she closed that door, but when she kissed him, she wasn't so sure. She couldn't deny feelings for Dan came flooding back a few days ago, and she couldn't pretend they left either. But before she got a chance to ask any of the many questions that plagued her, Dan spoke up.

"I know you are probably wondering where that came from," he said.

Karina profusely nodded. "Yeah, that would be a start," she said with a laugh and sat up a little taller on his couch.

"As you know, my breakup with Tina left me in quite a tailspin. She was the first person, the only person besides you, whom I saw my happy ending with, I guess." Even though it was only two sentences, the words came out a few at a time with plenty of awkward pauses in between. It was at this point Dan craved the opportunity to curl up into a ball and never speak to another person again, but he continued through his painfully slow speech. "I distanced myself a lot because I was angry at you, but I think I was really angry at the connection we had; that's what caused a divide between Tina and me."

Karina took a deep breath. While she understood the dinner had somehow spurred Dan asking point-blank if she was in love with him, she did not know the extent of her role in his relationship with Tina. Her initial reaction was to feel guilty, but she ignored that feeling and reminded herself the situation with Dan and Tina was out of her control.

This process in Karina's mind had to happen quickly because Dan continued to speak, and Karina wanted to be fully focused on what he was saying.

"Now I realize I never should have gotten angry at you. I probably shouldn't have kissed you either, if I'm being honest. But what I do know, Karina, is that I love you." Dan's voice got quieter as tears started to well up in his eyes. He had said those three words to her thousands of times before, but this time they had an entirely new meaning. So, he paused for a few moments to let the weight of the words sink in for them both. Then, he continued. "I have never stopped loving you, and since things ended with Tina, I have fallen in love with you again."

Karina opened her mouth to speak, but Dan stopped her. "Before you say anything, trust me, it was the last thing I expected to happen. But that is where I am, and I guess I'm hoping you feel something similar."

Karina always wore her heart on her sleeve when it came to Dan, and this was no exception. By the time he had finished talking, tears had already appeared on her face. "I love you too," was the first thing she replied.

This gave Dan an ounce of hope, but she knocked it down quickly.

"But I don't know what you expect to happen here," she remarked. "We have Bethany and Kayla. What would we tell our girls? That our divorce was for nothing? And what if we realize we aren't the best thing for each other? Are we going to destroy our friendship?" She traced her fingers through her hair as all the different ways this could go wrong filled her mind. "This wouldn't be a normal relationship, Dan. We have kids together. If things ended badly, we would still have to see each other for the rest of our lives. It was hard enough to get to a good place after we got divorced. Would we really be able to do that again?"

While Dan wanted to argue with her, he couldn't. These were all things he was not thinking about when he kissed her. The only thing he was thinking about then was what he wanted. But she was right. They had to account for a lot more than just what either of them wanted.

But Dan couldn't help asking her one question: "If the girls weren't a factor, would you want to give us another shot?"

Her answer to this would blow open the entire fantasy he created in his head of the two of them coming back together and being a family again. This one answer had the ability to change everything for him, for better, or for worse.

"I don't know, Dan," Karina started. "All of this has been really overwhelming for me. That kiss came out of nowhere, and I feel like I'm still feeling the whiplash of that."

"I understand," he softly responded with his head down. "I'm sorry for putting you in this position. I didn't want to complicate things even more for us. I—"

"Yes," Karina's delicate voice broke Dan's apologetic ramble.

"Yes?" he questioned to make sure he heard her correctly.

"If the girls weren't involved, then yes." Before Dan could rejoice in her response, she continued. "But that isn't our life, Dan. We do have two other human beings to consider."

"Then what if we just kept things between us? At least for a little while. The girls don't need to know anything," Dan suggested and looked up at Karina with hopeful eyes. Once he knew that having her back was even a possibility, Dan's mind became solely focused on that. He would do whatever it took to win her back, and this was his first suggestion on a long list of different ways Dan thought they could make it work. All that mattered to him was that they found a way. Even if it didn't last, Dan wanted now more than ever to give their love story one more shot. They had both grown in leaps and bounds over the past few years, and now they could try again with more experience (and pain) in their toolbox.

"You want us to sneak around?" Karina asked with her eyebrow cocked.

"Just until we figure out if we still work together. That way we aren't putting anyone's feelings on the line except our own."

As much as Karina wanted to hop into Dan's fantasy (something she didn't realize she even wanted until he kissed her), she also needed to be realistic. If she had learned anything in the past couple years it was to not act on impulse. She already did that when she kissed Dan back. Now she needed to keep the rational part of her alive and kicking. "If we are going to do this, then we have to promise if things don't work out, we are not going to let that get in the way of our responsibilities as parents."

Dan held out his hand with his pinkie raised. It was a tradition that they started two months into dating. They had only broken one pinkie promise: the one where they would stay together forever. "I'll swear if you will," he said. Then, they locked pinkies and made another promise they both desperately hoped they would be able to keep. Or, in Dan's case, that they would fix the first promise they broke.

Dan had learned one thing in the past three weeks: dating his ex-wife in secret was not easy. That night could be called Karina and Dan's third date. Dan was having her over for dinner at his apartment, although all Bethany and Kayla knew was that their mom was going out with her friends for the evening.

Karina hated lying to them, but she wanted to keep her promise, not only to Dan, but to herself, to wait and see how things went before throwing another life change onto their daughters' laps.

Karina knocked on the familiar door wearing a long, navy-blue dress and freshly curled hair. To say it was strange for Karina to get dressed up to go on dates with her ex-husband was an understatement. She only did it because she didn't want to fall into normalcy with Dan, which they already struggled not to do. The pair was overly familiar with each other. They knew everything about each other's pasts, their habits, weird quirks, and even random things the other one forgot about. With all this information already at their fingertips, it made it easy, and incredibly tempting, for them to fall right back into what their life looked like when they were married.

There were moments when Karina felt as though she was wearing an old glove out of the back of her closet that she hadn't worn in years. But that was the exact thing they were trying not to do. Karina, and Dan for that matter, had no desire to go back in time. Something in their marriage didn't work, and it wasn't just the distance. If they were ever going to have a fighting chance, they had to start forming new habits. Therefore, Karina went shopping for a new dress. When they sat down at the table and raised their wine glasses in the air, Dan toasted for their third date even though they had been on hundreds. Every acknowledgment of their new beginning set them a little further down a new trail that branched from the familiar path.

Luckily, they were never at a loss for things to talk about during their dates. If all else failed, they would just talk about Bethany and Kayla.

Karina casually talked about Kayla's new interest in computers, and then they remarked on how crazy the new technological advancements were, and then somewhere along the way the conversation shifted and Karina found herself talking about the ways she had grown in the past few years. Even though they saw the ways the other had grown and changed, they still needed to know what those changes looked like in a relationship, as opposed to their previous purely co-parenting lifestyle.

Dan recently learned Karina had become a bit more of a risktaker, which was a welcome surprise for Dan. On their second date, they went to an Indian restaurant and picked out the spiciest thing on the menu. This was completely outside of both of their realms, which was evident by their aggressive chugging of water and tears rolling down both of their faces. Karina's desire for risk taking and branching out allowed for both to experience something new amid the kinship they already had.

Dan was also happy to share the ways that he had grown too. While Karina knew vague details about his counseling, Dan took this date as the opportunity to impart some of the things he had taken from his counselor. "I definitely realized how stubborn I am," Dan said with a laugh, and Karina nodded.

"We both are," she chuckled.

"That's true," he agreed. "But my counselor made me notice how much my stubbornness got in the way of hearing other people," he admitted. "Sometimes I was so set in my own way I didn't have the capacity to listen or consider other people's points of view. But now that I have, I learned how wrong I am sometimes," he told her, and she laughed.

"I guess one of the biggest things is how much guilt I carried around." Karina looked down at her half-eaten plate of spaghetti and twirled a few noodles with her fork. "It took me a really long time to let go of all the guilt I felt about our marriage, about what kind of mother I was, about all my decisions, really."

"And now?" Dan asked.

"Well, I'd be lying if I said I haven't still had to work through some of those feelings of guilt. But I'm not carrying around the same worn-out baggage I lugged around for so many years."

"I'm proud of you," he told her, and her face grew flush.

"Thank you," she sincerely and shyly responded. "I'm proud of you too, you know." She looked down at her plate again. "If I'm being honest, when you first moved back, I was jealous of how great a father you became and the ways you stepped up for the girls. I resented you didn't do that earlier with us." She shook her head as she relived her past pain. "But now, I am so glad they have you in their lives."

"I'm sorry for not stepping up a lot sooner," he said, and reached his hand to hold hers. "Truly."

"You don't have to be sorry anymore," she whispered. "I've already forgiven you."

They both nodded, and before they knew it, the conversation shifted back to other trivial things.

The four of them awkwardly sat around the kitchen table and no one knew where to start. Dan and Karina had been dating each other in secret for the past six months, and they believed it was finally time to tell the girls about it. Well, Dan hoped to tell the girls months ago, but Karina's new, smart cautiousness told her they should wait longer. It wasn't that things weren't going well; things were going better than either of them expected. However, she also knew how much her past decisions affected her daughters and didn't want to make the same mistakes again. She wanted to ensure when she did tell them, whatever emotions followed wouldn't be for a waste. Of course, the results of her relationship with William lingered in her mind. While she didn't regret being with William, she still recognized she put her girls through a lot of unnecessary and confusing heartache that neither of them deserved, at least that was what Karina's mind told her.

Since they had been together for so long now, it felt almost ludicrous not to clue her daughters into what was happening. After all, she already suspected they had figured out something was going on, but neither said anything, so they danced the quiet dance of two parties knowing something and both refusing to acknowledge it.

Dan, on the other hand, was oblivious to what his daughters had caught onto.

Ironically, the girls were more suspicious of their father than of their mother. Dan was not good at hiding secrets but he was even worse at hiding his emotions, and Bethany and Kayla quickly caught onto their father's chipper mood.

A small part of Kayla secretly hoped Dan had gotten back together with Tina. This wasn't because she particularly missed Tina, but because she recognized how happy she made her father. Plus, she missed playing the guitar with Cassian and the adventures the five of them went on together. But, in all reality, Kayla knew too much time had passed, and that part of her life was over whether she wanted it to be or not. However, what Kayla didn't know at that moment was her conception of "time passed" was about to be flipped on its head.

Dan cleared his throat to start saying whatever it was he was going to say. After all, how was he expected to tell his teenage daughters their parents had fallen in love again after five years of being divorced? Well, Dan had no idea, but he was ready to give it his best shot, at least he thought he was. "Girls… Well…your mother and I…" Dan's start was not going as smoothly as he had hoped. "Let me start over," he said awkwardly. "We didn't want to tell you this until we were sure about things ourselves but…"

Dan hesitated long enough for Kayla and Bethany to glance at each other in panic. There was an endless list of things that could come out of their father's mouth at that moment, and the horrifying possibilities immediately flooded both of their minds.

But it didn't take long for Dan to finish his sentence. "Your mother and I have started seeing each other again." As the words came out of his mouth, his voice grew quieter, and his demeanor shifted to a cautious one.

The first thing that broke the void the sentence created was a laugh from Kayla. For a moment, she genuinely thought her parents were pulling a prank on them. But when her dad didn't burst into laughter and he still looked at her with a deer-in-the-headlights expression, the ghastly reality came to light: he wasn't kidding.

You see, when this simple sentence came out of Dan's mouth, it would have a very powerful effect on the two girls who sat in front of them. Immediately, Kayla was in disbelief. Then, a silent, seething anger overcame her. But above all, she was filled with a deep sense of injustice.

Bethany was not as surprised as her sister. Even though she was sad her parents got divorced and didn't believe they would get back together, she couldn't deny she saw her parents develop a solid friendship with each other in recent years. Even though she wasn't surprised, she wasn't pleased. A big part of her dissatisfaction was due to how it would affect her sister. Bethany knew better than anyone how terribly the divorce affected Kayla. But it didn't just affect Kayla, it affected Bethany too. She went through years of coming from a broken home. While most of the time she didn't care what people thought of her, Bethany's insecure teenage mind feared the judgement and possible ridicule she might face from her peers if they found out her broken home was even more complicated than divorced parents.

Wrapped up in this insecurity was the fear she would lose a friendship. In the past year, Bethany had kindled a close friendship with a girl in her grade named Kylie. In fact, Kylie had become one of Bethany's closest friends. They initially bonded over coming from families of divorced parents. There was an understanding that came from hopping from house to house, having two different rooms, and watching their parents go through different cycles of friendship (or lack thereof), and they were able to find solace with each other. While Bethany's young mind was being overly anxious, to her, she believed she was losing a piece of her identity. Coming from divorce allowed her to empathize with people in a way she couldn't before, and she was fearful she would lose that ability.

However, Karina and Dan were completely unaware of the multitude of emotions their daughters were feeling, because all they received in response was silence.

When the silence became too much to bear, Karina was the one to speak up. "I want to know how you girls are feeling about this," Karina assured them. "I can imagine this is all very confusing and shocking for you both. I want you to know your father and I waited to tell you because we wanted to make sure we were serious about each other. Now I want you to know I have fallen in love with your father again, and we hope we can become the family both of you dreamed of having."

At this point, Karina reached out both her hands to touch her daughters. When her hand touched Bethany's, it flinched and tightened, but she allowed it to stay. But when she touched Kayla's hand, her daughter instantly pulled away.

"Kayla—" Karina started, but Kayla quickly stood up out of her chair and interrupted her mother.

"Don't!" Kayla stopped her. "I don't want to hear any more excuses. I just want to know why."

Karina and Dan both looked at her with puzzled expressions.

"Why what, honey?" Dan asked her carefully.

Kayla scoffed. "Why get divorced in the first place? Why put us through hell for five years just to get back together?" Kayla raised her hands but didn't say anything else.

Karina and Dan both glanced at each other at a loss of what to say.

"Things were different then," Dan tried to explain. "Your mother and I weren't in the best place, and I think it took us being apart to realize how much we needed each other in the first place."

Kayla shook her head aggressively. "No. That's wrong," she boldly stated. "You both were fine, until you weren't. Something happened, and the least you can do is be honest and tell the truth. Why did you split up in the first place?" she questioned them. There was only silence to meet their daughters' questions. Tears teased at Kayla's eyes but she swallowed them down, letting the anger and injustice pulse through her veins. If they weren't going to answer her, she would have to try a different approach.

"Dad," she started, and looked her father dead in the eyes, "I was young, but Bethany and I both remember how broken up you were about the divorce. I know you tried to hide it, but it was obvious it wasn't something that you wanted. Please, just tell me what happened. I need to know," Kayla pleaded with her father desperately. The thing was, Kayla didn't grasp how much she needed to know the truth until that moment. While she had always believed her parents were withholding something about their reasons for splitting up, Kayla grew to accept and forget about it...until now. Now she questioned everything that occurred in the past five years, and perhaps before then.

It was torturous for Dan to have to lie to her daughter because, in his heart, he knew exactly what she needed to know. But he also knew he couldn't be the one to tell her. Even still, it was too much for him to look at her beautiful, yet broken, gaze, so he hung his head in shame. There was nothing he could give to her that could provide the answers she needed.

Karina could, and she knew that. She had been honest with everyone else in her life about the bad decisions she had made. There had even been times when she considered telling her daughters the truth, the whole truth, but it never seemed like the right time. Now, she supposed, was as good a time as any. "Okay," Karina said, and Dan quickly turned to her.

"Karina," he said in a tone that told her to stop what she was about to do.

But she didn't. Instead, she plowed forward with the courage she had built in the past few years. Before Karina opened her mouth, she took a second to acknowledge her past self would never have been willing to own what she was about to own, and for that she could be proud.

"You're right. There was more to why your father and I separated than what I told you."

Kayla, still standing, crossed her arms with pride. She had no idea what was coming, but felt relief that she was finally going to hear the truth.

Karina took a deep breath. "I cheated on your father," she blankly stated. "And I developed a strong emotional bond with William while your father and I were still together. While I did end it when things had gone too far, I was still persuaded to pursue separation from your father because of my feelings for William."

Dan held Karina's hand and admired her bravery. Even though they had an extensive conversation about William a month after they started dating, it was still painful for Dan to hear the past being drudged up again. And if it was painful for him, he couldn't imagine how difficult it was for Karina.

But Karina wasn't the one feeling the most intense emotions at that point. While she was feeling some residual guilt and was scared about her daughters' responses to her choices, she had also come to a healthier place in her life and now believed she could handle however her daughters reacted.

Kayla was in a state of complete disbelief and utter disgust. How could her father ever take back her mother after what she did? That was one of the main questions in Kayla's mind. But mostly, she couldn't form any thoughts because a piece of her reality had been shattered.

But even she wasn't the person feeling the most intense emotions. No, it was Bethany who sat in silence. Bethany was in the most dangerous place she had been in her whole life. Now her sister knew the truth, the truth Bethany had known for years. True, Bethany never confronted her mother about William, but she knew, which was why her mother's announcement came as no shock but only greeted her with an abundance of fear. No, after her mother admitted to her affair, Bethany's mind was on a fear-induced recon mission. She weighed what path she should take next. She could either continue lying to her sister about already knowing about the affair, or she could come clean and risk her sister pushing everyone away. Kayla was a highly emotional person and viewed betrayal as the most serious offense. This was the only secret Bethany kept from her sister, but now the thing she had worked so hard to forget about was going to haunt her.

Kayla, still standing, did not just storm out of the dining room. Instead, she grabbed the arm of her chair and threw it to the ground. She stormed into her bedroom and heard the *thud* of the chair crashing onto the floor. Her eyes were dry, but her heart was grieving. And this...was just the beginning.

There were four soft knocks on Kayla's door.

"Come in, Bethany," she replied.

Bethany gently opened the door. "How are you doing?" she asked as she settled on the corner of her sister's bed.

"I just can't believe it. I can't believe they hid this secret for all these years and didn't tell us."

"I know," Bethany softly replied.

"Why aren't you more upset about this?" Kayla questioned. Bethany looked down at the carpeted floor. Kayla knew her sister well, and when she didn't reply, Kayla looked up at her. She didn't need to make eye contact for Kayla to realize the truth. "You knew," Kayla stated. Bethany slightly nodded as she continued to avoid eye contact with Kayla. Kayla's mind was racing as she tried to piece together the betrayal of her family and of her sister: the one person whom she trusted more than anyone else. "How long have you known?" she asked, scared of what the answer would be.

"Kayla, it's not what you think," she replied, and the dodging of the question made her even more upset.

"How long have you known?" she yelled, and stood up from her bed with her arms crossed.

Bethany searched the floor for an answer she couldn't find. "I've known for a couple years."

"A couple...Oh my God!" Kayla wailed and tears poured out of her eyes. She covered her face with her hands in grief. "You've known for years and you didn't tell me?" she said, barely able to speak. She couldn't believe it was the truth.

"Kayla, I was just trying to protect you," she replied and moved slightly closer to Kayla, but Kayla backed away boldly.

"You're a liar!" she exclaimed.

"Kayla," Bethany softly replied, and tried to keep her cool as she felt her heart start to break, "I just put some pieces together, and I didn't want you to have to carry that pain with you. The divorce was hard enough for you ..." she tried to explain.

Kayla couldn't hear her. All she could hear was betrayal. The trust and relationship she had with her sister was slowly starting to burst at the seams. Kayla's breath was shaky, but she just wanted to get one more thing across before she completely lost herself to the grief. "You," she started, and took another deep, shaky breath before continuing, "You have spent my entire life trying to protect me, and I didn't need your protection! All you have done is lie to me FOR YEARS about something I deserved to know! That wasn't your call to make! I deserved to know. Every time I had questions about the divorce, and every time I told you how confused I was about their relationship, you knew the whole time what had split them up in the first place! You pretended and played dumb! And you just sat out there and let her confess something you already knew!" Kayla's throat burned from all the yelling, but that didn't stop her from continuing. "How many times have I cried in your arms because I didn't understand? None of it made sense, and you had the missing piece I've been so desperately trying to find the whole time! My own sister."

Tears rolled down Bethany's face; she was filled with more regret than she could bear. "I never meant to hurt you," she whimpered.

"Get out," Kayla said sternly. When Bethany didn't move, Kayla stomped over to the door and swung it open. "Get out!" she screamed, and Bethany walked away in shame. Kayla paced around her room with no idea what to do with all the anger and pain she felt in her heart. She had trusted her sister with everything, and this was what she did? Lie? And told herself it was to protect her? It was all so selfish she couldn't bear to think about it.

Kayla's mind was racing and her body was hot and throbbing. The physical response could not begin to express the emotional turmoil she experienced inside. She continued to pace around the room until she picked up a framed photo of her and her sister that sat on her desk. She gripped it so tightly in her hand her knuckles turned white. Then, she threw it against the wall with all her might and watched the glass shatter into pieces. The relief felt good for a moment, but then the feeling of entrapment set in. There was nowhere she could go. Kayla couldn't just escape her own family. Now she had to learn how to survive with someone she could never learn to forgive.

On the other end of the hall, Bethany sat curled up in her bed and sobbed. She didn't know what to say, or think, or feel, other than just bad. She had told herself for so long she was doing the right thing, and for a while, she didn't think about it that much. It wasn't until her parents showed interest in each other again that she remembered the secret she held on to.

She heard glass shatter in the room across from her and jumped in fear. As Bethany sat in the fetal position alone and sobbed, a dark reality seeped into the cracks of her mind. There were some choices relationships just couldn't come back from, and Bethany now knew with stark clarity she may have just made hers.

Chapter Twenty-Two: Now

Kayla found herself alone in a room that wasn't hers for yet another long day. It had been five days since the funeral. Each day felt as worse as the last. No matter how hard she tried to fight it, every single day she was pushed further away from the last time she saw her father alive. It was inevitable, and that was what made it so intolerable.

Even though she spent a few nights at her sister's, Kayla never imagined spending so much time at Cassian's house, especially for this long.

Cassian also wasn't expecting it, but he wasn't upset about it. While Cassian had learned to enjoy living alone, he also found himself grateful for the presence of another life in his house, even if it was a grieving one. It was an odd place he found himself in. He was comforting someone who felt familiar yet a stranger at the same time, which meant there were many times he had no idea how to be there for Kayla. He often sat with her in silence or listened to her tell stories about her dad. He even added a few of his own, but sometimes he was just lost. He found himself at a lost place that day.

It was the middle of the afternoon, and Kayla hadn't come out once. Cassian finally decided he had waited long enough and walked to the door to knock on it. Before his fist met the wood, Kayla swung it open and startled them both.

"Oh!" she said in surprise and took a step back.

For a moment, Cassian looked white as a ghost, but then regained his composure and they both laughed.

Unfortunately, the laughter only lasted a moment before the grief came rushing back into Kayla's mind. She learned it didn't like to stay away for long.

It didn't take long for Cassian to realize he lost her again. But this time, he had one more idea to bring her back, even if it was only temporarily.

"I have a surprise for you," he cautiously said, and she looked at him with a bemused smile. "Come into the living room and close your eyes. I'll be right back."

Kayla followed his instructions with an unenergetic pace. The old Kayla would have pestered Cassian impatiently and probably yelled a witty remark when she heard a clattering sound in the garage. The new Kayla found herself absentmindedly staring out the window in silence. For the first time since her father's death, Kayla's face lit up when she saw what Cassian proudly gripped in his hand. "Your guitar?" she questioned as she traced her hand across the familiar strings.

"It always kind of felt like our guitar," he admitted. It was true. Cassian only fell in love with his guitar again after he started teaching Kayla those many years ago. He always credited her for getting him back into it.

Kayla, on the other hand, had stopped playing guitar once Dan and Tina broke up. She didn't want to teach herself, and her mom seemed to resent the guitar's existence once she learned who it was tied to. Kayla thought it would be easier for everyone, including herself, if she just dropped it.

As Kayla lamented her own loss of a once loved hobby, Cassian started strumming a tune on the guitar. It wasn't one Kayla recognized, but it was beautiful. The notes strung together in a way that made it sound like they were always meant to be played together. He continued strumming and humming until he struck the final note and looked up at her with shy eyes.

"I've never heard that before. It's beautiful though," she remarked.

His cheeks grew flush. "I wrote it, actually," he nervously admitted to her.

Her eyes widened and a smile grew on her face. "Really? It would make an amazing song. Do you think you'll write lyrics to it?"

"Maybe…" his voice drifted. "I just haven't been able to find the words to describe you yet."

To say Kayla was caught off guard would be a drastic understatement. While someone else may have seen this coming, Kayla certainly did not. "Me?" she questioned, still unsure if she had heard him correctly.

"Yes, you," he responded, clearly believing his statement warranted no further explanation.

Kayla disagreed. Kayla felt panic bubble up inside of her. Instead of letting him see her like that (even though he had seen her in practically every emotional state at that point), she excused herself and walked outside.

Cassian had little of a porch or front yard, so Kayla sat on his front steps. When he found her, she had her head buried in her hands, and he could hear quiet sobs that slightly shook her body. He sat down next to her, wrapped his arm around her, and ran his fingers through her hair until she was able to take a breath.

When Kayla looked up, her face was wet and red and snot ran down her nose. The messes Cassian had already seen her in embarrassed her, but seeing her like this again certainly didn't help her self-confidence. "I'm sorry."

"You don't have to be sorry," he assured her. "I'm sorry. With everything you are going through, I never should have said anything. It was selfish on my part."

Instead of responding, Kayla wrapped her arms around him and pulled him into an embrace. "Thank you, for who you are," she said and another tear fell down her cheek. But this wasn't a tear of sadness; it was one of gratitude. "You are exactly who I needed by my side in this." When she said it out loud, she realized how true it was. Which meant, she faced a crossroads. The person she needed was settled in the place she hated the most. But this was the glaring question ahead: Could she be happy somewhere else without Cassian? Or could she be happy in Marshfield? She already knew the answer to both was no. Thus, Kayla kept her arms wrapped tightly around Cassian, because at that moment, she couldn't let go.

Bethany and Kayla both knew if they ever wanted to move forward in their relationship, really move forward, they would have to talk about the thing that divided them in the first place. After the funeral, the two found themselves spending a lot more time together. Sometimes they sat in silence, both were unsure of what to say. Other times they thought about memories of their father, and even their mother. Sometimes they even talked about themselves. They had a lot of years of a broken relationship to make up for, but they were all that was left of their childhoods. Even though neither of them said it, they had moments when they decided they wanted to be better for each other. They wanted to be the sister the other one needed.

Kayla's moment came shortly after she learned her sister was pregnant. She would be the first to admit she was not a good aunt to Henry. She let her bitterness with her sister pour into a relationship with her nephew, and she couldn't get that back. But with a new baby, Kayla had another chance to be a good aunt, and to do that, Kayla wanted to be a good sister first.

Bethany's moment came a little more unexpectedly. It was a few days before their dad died and Kayla was sitting next to him reading a poem from a book he used to read to them as children. In that moment, she saw a tenderness in her sister she hadn't seen before, and it made her realize how much she had grown since they were teenagers. Seeing that new side of Kayla fostered a desire in Bethany's heart to get to know and get to love her sister for who she was now, not who she always believed her to be.

So, the two set to work on talking out their issues. In the past weeks, they had casually tackled some of the smaller incidents that took place over the years. They weren't trying to live in the past, but each still harbored anger and resentments towards the other one for things that happened years ago. Neither brought up *the* thing, not until that day.

It had been on Bethany's mind all morning, and she assumed it had been on her sister's too. She supposed they were both too afraid to bring it up as there was so much emotion tied to it, on both of their ends.

"Why are you here?" Kayla sighed as she opened the door. She had given her family her Chicago address because her dad had wanted to send her something. Never did Kayla imagine seeing her sister standing on her doorstep without a call to let her know. If this was what her father wanted to send, Kayla wanted it returned immediately.

"You know, I'm trying to be like dad. Big gestures and all," Bethany jested, but Kayla did not laugh.

"I guess I have to invite you to come in," she said facetiously and left the door open as she walked back into her apartment.

Bethany uncomfortably stepped inside and looked around at her sister's new life. The apartment was barely furnished, with only a well-loved couch in the living room and a rug that didn't match on the floor. The only wall decor was a large map that hung up on the wall adjacent to the couch and a small TV on a stand that looked ready to break any minute.

"The map is pretty," Bethany remarked, and her sister gave her a half-hearted "Thanks."

"Are you going to tell me what brings you halfway across the country without letting me know?"

"I thought if I told you, you wouldn't want me to come," Bethany responded quietly.

"And you would have been right," Kayla scoffed. "So instead, you bombard me, and I don't have any option but to let you in." Kayla rolled her eyes at her own reality. She had moved halfway across the country and still couldn't avoid her sister's agenda. "Always like Bethany, only thinking of herself."

"Kayla, I—" Bethany started.

"Really?" Kayla questioned. She was going to say more, but for Kayla, nothing else needed to be said.

However, Bethany had a laundry list of things she wanted to talk about. "Everyone misses you, Kayla. Why don't you just quit your big act of defiance and come home?" she asked with more sass than intended.

"Wow," Kayla started with a resentful fake smile plastered on her face, "you are unbelievable." She stood up from the couch and walked into her kitchen. She grabbed a soda out of the fridge, cracked it open, and leaned against the counter. "You know, you didn't have to travel all this way to offend me. You could have just called." She took a drink of soda and slammed it on her counter. "Honestly, did you think this was the way to get me to come back home?"

Bethany sighed. "I didn't mean it like that. How many times do I have to say I'm sorry? I'm sorry for not telling you—"

"Stop!" Kayla loudly interrupted her. "I don't want to hear it."

"It's been years. I was sixteen. You have to forgive me some time."

"Do I?" Kayla laughed. "You spent two years lying to me, I think I should at least be allowed twice that much time to be angry about it. Don't you?" Bethany's lack of *response only provoked Kayla further. "Oh, and do we want to talk about what happened in the months that followed my discovery of your lie? Because you can say that it was you apologizing, but it was really you giving excuses as to why your lie was okay. Now you feel guilty because you know how badly you screwed up." Kayla sat back down on her couch. "But here's the thing, Bethany. I didn't leave because of you, I left for me. You always knew I wanted a life outside of that crappy town you are so dead set on staying in. I'm happy here."*

"How could you be happy with no one?" Bethany questioned aggressively.

"I would rather have no one than live with a family of screwed up liars."

"You still talk to Dad. Isn't he one of those screwed up liars?" Bethany snarked.

That was a question that did surprise Kayla, but it only took a moment for her to respond with the same harsh tone that engulfed the entire conversation.

"Dad was a victim too. He didn't ask to be cheated on, and it wasn't his place to tell me."

"And you think it was mine?" Bethany angrily questioned.

"You're my sister!" Kayla yelled. "I told you everything. I trusted you with everything, and look how well that turned out for me."

"Kayla, it was one lie. Obviously, if I could take it back I would, but there is nothing that I can do now."

"That is where you are right, Bethany; there is nothing you can do."

"Was there anything I could have done?" Bethany gently asked her.

When Bethany initially brought up the situation, Kayla did not have any interest in talking about it. But it didn't take long for Kayla to admit her sister was right. They had to have an honest conversation about this or it would always be the elephant in the room.

"You could have told me the truth," Kayla softly responded. "And I was tired of hearing the excuses, B. Every time it came up, even when you came to Chicago, you still had excuses for why you did it. I just wanted you to own what you did without any excuses tacked on."

"I tried, Kayla. I sent you letters. I tried to talk on the phone...you wouldn't hear it."

"Once again, blaming me," Kayla sneered and rolled her eyes. "I don't know why I expected this time to be any different."

"No, it is different," Bethany quickly interjected. She had gone long enough carrying this terrible conflict, and she was not about to let another conversation about it go badly. "I want to own that what I did was wrong. And, in a lot of ways, I felt justified in my decision, which is why I made so many excuses. It's true, I thought I was protecting you. But there also came a time I knew I had gone too long without telling you, and at that point, I was just protecting myself," she admitted.

It was an affirmation Kayla had waited many years to hear. With it, she felt ready to own up to her own faults in the situation.

"I should have moved forward a long time ago," she admitted. "I think it became bigger and bigger in my head, and I just got used to being angry. I think some part of me was scared to forgive you because I closed myself off to that kind of vulnerability. After seeing Dad get sick, and after things ended so terribly with Peter, I swore off having a deep relationship with anybody. And you were the person who knew me best! It was terrifying to have that kind of relationship again. I was scared to rely on anybody. But I never should have held it over your head for so long."

"Well, I gave you a lot of reasons to be scared," Bethany added. "I should not have pushed you so hard to come back here when Dad got really sick. I wanted someone to go through it all with, but ultimately, it was your decision. I also admit I put some of the burden of taking care of Dad on myself. Probably some pride thing. But when I understood it was a lot harder to take care of him than I thought it would be, I wanted help. But I shouldn't have asked you to give up your life because of the decision that I made with Dad. And while I'm at it, I should have included you in that decision."

"I didn't want to be included," Kayla responded. "It was terrifying to see Dad get worse, but I shouldn't have put that all on you," she confessed. "I don't think I should have moved back. I don't think that would have been a healthy decision for me, but I shouldn't have left you to deal with all of it, in every way, including financially. I know that was a big burden to force you to carry, and I should have shouldered some of it myself."

"I think we both screwed up a lot," Bethany remarked with a sigh.

"Yeah," Kayla's voice seemed to fade in the silent sadness the two sat in. It was Kayla that broke it. "I forgive you," she quietly said. "I don't agree with the decision you made about the affair, but I want you to know I forgive you. I don't want you to have to carry that anymore."

Tears fell down Bethany's face. "Thank you," she responded. "I am so sorry. I know you don't want me to carry it anymore, but I will regret lying to you for the rest of my life."

When Bethany said that, it made Kayla realize how many regrets she carried in her life and how desperate she was to not carry them anymore.

Bethany interrupted her stream of consciousness. "For what it's worth, I forgive you too."

In a perfect world, this would be the last time the past would haunt Bethany and Kayla. In that world, the two sisters would be able to move forward without any regrets or resentments. Unfortunately, none of us live in that perfect world. It would take many more times of them hashing out things of the past to really move forward. But, luckily, none of those would result in closing each other out. It would make each conflict more painful but more important and healthier. They had finally done what their teenage selves couldn't: forgive each other. Really forgive each other. And that would make all the difference.

"It still feels weird to be here," Bethany remarked as they looked down at the two pieces of granite that silently lay before them.

"It feels weird for Dad to have one at all since there isn't anything buried down there," Kayla remarked, even though she supported their decision to have a gravestone to rest next to their mother.

The sisters decided it only felt right if they both were remembered together. After all, their love story was quite the roller coaster to be remembered.

Kayla had only visited her mother's gravestone a few times, but every time she came, the same memory played in her head.

"Don't blame me for harboring a grudge over your sister for all these years. And now look what you've done. Your sister is never going to see anything beyond Plymouth because she is too terrified to split this family up even more than you already have!"

238

"I'm not the one who had an affair. All I did was move away from home! That's it! Something most kids do after they graduate high school. And Bethany is happy here. Why can't we just be happy? Why can't that be enough?"

"I love you girls. I just want the best for you, and I don't think this is it."

"Well, if this is your way of showing love, then you are even more screwed up than I thought."

The sound of the door slamming behind her echoed in Kayla's mind. "It was just so stupid. We never should have gotten in that fight in the first place," Kayla told her sister as they sat with their legs crossed in front of the stones.

"We both got in stupid fights with Mom. Even though we were close, Mom and I had a few screaming matches of our own. I don't think she holds it against us," Bethany joked, and Kayla gave a weak smile. "Maybe instead of remembering that day, you can pick a different one," she suggested.

"What, and replace my last memory with Mom?" Kayla teased, but Bethany only nodded.

"Why not? Who says that's what you must remember? Maybe you should let go of the fight entirely and focus on something else. What's your best memory with Mom?"

Kayla pondered the question. She had spent so long with that stupid fight in her head she hadn't taken the time to reflect on good memories in a while. When she did, it was mostly about watching her mom and dad fall back in love. But her favorite memory with her mom? She couldn't seem to find anything worthy of being her new last memory of her.

"Do you remember when the three of us went to Boston together?" Kayla asked as memories of their trip started to flood her mind.

"Is that the trip that our canoe flipped over in the Charles River?"

"And you complained the entire rest of the day about being wet? Oh yes," Kayla responded with a laugh. "But that's not the memory I'm thinking of. Do you remember when we sat at that park in front of the skyline and just waited until it got dark so we could see it all lit up?"

It took Bethany a minute to dig out the specific memory until she could see it in her mind: the three of them wrapped up in a blanket and Karina grabbing their hands and pulling them in closer when a loud, and surely high, person started yelling at no one on the other side of the park. They probably shouldn't have stayed out so late, but Karina didn't take the girls out of Plymouth often, so she wanted to make it worthwhile. Besides, as much as Karina loved Plymouth, seeing the lights of the small city filled her with an excitement that couldn't be found on a small-town street.

"I loved that trip," Kayla wistfully remarked. "I love Boston. I should really go back some time," she casually stated as her mind shifted away from her mother and onto the various trips she had made during her time in Massachusetts.

"Yeah, it's fun to visit. I don't think I could ever imagine living there though," Bethany joked, but Kayla remained silent.

"I could," she said after a while. Bethany's shocked face spoke for her. "I don't know, maybe a life in Boston wouldn't be so bad," she slightly elaborated, but didn't say anything else on the matter.

Bethany wanted to press her further, perhaps even persuade her to let this thought become a possibility, but she didn't. Instead, she stood up and decided it was time for them to go home.

Before they left, Kayla grabbed her sister's hand but didn't say a word. As they held each other's hands at the tombs of the two people who shaped their lives the most, they couldn't help but remember how much they had lost. It wasn't just the loss of their parents; it was the loss of each other for so many years. That loss wasn't one to be taken lightly. It was time they would never get back, and as they had both learned the hard way, time was a gift no one, not even the richest or most successful person, could buy. Almost every person in their life will wish they had more time for something: more time to love someone, more time to be somewhere or do something...

Bethany and Kayla both had a list. But, most of all, they wished they had more time to be a family. Even though they had gotten to a place where they felt like they were a family, in many ways it was too late. They had already lost that time with their parents, and they were both to blame. Now all they could do was try to love each other the best they could, and that would have to be enough. And it would be.

Chapter Twenty-Three: Then

"Let's go, girls!" Karina yelled in a sing-song voice to encourage the girls to come out into the living room. Karina and Dan decided they wanted to go on a family picnic.

If this suggestion had been made a month ago, the girls would have been slightly annoyed to leave their teenage antics, but would have ultimately accepted and enjoyed the idea of a family picnic. But circumstances changed. Faster than they could have imagined, their father was hanging out at the house more and more and they noticed slowly his belongings became permanent mementos within the walls of the home. This in and of itself wasn't a bad thing for Bethany or Kayla. In fact, Kayla had made her peace with her parents getting back together. However, she was nowhere near making her peace with the lies, not only her mother kept from her, but her sister as well.

As an adult, Kayla would have a deeper understanding as to why her mother didn't tell her. She was a kid. She didn't need to know. But in her teenage mind, she couldn't wrap her head around how her mom could lie to her for so long. But what cut far deeper, and what affected the family in a way none of them could have foreseen, was Kayla had no interest in continuing a relationship with her sister. There were many fights that ensued over the past month and would continue to ensue until the day Kayla moved out in three years. Unfortunately, no matter what Karina or Dan said to Kayla, she was firm in her beliefs.

It was more traumatic than Dan expected to watch Karina find out her daughter already knew about her affair. The fact Bethany already knew about her mistakes and held onto that secret for so long was enough to send Karina into a deep depressive spiral. No matter how hard she tried, she couldn't move past and reconcile the shame she felt. Not for her mistake, but that she had been so careless and blind to the burden her daughter carried. Most of all, Karina felt an immense amount of guilt and shame over how her secret had divided her children. The last thing in the world Karina wanted was for her children to not have a relationship. In fact, she would have rather lost relationships with both of her children if that meant they continued to have a connection with each other.

Karina admired their beautiful friendship their entire lives. They had a bond that, as an only child, Karina would never understand. However, now she took the entire responsibility for the rupture in her children's friendship as her own fault. She even begged Kayla to let her anger out on her, not Bethany.

That only served to make Kayla even more upset. She felt her mother didn't understand why she felt betrayed by Bethany, and with that pain compiled on the deep betrayal she felt, left her feeling completely lost. Not only had she lost her sister, but she pushed herself away from most of her friends, because most of them were mutual friends with Bethany. She had no interest in asking them to pick sides or, more accurately, she feared they would all take Bethany's side and she didn't want to deal with that kind of rejection.

Finally, the girls came out silently from their bedrooms, and they all loaded up in the car to have another awkward family gathering. Family dinners, which they still tried to do a few nights a week, had been a huge struggle.

Kayla had no interest in pretending everything was okay. This meant numerous dirty looks and snarky comments during casual conversations.

Today, they all sat on the ratted picnic blanket and ate the sandwiches Karina had made for them earlier. Karina attempted to make small talk with her daughters, asking trivial questions about school and their friends and anything else that would require more than a one-word response. Still, that was most of what she received from them.

While Kayla was silent out of bitterness, Bethany was silent out of shame. As Bethany journeyed into this new world without her sister by her side, two moods tended to flow in and out of her. The first was one of vicious anger rooted in a defense when the girls would engage in the same argument repeatedly. The other mood was quieter, but volatile all the same. Most of the time, Bethany felt overcome by a deep sadness. While she tried to pick out happy moments with her friends, or brief euphoric feelings after getting a good test grade back, the sadness was never far away. All she wanted was for things to return to normal, but she knew no matter how things went with her sister, that would never happen. There was a great divide that couldn't be erased from their story. But Bethany could not come to grips with this fact. And who could blame her? Kayla was her best friend, and now she felt the crippling weight of isolation for the first time in her life. The worst part of all of it was the only person Bethany could be angry with was herself (that was, until the other mood overtook her, then she was angry at her sister for being angry with her). Even in those moments, she still resented herself for getting them into this mess in the first place.

Karina decided to use this family gathering as an opportunity to announce Dan would be moving in with them. But this news came as no surprise to either Bethany nor Kayla. They both knew it was coming sooner or later, and they were too caught up in their own pain to have any opinion about it.

Bethany supposed she felt happy for her parents, but, in all honesty, she struggled to feel anything but that horrid sadness.

Kayla couldn't have cared less. She still loved her father as much as ever, and even though she was angry at her entire family, it was her father's and her relationship that held up the best through the storm. That was because Kayla felt sympathy for her father.

If Dan was being honest with himself, he knew this and didn't fight her sympathy because he couldn't imagine losing his daughter. He also believed Karina and Bethany hadn't lost her either. In a rare flash of optimism, he strongly hoped Kayla would be able to forgive Karina and Bethany sooner rather than later. But, as he would see, his optimism was sorely misplaced.

To fill the silence, Dan found himself going on a rant about a minor work inconvenience and then noticed the only person listening was Karina out of politeness not genuine interest. He searched for something that would catch the girls' attention, and then an idea popped into his mind. "Maybe we should all go on a vacation," he suggested. In all honesty, Dan knew a vacation was not what their family needed (what they really needed was some family therapy), but Dan was desperate to find anything to get his daughters even the least bit excited. "What if we all pick a destination, put it in a hat, and whichever one we pull out, that's where we go? Nothing too crazy, though," he added as he imagined his daughters putting in some international vacation none of them could afford.

The girls haphazardly agreed and, before they knew it, their father was handing out napkins and pens he fished out of Karina's purse.

At first Kayla considered writing a snarky comment like "anywhere but here," but as she thought about it, she had a 25% chance of going anywhere she wanted. After careful consideration, she scribbled down an answer and placed it in her father's Angels baseball cap.

When all the napkins found themselves in his cap, Dan gave himself the honor of pulling out the winning answer.

"Oh boy," Dan said when he saw the three words on the napkin. "Looks like we're going to the Big Apple," he remarked.

Karina's eyes widened as she panicked about traveling to the biggest city in America.

A large grin grew on Kayla's face. Looked like that 25% chance had paid off after all.

Karina racked her brain to figure out what in the world she was expected to pack for this excursion she had no interest in going on. It couldn't have been Karina's pick to go to Cape Cod or Dan's pick to go to a beach. No, of course it had to be her wild daughter's choice to go to a city that did not just intimidate her, but terrified her. However, she was the only one dreading the trip.

In fact, even Bethany had something to look forward to and find some peace and joy in. Although she knew things would still be tense with her sister, she hoped the distraction of going on a new adventure would create some sort of joy within their family again.

They all loaded into the car and drove the four hours to the place Karina had avoided, Dan and Bethany hadn't given much thought to, and Kayla had dreamed of going. And it was about time. They were so close to the city it seemed almost ludicrous they hadn't gone yet.

It had taken Kayla fifteen years before she would finally get to see the wonderful and magical city that never sleeps. As they came closer to the city, all their jaws dropped in wonderment. A smile didn't leave Kayla's face the entire time they drove through the skyscrapers as they made their way to their hotel located in a place called Chelsea; Kayla couldn't help but laugh at the strange name.

Once they got to the room, Kayla threw her bag onto a bed and anxiously stood by the door, eager to get back outside and go to the first place on their agenda: the Empire State Building.

Kayla's bossy tone irritated every other member of the Fitzpatrick family, but eventually they were ready to go back out and face the eight million people that awaited them. Karina was dead set against going on the subway and insisted they take a taxi.

Once they got outside and rode the elevator to the top of the tall building, Kayla rushed to the railing so she could look at the city that greeted her. It was amazing. It made her realize how desperately she wanted to get out of her small town and be somewhere more interesting.

Their day was filled with trips to Times Square, a free ferry to look at the Statue of Liberty, a peek at the Stock Exchange, and the night ended with seeing a Broadway show that Dan had found cheap tickets to (well, cheaper than the hundreds of dollars they typically cost).

The next day was filled with more touristy things and soon they found themselves standing in a beautiful gazebo in Central Park. Karina noticed music playing in the distance, and then it came closer to where they were. Soon she recognized the song to be one of her favorite Beatles songs. A smile grew on her face as she tapped Dan on the shoulder. "They're playing our song!" she exclaimed, and a toothy grin appeared on Dan's face. Karina was oblivious that earlier Dan had snuck off to slip the street players $50 to play this exact song. Even more of a surprise was her ex-husband getting on one knee as the band came into sight.

"I promise I'm not going to say anything cheesy, but I hope you feel the same way I do. I'm convinced a day without you is a day I do not want to see. You can make fun of me for this later, but Karina Ann Fitzpatrick, will you marry me…again?" he nervously asked as he held a small diamond ring in his hand.

In the brief speech her ex-husband gave, a flood of emotions came over Karina. First shock, then a quick flash of anger for making a public spectacle, then joy, then fear, and then joy again. If she was being honest with herself, she wasn't sure if she wanted to get married again at all. But the moment she saw Dan on one knee, he was right. She had no interest in spending a single day without him, so why not seal it with a ring and a familiar piece of paper?

"Yes, I will marry you again," she said with a grin. "Let's hope it goes better this time," she joked, and Dan laughed.

They kissed and embraced each other tightly, and then they opened their arms to invite their shocked daughters into a group hug.

Even though Kayla had a bitter resentment for her sister, she chose to embrace this moment for what it was: a beautiful time for her parents. So, they all hugged each other warmly, and allowed for all the pain that had occurred in the past months to become irrelevant for a few minutes. What replaced those feelings was an abundant amount of love.

And love was exactly what was present on the beautiful sunny day in their backyard. There were no chairs or decorations. There were merely scattered rose petals that resembled something of an aisle and a nervous Dan dressed in his nicest suit. Standing next to him was Antonio Cardenas, Angela's husband, who also happened to be an ordained minister. Dan and Antonio got along well as the two couples found themselves going on many double dates in the past year.

Karina had found a beautiful, long, lace, white dress at the thrift store and knew it was perfect for the occasion. Her freshly curled hair fell gently down her shoulders, and a flower crown adorned with small white flowers Bethany had picked out, rested on her head. She carried a bouquet of soft, pink roses in her hand and walked towards the beautiful man she couldn't wait to spend even more of her life with.

There was not a large audience to hear Antonio's opening remarks and cheesy jokes. It was only Angela, Karla and her husband Thomas, Emerson, who insisted on flying across the world to watch this crazy love story come to fruition, Bethany, Kayla, and of course Karina and Dan. But when Antonio asked them to do their vows, for both Karina and Dan, they were the only two people in the whole world.

Karina looked at Dan's soft green eyes and couldn't help but smile. She took a deep breath in preparation, knowing she would surely cry as she unfolded the piece of paper to begin.

"Dan, the first time we did this, we didn't understand what true commitment meant. Through losing each other, we learned about sacrifice, friendship, co-parenting, and finally, what loving each other truly meant: which is all the above. You are a truly wonderful man, and every day I watch you be a father to our girls, a friend to many, and a support system for me, it pushes me to be better. You not only inspire and amaze me, but you also love me so well. I hope with the time we have left that I am able to love you with as much love as I daily feel from you. You were right all along Dan. You were always meant to be my happy ending."

Tears rolled down Dan's face as he looked at the beautiful woman standing before him. If someone would have told Dan two years ago this was where he would be standing, he never would have believed it. In fact, he wasn't even sure if he would have wanted it. But now he saw a glimpse of how their complicated story had come together perfectly for this moment. With that realization, he was ready to say the vows he had stewed over for hours and finally threw away in the trash all to hope he would have the right words to say when the moment came. He would.

"Some people might say we lost a lot of time during the years we were apart, but I don't count those years as a loss. We were broken, and it took those years for us to find healing within ourselves, and I think only after we did that were we truly ready to love each other well. When I first fell in love with you, I was young and dumb and didn't know what I was doing with my life. Now, I'm a little less young and dumb, and even though some days I don't know what I'm doing with my life, I know I don't want to live a single day without you in it. Every day I look at you, I see the greatest gift that being with you has given me: hope. Hope that no matter how screwed up life gets, sometimes people are just meant to find their way back to each other. And I'm really glad we found our way back to each other." Dan's hand shakily put a silver band on Karina's hand. "I love you, Karina, and I am committed to you from now until the last of my days."

"With that, I now pronounce you husband and wife, again," Antonio said with a laugh.

Despite the dig, a big grin grew on Dan's face as he grabbed Karina to kiss her. When he did, it was like no time had passed at all. They were back to being the giddy kids who had deeply fallen in love for the first time. But when he pulled away, he saw how much they had grown since then. He looked at their two beautiful daughters and was filled with pride at who they had raised. Dan looked at his wife, the woman who had been and would continue to be the greatest part of his story, and couldn't think of a happier moment. In fact, he would always cherish that moment as his happiest.

After the ceremony, Karina and Dan walked over to their daughters and grabbed their hands. Bethany reached out her hand for Kayla to grab, and in that moment, she decided to give her parents a special moment as the family they used to be. Kayla put her pain aside and grabbed her sister's hand.

"I know we have been through a hell of a lot as a family," Dan started with an honest chuckle, "but I hope you girls know how abundantly loved you are, and how grateful I am for the beautiful family we have made." He glanced at the woman he did not feel deserving to be his again, and she greeted him with a warm familiar smile.

"Even with all the bumps and bruises we've incurred along the way, I wouldn't have it any other way because that is what brought us to right here."

"I love you, Dad," Kayla tenderly replied.

"And I love you. I love both of you," Dan said as he looked at the two young women who had grown up much too fast for Dan's liking. "I love you both more than you will ever know," he whispered.

"We are going to be okay," Karina assured them and pulled all three of the people she loved most into an embrace. She wasn't sure if she believed it, and while she wouldn't live to see it herself, they would be okay.

It would take a lot longer than Karina would have imagined, but just as her husband said that day, she would have been okay because that was exactly the way it was supposed to happen.

Sometimes even amid the greatest brokenness, people could have good days, or at the very least, good moments. And the moment the Fitzpatrick family hugged each other with as much love as they could muster was just that: good.

Chapter Twenty-Four: Now

"I will miss you," Melinda said as she pulled the packing tape across the stuffed box.

"I know, but it gives you an excuse to visit Boston!" Kayla exclaimed and grabbed another box that was heavier than she imagined.

As she steadied herself, Bethany came up behind her to try to grab the box.

"Heck no!" Kayla aggressively said and yanked the box back into her grasp. "If you think I am letting my six-month pregnant sister lift anything but pillows, you are wrong."

Bethany rolled her eyes and picked up the box boldly marked "pillows," and marched it into her van.

Once they loaded the last of the boxes, Kayla had a tearful goodbye with the friend she never expected to gain. "Have I mentioned that I'll miss you yet?" Melinda asked and they both laughed as tears filled their eyes.

"I'm telling you. The best way for Ben to make it up to me would be for you to visit frequently," Kayla teased and they found themselves laughing through the tears again.

"Drive safe. Text me when you get settled," Melinda told her.

Kayla nodded. She hopped into the passenger's seat of her sister's van, but before Bethany drove off, she handed her sister an envelope. Kayla tore it open and found three round trip train tickets from Boston to St. Louis.

"Three?" Kayla questioned and wondered if Cassian was somehow part of this surprise.

"One for you, one for me, and one for Danielle. I want her to see some of the world outside of Massachusetts," Bethany said and set her hand on her belly.

Kayla's face lit up at the name. "Dad would love it," she told her.

Bethany squeezed her hand. "You ready?" she asked, and Kayla shook her head. "It's okay, we never are," she said and put the car in drive.

"Surprise!" Cassian exclaimed when Bethany and Kayla walked through the door. Above him hung a banner that read: "Welcome to Your New Home, Kayla" in big, blue letters.

Kayla's heart skipped a beat when she saw the banner and Cassian, Huxley, and Henry there to greet them. Behind Cassian stood a shy seven-year-old boy who didn't say a word until Kayla knelt to meet him.

"You must be Benji," she said gently. He didn't verbally respond, only nodded and avoided eye contact with the stranger. "My name is Kayla. I just moved to Boston." Benji was still silent and Kayla looked up at Cassian with disappointed eyes.

He knelt beside the two of them. "Maybe the three of us can get ice cream sometime," Cassian suggested, and Benji's eyes lit up. He nodded quickly, and Kayla sighed, relieved.

Cassian had mentioned Benji was quiet, but she still hoped that with time, he would warm up to her. After all, now she only lived forty-five minutes away from them, and besides her sister, Cassian was the only person she had on the East Coast. Even still, Kayla was at peace with that. She would be starting a new job at a coding company, she had a beautiful apartment, and most important of all, she had her sister.

For a long time, Bethany and Kayla did not know what the stars their father told them about really meant. For a while, Kayla believed the stars were getting a job and seeing the world and going on new adventures.

Bethany thought the stars were settling down and starting a family. All these good things were stars in their little worlds, but it took completely falling apart to finally realize they had been denying themselves of a bright star in their galaxy: each other.

Sisterhood had meant so many things over the years for each of them, and in recent years, those definitions were not positive ones, but losing their dad and losing each other over the years made them both recognize how much they loved each other. That was sisterhood: loving your sister. For so long it was always: loving your sister but something else. Loving your sister but resenting her, loving your sister but still jealous of her, loving your sister but not agreeing with her choices, loving your sister but not liking her. Now, they were both so broken they didn't want to carry any of the buts, and so they laid the first stones on their path towards loving each other again without any strings attached. They would stumble and hurt each other and crack many stones along that path, but they never denied the brokenness that brought them together.

"I'm still terrified about all of this," Kayla told her sister as they sat on pillows in the middle of the living room floor. Tomorrow they would go and find some cheap furniture to fill the apartment, but today, decorative pillows would have to do.

"I know," Bethany replied. "But things will be different this time. We have each other. We are going to be okay."

"Yeah?" Kayla asked, still questioning what okay even meant for her.

"Absolutely." Bethany squeezed Kayla's hand as she laid her head on Bethany's shoulder.

Life still went on faster than either of them anticipated it would, and unexpected changes hit them left and right, but there was a newfound completeness in knowing they had each other. Somehow, someway, a broken family found a way to be enough for each other. And that is what made all the difference.

Acknowledgments

This book was written after one of the most tragic losses in my life. Yet, out of that loss came the greatest joy of my life, my husband. For that entire experience, and for everything in my life, I thank God. I am nothing without His love for me.

My husband, Abel, I adore you so much. Thank you for supporting me and loving me through all my mess.

Mom, thank you for seeing me through the worst times in my life, and for being my biggest fan. I hope this labor of love will make you proud.

Taya, my best friend, who also happens to be my niece, thank you for everything you have given me. You teach me daily what family means.

Kinley, thank you for teaching me to not be afraid to ask for what I want, and to go out and get it. I love your boldness.

Sara, my sister, I love you. I didn't know it when I wrote it, but a lot of this work was written for you. Dustin, thank you for being the best bonus bridesmaid a girl could ask for, and for supporting me.

Dr. Hershey, thank you for being the best professor and supporter a girl could ask for. I'm so lucky to have you in my corner. Sierra, Spencer, Daiya, Claire, Holly, Shelley, Briana, Stephen, Meredith, Koshal, Felix, and Max, I am indebted to you, my friends. I love you more than you will ever know. You are my people, and I am so glad God gave me the gift of your friendships.

My team at Dorrance, thank you for helping me to publish something so close to my heart.

Finally, to anyone who has what the world defines as a "broken family." You are not alone, and your family is not broken. I've learned family is truly defined as the people who love you most, and that isn't always blood. You can have a whole and complete family, even if it doesn't look exactly how you might have imagined it to. Whomever that is for you, hold them close.

Thank you for reading.

Love, Marisa.

CPSIA information can be obtained
at www.ICGtesting.com
Printed in the USA
BVHW032139280722
643316BV00012B/236